THE KING OF CARENTAN
Carentan – Book 2

FG and DC Laval

THE KING OF CARENTAN
Carentan – Book 2

Dedication

In memory of
Martin Alexander Laval

With continued thanks to Charlotte Laval for her support in reading, editing and suggesting changes and just being there in more ways than anyone could hope for.

To Billy, William and Damien for their love, support and encouragement, as always.

Thank you to all our family and friends for their continued enthusiasm and interest and of course, the authors would like to thank You, the reader, for coming along with us on this journey.

It is with great sadness I write that my Dad and writing partner, DC Laval (Derek Clive), passed away in January 2016. The Carentan Series is his brainchild, and we have collaborated for many years on this project. We have had great fun writing these books and his memory will always live on in the characters and stories published here and in those yet to come. I hope you enjoy reading them as much as we enjoyed writing them. (FG Laval)

CHAPTER ONE

Tennengaul

Jehanna stifled a sob as Sardi entered the front room and shut the door. She was cleaning the window that looked out into the back yard as she had promised she would. Unfortunately, her eight-year-old arms could not quite reach the top panel. Had Sardi not been in the room, she might have climbed up on the ledge, as she often did. She had walked every ledge and rafter in that house with an agility that would make a spider envious, but climbing was forbidden in the house. He moved behind her and the bile rose in her throat, the hairs pricked up on her skin.

The others were in the village, shopping, so as far as she knew the cottage was empty. This thought made her more wary than ever of his encroaching presence. In the distance, she could see the blue ocean. She loved the water and the salty scent that hung in the air. A winding dirt track trailed its way down towards the village and she squinted into the distance, hoping that soon she would see the others amble into view. In vain, she reached up to the top panel pretending not to have noticed Sardi's presence.

"Here, let me help you," Sardi said, his words a little slurred. His big clumsy hands fumbled around her waist and he lifted her up so she could reach the highest pane. She gasped and could have kicked herself as Sardi chuckled, reading excitement into her reaction. He squeezed her a bit tighter, pinching the skin around her middle. Jehanna froze.

She had always been Sardi's favourite; he had constantly picked her up and doted on her like any new parent. Except, Sardi Mantar wasn't her real father. He had adopted her and her twin brother when they were just four years old. She and Jehan were different. Their skin colour was darker than that of the Mantars and of most of the villagers who had always treated them with a measure of suspicion. But the Mantars had happily taken them in and for that alone she knew she should be grateful.

As Sardi lowered her to the floor, he lingered a little too long, holding her just level with his face, his thick tree trunk arms circling her from behind. The stench of ale on his breath made her pinch her nostrils and take short shallow breaths through her mouth like a panting dog. He nuzzled his nose in her long dark curls, oblivious to the fact that her body was rigid with fear. He easily held her imprisoned in one huge arm, leaving the other hand free to slowly snake down her body, pulling with a sudden urgency at her clothes. Jehanna's fists clenched and unclenched as she tried to think what she could do to get out of this.

Jehan had once told her that if you punch or kick a man hard enough just below their belt, that they would fall to floor and not get up again for a long time. She could never reach him from that position and if she didn't hit hard enough, that might just make Sardi angry. A drunk Sardi, she could maybe deal with, but an angry drunk Sardi was too much. She could just poke him in the eye, then he might let her go. But again... one squeeze with his arms and he could crush her bones or throw her to the wall like a rag doll. She wanted to scream. Jehan would know what to do. Where was he?

There was a loud bark from the yard from Lobo the guard dog. Was it the others? Her heart fluttered. Sardi sighed and released her. The moment her feet hit the ground, she sped out of the room, leaving the door swinging on its hinges. She raced into the yard just as Jehan, Monie and the kids came around the corner laden with wares. Her brother stopped in his tracks. His eyes sharpened at the sight of her and Jehanna skidded to a halt at the same time, just a few yards away. They exchanged a glance. His eyes flickered to her fists which were clenched at her side and he nodded before striding off towards the cottage. Jehanna took in a deep breath and let it slowly out again. She was shaking, but tried not to let Monie and the kids see that. She smiled at last and took some bags from Monie, helping them into the yard.

***

It was early evening and the sun was setting, but there was enough light to be able to dig a large hole for Jehanna to plant some seedlings. Sardi was a fisherman, so he was up and out early in the morning and back by midday. The evening was usually spent in the local tavern, drinking away any profits from the day's catch. He always made sure that Monie had enough meat or fish to feed them all, but vegetables were expensive to buy from market, so one of Jehanna's many tasks was to tend to their vegetable garden.

By the time Jehan found her, she was digging so furiously that the hole had become too deep for the little bean plants she intended to transfer. She looked up at her brother, sighed and began to shovel some of the dirt back. Her face was a dirty grey colour where she had wiped her soil covered hands across her brow and her skirt was covered in round patches of dirt where she had used it to protect her knees as she tended to the garden. Jehan put a hand on her arm and prised the little shovel from her grip. She looked up at him at first in anger, until she registered the empathy in his eyes, then a lump formed in her throat and her bottom lip began to quiver.

"I can't do this anymore," she said. Fresh tears spilt from her eyes and left a watery track as they ran down her cheeks.

"Shhh," Jehan said. He took her into his arms and softly patted her back. "We'll be okay. He's at the tavern and Monie is with the children." Her chest shuddered as the tears began to subside.

"I'm scared, Jay. His hands are... horrible." Jehanna felt her brother tense. He released the embrace and held her at arm's length, looking into her eyes.

"I won't let him hurt you. We'll think of a way. What about Monie? Can she do something?" He said. Jehanna pulled a face.

"She won't do anything, she's scared too."

"I could kill him," Jehan said. For a moment Jehanna thought he was joking, then she saw the serious glint in his eye. "It would be easy, you know. He's always drunk. It would be like an accident, he could fall downstairs."

"We can't. What about Monie and the children? What would they do without Sardi?" she said. Jehan grunted. "I know you don't like Kherula and Lanni, but I don't want them to die too."

"And what about us?" Jehan said. Jehanna dropped her head. In her mind's eye, she could only see Sardi's drooling, grunting face and the smell of his mouldy, ale ridden breath. She wanted to vomit. "I can show you a few things for now, but we must get away soon." Jehan took her hand in his and turned over her palm. "Take hold of my hand...like this." Jehanna grinned and grabbed hold of Jay's hand. She was used to his little lessons in survival, but until now had not been able to try them out for real. "If he grabs your hand, all you have to do is press your knuckle down on the back of his hand just here..." He pressed down on her hand and Jehanna felt a sharp pain, like a needle stabbing her hand.

"Oww," she squealed and snatched back her hand. "That hurt."

"Isn't that the point?" Jehan said with a sigh. "The idea is to get him to let go, so that you can run."

"So that he can beat me, more like," she said.

"He won't beat you. Trust me. You just have to get him to let you go. You try." Jehan grabbed hold of her hand and she pressed down with her knuckle as he had shown her and nothing happened. He took her finger and moved it a fraction to the left, so that the knuckle sat just between two bones on the back of his hand. "Try there." She pushed and he withdrew his hand, grinning. "See. You can't help

11

but pull away - it sends shooting pains right up your arm."

"Where did you learn that?" Jehanna absently picked a doc leaf from her garden, split it in half giving one half to Jehan, then rubbed the remaining half over the sore spot on the back of her hand.

"Same way you learnt about the leaves," he said rubbing the broken end of the leaf into his hand. "Trying to find out how things work. Like Kherula. Yesterday, I was in the yard chopping wood, when he came hurtling up behind me with a large stick and whacked me over the head without any warning. Lucky he is only four, otherwise you would be bandaging my head and sticking on one of your yucky poultices." Jehan pulled a face and Jehanna batted his arm playfully.

"What did Sardi do?"

"Sardi just laughed. So I have to find ways to keep Kherula away from me so he doesn't get hurt or split my head open or something stupid."

Jehanna jumped to her feet. "Show me some more moves," she said. "What if he grabs me from behind?" Jay stood up, turned her around so that she was facing away from him, then wrapped his arms around her shoulders pinning both of her arms to her side. Jehanna laughed and wriggled, but couldn't free herself from his embrace, despite Jehan weighing far less than Sardi and having about a third of his strength. "Okay, so what now?"

"Can you reach behind you with one hand?" Jehan said pulling her tighter still. She could easily shift one hand behind her back. "Now take a large pinch of whatever you can grab hold of, best place is just inside the thigh, now squeeze and twist as

12

hard and as fast as you can. Jehanna didn't want to hurt her brother, but managed to take a fold of skin beneath his trousers between her fingers and twisted. Jehan let go with a squeal. "Good," he said rubbing the inside of his thigh. "And again." He grabbed hold of her from the front this time, so that she was looking over his shoulder. Just as he began to tighten his hold, Lobo, the guard dog came pounding into the garden and stopped dead in front of them. His ears were flat to his head and he was bearing his teeth in a low rumbling growl.

"Err... Jay? Hold very still. Don't do anything sudden," Jehanna said smiling at Lobo.

"It's that dog again, isn't it?" Jehan sighed but followed his sister's instructions.

"Slowly drop your arms away from me and take two steps back with your hands in the air," Jehanna said. Slowly, Jehan retreated, being followed all the time by Lobo who looked like he was about to leap onto him and rip his throat out. Once Jehanna was sure that Jay was no longer a threat in Lobo's eyes, she said, "Lobo, lie down." The dog did as he was told and Jehanna went over to ruffle his ears. Lobo whimpered softly and lost all interest in Jehan.

"I don't know how you do it," Jehan said. "That dog never does what I tell him to do." He sat down, defeated, in the middle of the vegetable patch.

The twins looked at each other and an understanding passed between them. They knew that they were going to have to leave Villan, sooner rather than later. They didn't want to abandon the place that had become their home, but they both

13

knew that sooner, rather than later, Sardi was going to hurt Jehanna.

That same night, while the household slept, the twins packed everything they owned into two small bags. Jehan stopped by the kitchen and signalled to Jehanna that he would follow on. They had agreed to steal what meagre provisions that could be spared, without leaving Monie and the kids with nothing.

Jehanna slipped into the yard. As she made her way to the stable, Lobo raised his sleepy head then pricked up his ears when he saw who it was. Jehanna made a shush sound, then went over to stroke his head. She wished she could take him with her but Lobo was too old to be going off on adventures. Besides, she already felt guilty that they were about to steal one of the pack ponies to ease their travel burden. Jehanna had been responsible for training their newest animal, Arion, who was not yet ready to accompany Sardi to port.

She slipped through the stable door. Their aging pack pony, Baku, lifted her head when she saw her coming in, but Arion was on his feet, neighing for attention. Jehanna reached into her pocket and pulled out two small apples. One she gave to Baku, with a kiss on her nose.

"I'm so sorry my love. I wish I could take you too, but Sardi needs someone to carry his fish. He will find someone new to keep you company." Baku chewed on the apple and remained lying in the hay silently accepting Jehanna's words. The other apple she used to coax Arion out of the stable with as little fuss as necessary. He seemed content just to be around Jehanna and didn't even complain when she

14

slid a bridle over his head. She slid easily onto his back, laying the bags in front of her, pannier style.

She waited for Jehan at the gate to the cottage. He was silent as he laid his bag across Arion's back alongside Jehanna's belongings. As he reached across the pony's back, Jehanna caught the glint of a blade nestling inside his jacket, the hilt within easy reach. An uneasy feeling settled in the back of her mind. Jehan had always said to her that a person should never pick up a weapon unless they intended to use it. She was also well aware that their journey could take them into unknown areas with unknown threats. She wasn't sure if it was unease at the thought of her brother wielding a weapon or at the realisation that there may be dangers ahead.

Jehan lead Arion out of the gate. There was a loud crack behind them, as the wind caught the gate and slammed it shut in the frame. Jehanna winced and looked at Jehan, but they carried on walking down the path. She held her breath, counted to ten and when nothing stirred in the darkness of the Mantar household, she let out her breath and her heart hammered in response.

"There's room up here for you too, Jay," she said. He shrugged. "We could move faster. Arion is stronger than he looks." Then they heard it. A loud, sharp bark. They stopped in their tracks and looked back towards the cottage. A light winked on. More barking. Then they heard shouting, doors banging and commotion in the stables peppered with intermittent barking. Jehanna's heart was racing. What would Sardi do if he caught them? Jehan was clearly thinking the same and he broke into a run, pulling Arion's bridle behind him. Arion was

15

stubborn at first, but Jehanna coaxed him into a trot and they sped down the path towards the coastal road. Before they disappeared out of view of the cottage, Jehanna looked over her shoulder and saw Lobo jump the gate, closely followed by Sardi. Lobo was fast for an old dog, but Sardi was too big and heavy for old Baku. He was waving a fist, digging his heels into the poor old pack pony and shouting.

"Thieves!" he said. "When I get my hands on you, I'll... you'll wish you were never born. Do you take me for a fool? Ungrateful little bastards. Thieves!"

"Get up here, Jay. Arion can easily outrun Baku, especially with Sardi on her back." Jehan didn't need any prompting as he leapt up behind Jehanna and Arion broke into a canter. But they weren't fast enough to outrun Lobo. The dog had run through the undergrowth to cut them off where the track went into the coastal road. If they had made it at least that far, they could have taken Arion into a gallop and put enough distance between them and Sardi that he would never have been able to catch them. But Lobo burst into view ahead and stood his ground, barking at them. They came to a standstill, Arion unable to move beyond the barking guard dog.

"Go away, Lobo," Jehanna said. "What are you doing here?" She jumped down from Arion and made shooing movements with her arms, but the dog stood his ground. He barked again, but it was a questioning bark and he hung his head to one side. "I can't take you with me. You have to stay and look after the cottage." But the dog was not taking no for an answer and carried on barking and pawing the ground in front of him. Arion was becoming restless and seemed to be trying to turn around. Then in the background they could hear Sardi's bellowing getting closer.

"Do something," Jehan said. He was reaching inside his jacket and Jehanna panicked. She picked up a small flat pebble and launched it at Lobo. It hit him on the head, not hard, but hard enough for the dog to feel it. Lobo stopped barking and hung his head, whining.

"Go away," she said. "You are not wanted here. Go and look after Sardi." Lobo whined again and let out another bark.

"Damn that dog. It's going to get us caught," Jehan said, pulling the kitchen knife out of his jacket and jumping down from Arion's back.

"No," Jehanna said. "Not Lobo. Go! Shoo, dog!" She picked up a handful of pebbles and launched them at Lobo. The dog turned around and ran off, back into the undergrowth. Jehanna jumped up onto Arion's back, closely followed by Jehan, then coaxed Arion into a trot, then a canter. Tears were streaming down her face. She hadn't wanted to hurt Lobo, but could see no other way. Even as they launched into a gallop for the coastal road, they could hear Sardi's swearing and shouting die away on the breeze. That was the last they ever saw of Villan or the Mantars.

CHAPTER TWO

The town of Lendholm lay halfway between Sternhelm and the capital of Tennengaul, Dern. The twins arrived there only five days after leaving their home. The road out of Villan was a rocky slope to begin with and Arion had lost his footing several times, terrifying Jehanna who nearly landed beneath his flailing hooves. As they had moved further inland, the terrain became gentler, with rolling plains and grassland meadows.

Mostly, they slept beneath the stars and only once had to make a quick escape from what looked like a band of robbers or barbarians. They hid in a nearby ditch until the threat had passed. Jehanna saw two young girls in the back of the wagon with hair like rat-tails and grubby faces pressed miserably against the wooden bars. Nausea stirred in the pit of her stomach and she reached instinctively for the comfort of Jay's hand. Jehan shifted his arm and when she turned to look at him, the hairs on the back of her neck prickled; the kitchen knife was in his hand and he had a furtive look on his face. He shook his head when he saw her looking at him and nodded in the direction of the departing wagon.

"I would rather use this than see you taken away in one of those," he whispered. She shuddered and held her breath until sure that all the bad men had really gone. She let out her breath slowly and they both sat in the ditch immobile until the sun went down and they were certain they would not be seen. They returned to the meadow where Arion was still gorging himself on grass. She ran to the pony and threw her arms around him, planting kisses on his nose.

The meagre amount of food they had stolen from Monie's kitchen had lasted only a day, so they used a combination of begging and bartering to maintain enough supplies to get them as far as Lendholm. People in the smaller villages judged them by appearance, so their dark skin and ragged clothes lead most to assume that they were stowaways from Sternhelm. The Gaullians were generous by nature and took pity on the twins, giving them their leftover bread and pickles. The larger towns were more difficult to penetrate, so they had to be more creative about how to get food. Jehanna picked wild flowers and herbs along the way; chamomile and lavender, which local healers would buy from her for the price of a meal. Jehan offered his services cutting wood or pulling carts with Arion to give them enough supplies to move on, in search of somewhere to stay.

Lendholm was a prosperous and bustling town and most people took little notice of the twins as they ambled into the town square and sat on a bench beneath a large oak tree. It was midday and the market was in full swing with traders shouting their wares and buyers haggling for discounts. A rugged looking man with hands as big as plates, sidled up to Arion and started stroking his back and feeling his rump. Jehanna stood up and took hold of Arion's bridle for fear that he would try to make off with the pony. But he just smirked at her and shook his head.

"I'll give you twenty crowns, though it's not worth more than fifteen, the way you've run it ragged."

"Arion is not for sale," Jehanna said. The man just shrugged and walked off.

A group of boys, a little older than the twins, appeared from the other side of the tree. They stood in a semi-circle, staring at them. Jay rose up and stood between Jehanna and the group. She could see his fist clenching beside him. But the boys just continued to stare. Eventually, one of them stepped forward. He was about twelve years old, with rusty coloured hair and a pale complexion. His face twisted into a grimace as he spat on the ground in front of Jehan.

"Go home, darkies."

Jehanna's heart began to beat faster and she too started to clench her fists. Her cheeks burned. People had known that they were different in Villan and they had been accepted. No one had ever called them that before. It wasn't so much the word, but the venom with which it was said that hurt the most.

"We are home," Jehan said.

"Go back to your own country," the boy said. He stepped up to Jehan and pointed a finger to emphasise his words, making a stabbing gesture with his index finger on Jehan's chest. Jehan looked down at the finger, then up at the boy who appeared to be enjoying his position of power. All the time, Jehanna was thinking that they would go home if they only knew where home was. It happened so quickly, that she could have blinked and missed it. Within seconds, Jehan had gripped the finger in his fist and twisted it back, causing the boy to shriek and drop to the ground to nurse his injured hand. The rest of the boys rushed forward, and Jehan's hand delved inside his jacket to retrieve the knife.

"What's all this nonsense?" A rough voice cut across the melee and the boys dispersed almost as quickly as they had appeared. There was an old ragged looking man standing in front of Jehan with his back to them, hissing at the group until the last of them had scattered across the square. He turned to look at the twins and Jehanna was intrigued to see that he was not that old after all. His hair was dark and matted to his skull, as though he had not bathed in a decade. His face was grubby, but fairly youthful underneath all the hair. His beard was tangled and spotted with bits of straw and stray crumbs. Jehan had not moved a muscle. He still had his arm crossed over his chest and his hand inside his jacket, but the knife remained hidden to view.

"I wouldn't do that if I were you," the man said in a thick Gaullian accent. Jehanna held her breath while her brother appeared to weigh up the situation before slowly taking his empty hand out of his pocket and showing it to the man. The man looked at Jehan's hand in front of him, wiped his own down his trousers, then held it out to shake. Jehan looked at the man's hand and glanced back at Jehanna, who pushed past her brother and curtsied in front of the man. The man nodded his head in return.

"I'm Jehanna," she said. "And this is my brother, Jehan. Thank you."

"Yes, well..." The man looked back and forth from one to the other. "You nearly did a very foolish thing, Jehan." Jehan shrugged and went back

21

to minding his own business on the bench. "I'm Lugus. You know... after the ancient god of life. Only most people around here see me more as a parasite. I think my mother was misguided when she named me."

"Well, you just saved a life," Jehanna said.

"Not ours, though," Jehan muttered under his breath. Lugus glanced at him and frowned. He looked as though he wanted to say something but kept quiet.

"Why are you so dirty?" Jehanna looked Lugus up and down, thinking he looked more like a street urchin than a god. Lugus smiled, revealing a row of broken and blackened teeth.

"You're not exactly the picture of cleanliness yourself," he said. For the first time since they had left Villan, Jehanna thought about her appearance. They had been so intent on getting far enough away from Villan to make a new start, that she had not had time to think about bathing or finding clean clothes to wear. Her skirts were grubby and starting to fray at the edges and she dared not guess what her face looked like. She hoped she didn't look quite as bad as Lugus.

"I do a lot of gardening," she said, wiping her hands down her skirt.

"Come on," Jehan said standing up and pushing Jehanna forward. She grabbed Arion's bridle and the pony fell into a slow walk beside them.

"Goodbye Mr Lugus," she said looking over her shoulder at him. He smiled through his crooked black teeth and gave a jovial wave. "I wonder why the boys were all so scared of him?" she said as they made their way across the square.

22

"He's just a beggar, Jehanna. Don't even think about it."

"Think about what? I was just saying..." She looked over her shoulder again as they made their distance and saw Lugus walk off through the crowd in the opposite direction. It seemed to her that people consciously stepped out of his way as he ambled about with little direction or purpose. "You could have got into trouble, Jay. And we've only just got here."

They stopped outside a large wooden door with a plaque marked with the words 'Apothecary'. "What have you got in your herbs bag that might buy us a meal and a hot bath?" Jehanna took the herb bag from Arion's backpack and peered inside, not holding out too much hope as she had sold most of the popular flowers with serious healing properties.

"There's this," she said, pulling out a small unremarkable shrub with bright red berries.

"What is it?" Jehan peered at the plant.

"Wolfberry," said a gravelly female voice behind them. Jehan swung around and a tall slim woman with bright red hair piled up on top of her head and pale white skin looked down on the pair of them. Jehanna jumped. "Where did you find it? And why did you pick it?"

"Who are you?" Jehanna said, suddenly aware of their vulnerability as outsiders. The woman smiled, clearly enjoying the advantage. She pointed at the plaque on the door that read 'Apothecary'.

"Herb mistress, healer, some prefer apothecary, but whichever way you look at it, I deal in products made from plants such as these." She carefully took the shrub from Jehanna's hands and inspected it. "I'm interested to know where you found this and whether you can help supply me with more. Clearly, you have some knowledge of plants. Otherwise you might have let this one stay attached to its bush. I see you have travelled far. Perhaps I can offer you somewhere to rest before we discuss a price for this rare specimen." Jehanna and Jehan looked at each other, slightly bewildered, though in mute agreement that they could do worse than accept some kindness from the village apothecary, however strange looking.

The woman introduced herself as Cassiel. She put the stable boy in charge of Arion, then ushered the twins into her roomy parlour, which had a connecting door to the shop overlooking the square. She left the door open to keep an eye on the shop.

"Wolfberry," she said, getting straight down to business. "Sometimes known as Lycium. A single berry can produce a tonic that can prolong the life of an elderly patient for over a decade. We have an aging population in Tennengaul, largely due to marauders from the North coming and taking away our children for slaves during the middle of the last century causing a generation gap. Credit to the Prince, he has successfully stamped out the worst of it, although I understand it is still wise not to travel alone these days, particularly at your age." She fixed Jehanna with a stern look, then shook her head. Jehanna thought of the wagon they had seen carrying off young girls and shivered.

"Lycium can be made into a blood tonic. Helps direct the flow of blood around the body and can relieve the symptoms of the wasting disease,"

24

Jehanna said. Cassiel raised her eyebrows. Jehan nodded and smiled to himself. "Also can help to improve eyesight and reduce fever in babies."

"Whose herbal have you been devouring for breakfast?" Cassiel went to her bookcase and pulled down a large tome with the title 'Herbal Lore', written by Airmid Junos, a well-known traditionalist named after the Gaullian goddess of healing and medicine.

"No one's," Jehanna said, calmly pulling out her own battered notebook from her baggage. "I'm writing my own. It's just an interest, really."

"I see," Cassiel said, standing with the book in her hand and staring at Jehanna in a strange sort of way, as though she had just performed some kind of parlour trick.

"Although I've never heard it called Wolfberry before," Jehanna said flipping open her book and making an entry with her short fat pencil rod.

"My, my," Cassiel said still standing with the book in her hand. "All of what, eight or nine, and writing already. You look like a pair of stowaways from the eastern lands that have just pitched up at Sternhelm and have been living rough for goodness knows how long. Who taught you to read and write?" Jehanna thought about Sardi and after suppressing her initial disgust at the thought of her adopted father ever teaching her anything, she reflected on life before Villan.

"I don't know," she said. "I don't remember."

Cassiel finally put the book down and returned to her seat. She sat for a while, every so often looking at the open door when she heard someone walk past the shop front. She picked up the branch of Wolfberry and inspected it, turning it over and over, silently appraising the twins. Eventually, she seemed to reach a decision.

"Well," she said turning to Jehan. "And what hidden talents do you have, young man?" Jehan shrugged, but Jehanna was quick to intervene.

"He is much stronger for his age than he looks and can easily chop wood, build things and with Arion, he can pull carts. If you want anything doing around the house, I can cook and clean and look after the shop for you while you make tonics. I even know how to make a poultice." Jehanna's words tumbled out and she instantly regretted sounding so desperate.

"Can your brother not speak for himself?" Cassiel said, her eyes remaining fixed on Jehan. Jehan just looked at the floor, drawing patterns in the dust with his feet. Cassiel sighed. "There is a loft in the stables where you can stay. Jehan can help with the horses and any work around the house. You, my dear, can be my assistant and help out in the shop. But before you do anything, you can both get yourselves washed up out back. The housekeeper will show you where." Cassiel stood up and took the branch of Wolfberry with her. Just as she reached the connecting door into the shop, she turned and addressed Jehan. "And you can stay away from that vagrant, Lugus," she said pointing the shrub at him. "Take my word for it, he is nothing but trouble." She turned and strode into the shop. The twins looked at each other. Jehanna shrugged. A smile tugged lazily at the corners of Jehan's mouth.

CHAPTER THREE

The housekeeper was a maternal sort of woman, named Maelsa, who fussed around the twins like they were her long-lost children. Her own children had long since grown up and left the comfort of the family nest to make their own way in the world and she seemed only too happy to have someone new to cook and care for.

They had to work for their keep, but it was nothing compared to the gruelling hours they had put in for Sardi and Monie. For the first time in her short life, Jehanna had some guidance from a professional herb mistress and had soon filled her notebook and was begging Cassiel to provide a new one. She often went on outings to gather herbs and the rare Wolfberry branches she had discovered on her journey to Lendholm. She never went alone and always took Jehan and Arion with her for protection, although Cassiel had protested when she had refused additional backup from the local smithy, which was run by her cousin.

As weeks turned into months, the twins were rewarded for their hard work by being given a room of their own and Jehan had kept himself far enough away from trouble to gain some trust from Cassiel and an introduction to her cousin at the smithy. The biggest commission for swords came from the local garrison at Castle Lendholm. The only downside to working at the smithy came in the form of one young man named, Kenric, one of the children of Cassiel's cousin, who took an instant dislike to Jehan. Kenric also worked there as an apprentice and looked tipped to be one of the future owners, so

Jehan kept his misapprehensions to himself and got on with the work.

It was only when he was working the bellows for Kenric one day, when he noticed that the index finger on his right hand looked slightly bent. It did not take him long after that to work out where he had seen that rusty coloured hair and pale skin, which had turned more of a mousy grey over time. The sneer on his face, unfortunately, had not improved since their first altercation in the village square, that first day the twin had ambled into the town.

The local boys mostly kept their distance from Jehan as he spent much of his spare time with Lugus. But as soon as the twins were on their own, the jibes began, often lead by Kenric and his cronies. Things like, 'Go home darkies,' and 'What do you call a mud slide on the bank of the river Stenn? Full of eastern promise.' It was hurtful, particularly for Jehanna who was more sensitive to such verbal abuse, but nevertheless harmless. They learnt to ignore it and the boys didn't come close enough to be of any physical threat. As long as it remained that way, the knife that Jehan carried with him at all times remained tucked away from sight. No longer a mere kitchen knife, he had been rewarded for his work at the smithy with a real hunting knife, which merely served to deepen Jehanna's concern, particularly the more she heard about Kenric's attempts to subvert Jehan's reputation in the eyes of Cassiel's cousins.

Jehan had promised to stay away from Lugus, but Jehanna was not surprised to see the two of them together on occasions when Cassiel was out on private visits. He insisted that Cassiel had the wrong impression of Lugus and that Jehanna should hear his story, but she felt a growing sense of loyalty towards Cassiel and didn't want to destroy that.

"Lugus teaches me things," Jehan said. It was late at night, the house was quiet and the twins were chattering quietly in their room. The only other sounds were that of Arion and the horses snickering to themselves in the stables outside their window.

"But Cassiel says he is a bad man. While we are staying at her house, you must do as she says. What happens if she finds out and we are back out on the street?"

"Shhh... that won't happen. Look, it is personal with Lugus. He is not a bad man, but Cassiel was once betrothed to marry him and he let her down. She has never forgiven him. He used to work for Count Lenden at Castle Lendholm. That is where he learnt his fighting skills, in the military guard. Unfortunately, Count Lenden is Cassiel's uncle. So when Lugus did wrong, he was thrown out of the guard."

"Oh." Jehanna had a picture in her mind of a clean-shaven Lugus with a bright future ahead of him thrown into despair and regret, outcast from his future wife's family. "But why did he stay here? Surely he could find work somewhere else, instead of living the life of a street thief."

"Oh Jehanna. Surely you of all people can't be so blind." She stared at Jehan, and then it hit her straight between the eyes.

"He still loves her..." Now she felt Lugus's pain. Abandonment was something with which both the twins could empathise. "He must have done a very bad thing."

"He did," Jehan said. "And there is no excusing it, but he was misled. Deliberately misled by a jealous woman who wanted him for herself."

"Oh, my. That is terrible." Jehanna had heard about women like that, who tempted men away from their loved ones for money or sometimes status. Sometimes, powerful men even kept such women around to use as leverage when a young man overstepped his mark. That kind of thing didn't happen in the eastern lands, where she had heard that men were allowed to have more than one wife. She wondered absently how many wives their true father had. The only memories they had before Villan was of a great many people looking after them and caring for their needs. Perhaps they had many different mothers. The thought seemed odd to her, though it explained why they could not remember their parents. She shook the memory away, like shedding a second skin. It left an aching hole in her heart. "What things does Lugus teach you?" she said.

"Look," Jehan said, springing to his feet. "Lugus says that before you can learn how to use a knife and a sword, you must first learn to fight empty-handed. He has taught me this routine, called 'Chinto', which means 'fighter to the east'." He cleared a space in the room and took up a stance in the middle of the floor. For moment, he stood stock-still and Jehanna held her breath waiting for him to do something. When he finally moved, it was as if the energy flowed through his body and he moved like he owned the space around him. His gaze was focused ahead and unwavering in concentration. His hands exploded from his hip, first crossing over, fists clenched, then twisting and releasing as though he was holding some invisible stick. His feet moved in an arc across the floor, bending at the knee, then straightening, turning at different angles to change direction. His movements alternated from smooth and elegant to sharp and fast, hands and feet striking out in a combination of blocking and punching moves. Jehanna could almost visualise her brother surrounded by the village boys, dispatching each, one by one in an intricate dance to the death. She was stunned.

When finally, Jehan stopped, he completed his routine with a deep bow from the waist. His eyes then refocused on Jehanna as he came out of his trance and the spell was broken.

"That was... incredible." She stared at her brother, seeing for the first time how he had grown in stature and how his muscles were gaining definition. "So that is what you have been doing all those hours when Cassiel is away."

"Lugus says it is an ancient art form, invented by the gods and handed down to the priests through the ages, who used to practise the moves in order to protect their temples from thieves and bandits. The movements were so elegant and flowing that they could disguise it as a dance. So it became known as a ritual dance for the gods. The practice has died out in all but a few of the temples in Tennengaul and most to the south, largely due to the popularity of the Church of the One God."

"Come," he beckoned to her. "Let me show you some moves." Jehanna jumped up, suddenly wide-awake. They walked through the first few steps of the routine, Jehanna giggling whenever she got a move wrong. It took a long time before they exhausted themselves enough to rest, but she felt good about herself. It was like a dance, but a dance with spiritual power. As they lay back on their beds, Jehanna thought about Lugus and Cassiel, feeling a strange tug of emotion pulling from both directions. She leaned over and nudged Jehan.

"As long as you keep your meetings with Lugus discreet, I'll cover your back," she whispered. "Provided you promise to show me some more of your routines." She felt Jehan turn towards her and scoff teasingly.

"Sister, I have only just got started. I have yet to show you what all of those moves mean." Jehanna smiled to herself. For the first time in her life, she felt that they truly had the gods on their side.

CHAPTER FOUR

The practice of fighting routines and the accompanying applications became a regular late-night ritual for Jehanna. The more Jehan learnt from Lugus, the more he passed on to Jehanna and they used each other as fight dummies to perfect their technique. They practised barefoot on the stone floor of their room, being stealthy to avoid waking Cassiel.

Jehan launched a vicious attack with a short, pointed stick, fashioned to imitate a knife. Jehanna sidestepped, blocking his knife hand with a sharp downward strike. She could see that her attack had struck home, but Jehan covered it well and stubbornly held onto the makeshift knife. He was about to counter strike when she gripped his wrist, twisted his arm in an arc over his shoulder, which forced his body to the floor. His body went limp and she knew that if he resisted, it would hurt him and potentially break his arm. She had him now. Jehanna always preferred to finish her opponents quickly, unlike Jehan who liked nothing better than to play around. If people could be likened to animals, then Jehan would be a cat. A sleek black panther, playfully smug and dangerously underestimated; you would not know until he pounced that you had crossed an invisible line.

She swung her leg up high and brought her heel down fast and sharp, stopping a hair's breadth from the bridge of his nose. She released her hold on him and batted his nose with her toes. Jehan rolled over onto his back and laughed.

"Very good, little sis," he said. He lay on the floor, one ankle crossed over the other, hands behind his head. "Soon, I might even be able to let you out on your own."

"Funny, Jay," she said digging him teasingly with her foot. She dropped down to the floor and crossed her legs.

They had learnt several routines and Jehan had more than proven his competence at using the empty-handed techniques before Lugus introduced weapons. The beauty of the system was that they didn't have to learn new techniques to accommodate knives, swords and sticks; it was all there in the routines, hidden amongst the intricate moves which through practice had become second nature to the twins.

"I told Lugus that you were learning to fight."

"What? Why?" Jehanna said.

"I thought he should know what I am doing with this knowledge. But it didn't go down too well. He says that women should not be fighters."

"Pah. What nonsense. What did the high priestesses do when barbarians came to ransack the temples all those years ago? Sit back and let them befoul the worship of their deities? I don't think so. There are plenty of stories told about female warriors in the eastern lands." Jehan was nodding and looking thoughtful. "It is not like I want to be a warrior or anything. I just want to be able to look after myself. One day, you might not be there for me, Jay."

"I will always be there for you, sis. But one day you might marry your own warrior who will take care of you and you won't need me anymore."

"I will always need you. Besides, I'm not going to marry." Jehan looked at his sister and frowned.

"You are the most beautiful young woman in the whole of Tennengaul. How can you say that?" he said. Jehanna felt her cheeks flush.

"I think that's a bit of an exaggeration," she said.

"Give me a girl with your dark, soulful looks and abundance of curls any day compared to the thin, pale Gaullians. The girls around here look like they have washed in pail of milk every morning." Jehanna laughed and tossed the wave of long dark curls over her shoulder. She was well aware that she looked different to the local girls and also well aware of the eyes that followed her around the village every time she stepped out of Cassiel's shop.

"I don't like the way Kenric and those boys look at me," she said. Jehan sat up and looked at her. She had seen that look of his before, years ago when she had first told her brother about Sardi's unwanted attentions and he had offered to kill him for her. "It's probably nothing," she said. "I'm not a little girl any more. I guess that sort of thing is normal, I just don't like it. Is there something wrong with me? Cassiel tries to talk to me about boys, but I don't want them to look at me like that. It reminds me of Sardi." She shuddered.

"I don't want you going out alone, Jehanna." He was scaring her with his serious tone. "Kenric is not like any normal boy. He has a vendetta against us. He tries everything he can to get me into trouble at the smithy. Yesterday, he let one of the fires practically die out before telling his father that I had been taking a nap at the bellows. It took me the best

35

part of the day to get it back up and running. I nearly got a thrashing for the money we could have lost; we have a big consignment from the garrison."

"Why don't you tell his father what he is doing? If you don't, I'll tell Cassiel. It's not fair." Jehanna tried to stand up, but Jehan grabbed her arm and pulled her back down.

"Shh. A lot of good that will do at this time of night. Besides, they all know. They turn a blind eye, because no one wants to believe that Kenric, who is tipped to take over the smithy when his father dies, is a good-for-nothing bully who will only ever amount to anything through inheritance. Things are never going to be easy for us. We are different. We've been lucky so far, with your healing skills, finding a home here and my apprenticeship to the smithy. But I don't intend to be satisfied with the life of a blacksmith. I have plans. Whatever we do, we will have to make our own way in the world. That much was determined the moment we found ourselves alone in a strange new world."

"Cassiel says that the eastern lands used to have a practice of kidnapping children from noble families and dumping them off the shores of foreign lands. It used to be a way of disposing of rival heirs without having to kill them." Jehan was shaking his head and smiling. He was always so firmly grounded in the here and now, it sometimes irritated Jehanna, who liked to indulge in fantasies of far off lands. "Do you think we are from a noble family?" she said. Jehan gripped his sister's arms just above her elbows and looked her in the eye.

"Of course we are. Wherever we came from and whoever we are, don't ever think we are anything less." Jehanna nodded, relieved that Jehan shared her most profound belief. They settled down to sleep, exhausted from the day's work and the night-time's training.

"Just keep away from Kenric," said Jehan lazily in the dark. There was a quiet 'hmmph' from Jehanna's side of the room, then silence as they drifted to sleep.

CHAPTER FIVE

Jehanna was in the shop preparing a tonic for one of their regulars when Cassiel came bustling in from the square.

"Look sharp, girl. It is the magistrate's wife, Mistress Altard. I saw her limping across the square. No doubt it is her knee again. Ah, Mistress," Cassiel said curtseying as the door opened to reveal a middle-aged woman with a rounded back and a pinched expression on her face. The years had not been kind to her body. Jehanna noted how she hunched over a thick walking stick. Her hair had begun to grey, though she looked not far from thirty years old.

"It's my knee," Mistress Altard said, looking at Cassiel. Jehanna began to prepare a poultice, clinking glass jars and opening cupboards. Mistress Altard glanced at her and frowned.

"Of course, Mistress. We shall have something prepared for you in no time. Please, take a seat here." Cassiel helped the woman to her seat, then turned to Jehanna, about to issue instructions for the preparation, when Mistress Altard interrupted.

"Not her," she said. Jehanna stopped, a glass jar in one hand and a wooden spoon in the other. "I don't want her to touch a thing. You, Mistress. You are to do it." Cassiel stood with her mouth open, about to say something, then thought better of it. She clamped her mouth shut, then took the preparation materials from Jehanna. "Make it a new one, make it a new one," said Mistress Altard. "Can't stand these foreigners, interfering where they are not wanted. That one in the square, always playing around with knives, he is. Will cause an accident one day, mark my words. Shoo girl." Jehanna flinched at her words and backed out of the shop into the waiting room.

"Now then Mistress Altard." She heard Cassiel address the woman. "Let us see what we can do for you."

She closed the door behind her. She had got used to the escalating abuse from the young people in the village, but somehow coming from an adult it felt different. If there was one thing that she had counted on it was the rationality of adults to see beyond the colour of her skin. She realised now that this was not a certainty she could consistently rely on. Perhaps that was why everyone seemed to turn a blind eye to the shenanigans of Kenric and his friends; they were merely acting on a feeling that everyone else, excepting Mistress Altard of course, dare not express in public. It was a blow to her confidence and she suddenly felt the need to talk to Jehan.

She left the shop from the back to avoid further confrontation with the magistrate's wife and hurried across the square to the blacksmiths. The air was heavy with heat from the fires and the scent of burning steel lingered on the breeze. As she got closer, the sound of metal clashing with metal rang out and there were men jostling to and fro as the business of the day stood still for no one.

Jehanna's heart leapt, as a tall young man stepped in front of her, barring her from entering the premises. After a moment's hesitation, she recognised Kenric's sneering smile as he stood with his arms across the doorway.

"May I speak with Jehan?" she said, making an effort to be polite.

"He's busy," he said, a glimmer of mischief in his eye. Jehanna hesitated, wondering how far she could push the young man, then decided it wasn't worth the effort.

"I see," she said, refusing to be drawn into a battle of wits. "Perhaps you could tell him I was here." She turned to go.

"What's it worth?" Kenric was smiling when she turned and looked over her shoulder. It was early, there were few people out and about in the square at that time of day, but still, what could he possibly do to her in such a public place? She turned back to him and planted her hands on her hips.

"Perhaps I shan't tell your father what a rude young man you are," she said. He leapt forward, closing the distance between them. She backed away but he stalked her, shadowing her every step.

"That's not quite what I had in mind," he said, then grabbed her. Before she had time to react he planted his lips on hers and was roughly feeling her body up and down. Her mind went suddenly blank. She knew all those defence moves, twists, locks, throws and holds, but when she needed it most, her knowledge deserted her. The bile rose to her throat. Kenric smelt of the coal fire forge and a man's sweat. She fought back a tide of panic before lifting her foot and stamping down hard on his toes. He squealed and released his hold long enough for her to scramble out of his embrace and run away.

It had probably been the shock more than the pain that had made him let go. Shock that a girl like her had fought back against him. She doubted that his foot had sustained any injury through the boots he was wearing; she had likely hurt her own foot more. When she looked back across the square, he appeared to have forgotten all about his toes and was waving his fist at her and pointing his finger as to say, 'I'm going to get you for that'.

Oh, gods. She had just made things doubly worse, as if it couldn't get any worse, what with the incident with the magistrate's wife. A few people glanced at her as she fled the square, probably thinking that she was responsible for disturbing their peace.

Back at the Apothecary, the shop was empty and she found Cassiel in the back, classifying the recent collection of herbs that Jehanna had brought in. Since the arrival of the twins, the supplies to the Apothecary had more than doubled and they had devised a system of notation to put each ingredient into storage with those belonging to the same family of plants. Every plant was put in the book – twice in Jehanna's case, as she kept her own herbal in addition to that of the Apothecary – then classified according to family before being bagged, bottled or hung out to dry depending on its required use. Each time Jehanna went out to forage for supplies, she kept a little sample of everything for her own. Cassiel was aware of this and appeared not to mind, since they now had such an abundance of supplies that it made no difference to the business of the Apothecary.

"Good gods, girl. You look like you've just had a tussle with a mountain tiger," Cassiel said as she noticed Jehanna's dishevelled hair and clothing.

Would that it were a mountain tiger, Jehanna thought. She probably stood a better chance of reasoning with a tiger's instinct than with the animal in Kenric. She smoothed down her dress and hair, then began helping Cassiel to bag the dried lavender flowers, taking a deep calming breath from the scent. Cassiel didn't push her further and Jehanna didn't volunteer any more information. They worked together in silence for the best part of the day, stopping only to see to the odd customer. No real serious cases; an elderly customer requiring a dose of Cassiel's 'miracle' tonic, various enquiries about coughing remedies. Later, a young child with his concerned mother came looking for a suitable poultice for a leg graze that had started to show signs of infection. It wasn't until the sun had started to go down and the light began to wane that they finally called a halt to their work and packed up the shop.

Cassiel was about to turn the locks on the front door when it burst open and Jehan came striding in. He ran to Jehanna and grabbed her by the shoulders looking her up and down.

"Are you all right? Did he hurt you?" He was tense and agitated. "Right. I'm going to kill him." Jehan turned and drew his hunting knife, making for the door but Cassiel was in front of him before he could get out. She kicked the door shut and stood with her arms folded across her chest.

"Well?" She said. Are you going to tell me what the devil is going on, or are you going to have to kill me to get past?" Cassiel said.

"Cassiel, don't make me do anything I might regret," Jehan said. The anger steamed from his body like a second skin and Jehanna's own heart beat faster in response.

"Jehan. Don't," she said.

"Just tell me why I shouldn't finish it here and now? They will never touch you again, I promise you that," Jehan said.

"And you will spend the rest of your days rotting away in a dungeon. Then you will no longer be able to protect me. And you certainly won't be able to protect me when I need it most. Which is not today. Look at me Jehan." He turned away from Cassiel and looked to Jehanna. She reached her hands out to Jehan, willing her composure onto her brother. "See? I am fine. I am not damaged or upset in any way. I used my judgement and my skill to get away from him. Just like you taught me." She didn't dare to admit that most of her fighting skill had deserted her in her moment of need. She saw Jehan's shoulders drop. Then his knife hand relaxed a little. After a moment's thought, he put the knife away and turned to address Cassiel who was still standing stubbornly by the door.

"I'm sorry, Cassiel. Kenric has been taunting me all day. I was starting to go mad with worry about what he had done to Jehanna."

"Well," Cassiel said, relaxing her arms. "As you can see, she is fine and you have fallen foul of a cruel jibe, exacted precisely to induce such a reaction from you." When Jehan turned to look at his sister, Cassiel shot a questioning look in her direction. "You have survived well enough over the years to keep out of trouble, despite going against my wishes and keeping in touch with Lugus." The twins looked at each other, caught off guard as they

43

realised that Cassiel had not been taken for a fool. "Don't look at me like that, do you think I don't hear you practising your fighting late at night? My disappointment was only tempered by the fact that I began to understand what a calming effect the training was having on you both. Well. Perhaps it has come to this now. I feared it could not last forever in this town, knowing how insular the locals are. Despite having family here, I was always treated like an outsider. That is, until they learned that my skill with healing would benefit their community. Lugus has not been so favoured, though not without reason, in my mind." Cassiel's voice was laced with a bitterness that stirred Jehanna's heart. "Perhaps it is time that you both moved on."

They stood in silence, lost for words. Jehanna had not really thought further than Lendholm. She knew that Jehan had 'plans' but as far as she knew his plans had not gone further than honing his fighting skills and learning the trade of a blacksmith. Cassiel broke the silence. "Maelsa is preparing supper. We shall sit and eat and discuss what we need to do next."

Cassiel had some connections with the staff at the garrison in Castle Lendholm, she explained over supper, and through her cousin she had on occasion been commissioned to provide some liniments for injuries sustained by the troops.

"The best I can do is to send word to my contacts and hope that they can find you some work. They always need new blood for the military guard," she said looking at Jehan. He dropped his eyes to his plate and Jehanna suspected that his plans had not included joining the military. "And, you my girl. You have a gift with healing. And not just people. Their greatest need is to keep the horses healthy and happy. Failing that, there is a big household at the castle and they are always in need of serving staff. I will put the word out and hope that your names will be put before the district suzerain, Count Lenden. He is my Uncle and a very fair and just man."

They ate in silence. Somehow the discussion about what to do next had been more like a decision that Cassiel was delivering to them already signed and sealed. Jehanna wondered how long Cassiel had been planning this. She chewed on the meat stew, hardly tasting the flavours that she knew Maelsa had taken great pains to create. What if they didn't want to go to Castle Lendholm? What if when they got there, it was just more of the same abuse they had encountered in the village? She knew that Jehan was running the same questions through his mind and underneath the table they linked hands in solidarity. She also knew that Jehan would be considering the opportunity that the military might present to him. Not only to practice his fighting skills and use of weapons but also as a means to progress. He was highly ambitious and would almost certainly be planning in his mind where this new turn of events might take him. And what of her? Could she be happy as a servant in the castle?

"Good then," Cassiel said, breaking their thoughts. The twins both looked up at her. "That is decided. I will send word first thing in the morning." She had assumed that their silence meant acquiescence and neither of them made any move to suggest otherwise. It was, apparently, decided.

CHAPTER SIX

Two days later, Count Lenden himself paid a visit to the Apothecary. He was a tall, fair haired man with sky blue eyes and a kindly smile that made the corners of his mouth and around his eyes wrinkle slightly. His strong personal presence when he walked into the shop made Jehanna lower her eyes.

"Count Lenden, my Lord Uncle. Please, may I introduce you to my ward, Jehanna Mantar." Cassiel glared at Jehanna and she duly curtsied, unaccustomed to being in the company of western nobility. The Count just smiled and used his fingertips to gently lift her chin so that she had no option but to look at him.

"My. You are a beautiful young woman, Mistress Mantar. No wonder you have caused a stir in our little town." Jehanna wondered how much he knew of what had been going on and where she and Jehan had come from. She felt no fear of recrimination from this man; his aura felt good and clean.

"Where I come from, my Lord, I am a woman of noble birth." A look of surprise flickered across the Count's face before he settled on amusement. Behind her she could feel the angst rising in waves from Cassiel, who couldn't resist making a 'tsk' noise in disapproval. It did not evade the notice of the Count, either.

"Mistress Cassiel, do not worry yourself so. Indeed, then I shall call you Lady Mantar." She wasn't quite sure if he was just humouring her, but felt that perhaps it was one small battle won. Jehan would have been proud of her. "And what of the boy?" The Count said.

"My Lord, I have sent word to the smithy," Cassiel said.

"No problem, I shall go there myself," he said still looking at Jehanna. "And I shall be seeing you in two days' time. That should give you and your brother enough time to say your goodbyes and pack up your things." He turned and left the Apothecary. Cassiel stood for a moment looking at Jehanna with her hands on her hips.

"Good gods, girl, are you out of your mind? The Count is offering you a lifeline; don't squander this opportunity with your fancy nonsense," she said.

"He is a good man," Jehanna said ignoring Cassiel's flapping about. "But I'm not so sure it is a good idea that he goes over to the smithy right now."

"Perhaps the Count will understand our need for haste when he sees how they treat your poor brother," Cassiel said. "The gods only know how he has put up with it for so long."

As it happened, the Count's visit went ahead with very little adverse behaviour from Kenric or the others. In fact, Kenric had been only too pleased to put in a glowing report for Jehan. It was only his obsequious behaviour towards the Count that made for a rather nauseating performance. Jehan later described how Count Lenden had tried to ignore Kenric on number occasions to talk directly to Jehan, only to be interrupted by a barrage of questions relating to Kenric's own affairs. The Count, apparently, had been irritated but polite and

47

had eventually left, telling Jehan that he would be expected to report to the garrison in two days' time.

Kenric and his cronies came for Jehanna early the next morning. They had been waiting in hiding for her to return from exercising Arion. It was before she was due to open the shop, Jehan had already left for the smithy and Cassiel was on a home visit. Jehanna had brushed down her pony and given the stable boy a crown to run and fetch a fresh bundle of hay. Minutes later she heard someone approach, hay scrunching underfoot. Thinking it was the stable boy forgetting something, she turned to put her hands on her hips and all of a sudden he was there in her face, holding a knife to her throat. Despite the fact that her reactions had quickened through training, she remained still, heart pumping, adrenaline rushing through her veins. There were three other boys, all taller and stronger. She might have thought about taking them on, but with the blade at her throat, her options were limited.

Kenric motioned her back into the stable, keeping the knife in contact with her skin. His eyes gleamed with intent; he meant to have what she had robbed him of some days ago. But it was clearly not just physical; his pride was at stake. At the sight of the knife her breathing had started out shallow and panicky, but now she screwed her eyes shut and forced her breath into a long slow rhythm. Tears squeezed out of her eyes and she fought back the lump that was growing in her throat. If she could just block it all out, block him out, she could get through this. Then she opened her eyes, ready for the moment he would lower the knife, for surely, if he intended what she thought, he would have to lower the knife.

He backed her into a corner and to her utter dismay, the other boys took hold of her arms and legs, pushing her down to the ground while Kenric used one hand to lift her skirts and release himself from his trousers. She wanted to scream, but knew that one slip with that knife and she was as good as dead. The other boys were laughing and jeering, working out between them who was going to be next, then suddenly the knife was down as Kenric put his attention to the task at hand. She screamed and twisted her torso from side to side trying to prevent him from his purpose. She pulled with her arms and thrashed from side to side, the smell of hay and manure filling her nostrils, but the boys held fast. She had one leg free, but she couldn't get any leverage to throw a kick as he was sitting on top of her hips.

"Bitch! Why can't you just lie still? It will be a lot easier for you." Kenric slapped her around the face. The blow stung her cheek and she shrieked, then felt her bottom lip start to ooze with blood and the salty metallic taste filled her mouth. He had the knife again and was tracing a line along her cheek. That's good, she thought. As long as he has the knife, he can't do much else. "Now," he said. "Shut your dirty mouth or I'll slice it from your face." He stared hard at her, just to be sure she understood, then lowered the knife to the floor and started fumbling again with his trousers.

"Let. Her. Go." The voice cut through the mumbling and jeering of the boys. Ice cold.

Emotionless. It sent a shiver down her spine. But then a beam of hope lit up inside her. Jehan.

There was a momentary pause of indecision, then Kenric reached for the knife. Before he had a chance to grasp its hilt, there was a thud and a strangled cry as one of the boys holding her arm fell over backwards in a spray of blood, the handle of a throwing knife protruding from his neck. The instant his hold released her arm, Jehanna swung her elbow round in an arc, smashing Kenric in the side of his head near the temple. Kenric didn't make a sound. His eyes rolled into the back of his head and he slumped on top of Jehanna, pinning her to the ground with his weight. The other two boys froze for an instant like deer before the hunter, then bolted out of the stable as fast as they could.

The stable boy returned, dropped the bale of hay, screamed, then ran for the house. Before long, the stable was heaving with people, from the staff at the smithy and the local shops to the market traders, up early to set up their wares. Many eyes saw first-hand the state of Jehanna and the unconscious Kenric lying on top of her before Jehan had a chance to roll him off to the incredulity of onlookers when they saw his semi-naked state. Jehanna was shivering with the shock and was relieved when Jehan wrapped his cloak around her and carried her up to the house.

CHAPTER SEVEN

Respite for the twins was short lived. No sooner had they made it to the house to tend to Jehanna's injuries than the villagers came crashing through the shop screaming murder. No one but the twins and the perpetrators had witnessed Jehanna's ordeal, but a crowd big enough to march them down to the village square had witnessed the aftermath.

One boy dead, through a knife injury to the neck and another one unconscious. And it was plain to see who had been at fault; the whoring foreign girl with her skirts hiked up to her waist. She had quite clearly tempted poor Kenric with her promiscuous eastern ways to the point of near death and very certainly caused her jealous brother to kill the other boy. There was only one way this would be dealt with; trial by the local magistrate. The boy was a murderer and the girl a whore. The villagers demanded a public hearing.

Jehanna was still shivering with the shock when her hands were tied roughly behind her back and she was shoved forwards, surrounded by angry people who spat and swore at her. Her head pounded and a slow steady tide of nausea crept from the pit of stomach up to her throat. She had no option but to move in the middle of the huddle, taking prods and pokes to keep her walking. She stumbled several times and heaved up bile by the road side, barely given time to pause before being dragged back to her feet. She saw Jehan being marched forward in a similar manner. She caught a flash of concern in his face as he sought to locate her, before he was buried again by a sea of angry faces. It wasn't long before they reached the village square.

They were delivered without ceremony to the local courthouse and tied to a wooden post outside. There, they were left to reflect on their crimes before the magistrate was ready to hear their case. Every so often, villagers would come by and throw something at them; mud, rotten food, eggs.

"This is it, then," Jehanna said, her voice wavering with fear and despair. She could just about reach Jehan's fingertips on the other side of the post and found some strength in his touch.

"Just keep to the truth. We can only say what really happened. We are only guilty of protecting ourselves. Remember that."

Though Jehan's words gave her hope, every time someone came past and hurled something horrid or shouted abuse, Jehanna's confidence came crashing back down. They stayed tied to the post for most of the morning, their faces away from the courthouse and looking out across the village. The bustle of the day's trading continued regardless, as though the capture and imprisonment of two young villagers was a normal daily occurrence.

By the time the magistrate had deemed them worthy of a hearing, they were tired, hungry and thirsty. But that was the least of their worries.

The courthouse was an open spaced area, which allowed a public audience. The magistrate sat behind a large table at the front of the oblong room. Benches all around the outskirts were filled with villagers who jeered when the twins were brought into the room. They were made to walk the length of the room to the table at the front, hands kept tied and forced to their knees before the magistrate. Jehanna was sickened by the eager crowd, hungry for the entertainment of seeing someone else suffer.

The magistrate was a middle-aged man with a pointed nose and a brow beaten look. He sighed and glanced to his left. Jehanna followed his gaze and saw what it was that bothered him. Mistress Altard, his wife, sat on the front bench to their right, smiling and nodding appropriate encouragements. Jehanna's heart sank. She scanned the crowds, looking for Cassiel, or anyone they knew who might be able to help them, but saw only the faces of people who over the years had either ignored them or remained indifferent to their presence. Surely there must be someone here she had treated, or had benefited from one of her tonics? For the first time, she thought about how much real interaction she had been allowed with the villagers. Cassiel had always been careful to finish most transactions and only let her treat someone under strict supervision. Perhaps she had meant only to protect Jehanna, but in the long run, it had not created any lasting favour for her amongst the locals. They didn't really know whom it was who mixed the tonics or gathered the supplies. There were a few faces she recognised from the smithy, but they were not friendly faces. This was the anger of a community that had been robbed of the life of one of their own.

She glanced at Jehan, who stayed with his head bowed, looking at the floor. He was not going to indulge the crowd with the desperation that must have been evident in Jehanna's face. She took strength from her brother's composure, then they linked hands as the magistrate called for order in the courthouse. The hall reeked of sweat, envy and retribution.

The magistrate held out a scroll in front of him with both hands, then unrolled it at arm's length and frowned at the words in ink.

"Jehan Mantar, you are accused here today of murder, for which the penalty will be hanging until death. How do you plead?" Jehanna gasped and there was a light cheer from crowd. Jehan lifted his eyes to the magistrate and said.

"Not guilty."

The magistrate sighed.

"Jehanna Mantar, you are accused here today of firstly prostituting yourself and secondly of grievous bodily harm, for which the penalty will be death by strangulation and burning. On the first Count, how do you plead?"

"No," Jehanna said, unable to stop herself. "You've got it wrong."

"Quiet." The magistrate gave her an angry glare. "You will speak only when asked to do so." Jehanna shook her head, tears streaming down her cheeks. "How do you plead to these charges?" The magistrate said.

"Not guilty," she said, her voice wavering and barely audible. Jehan tightened his grip on her hand.

"Very well," the magistrate said. "We shall hear from the witnesses."

Jehanna recognised the two boys who had held her down in the barn. They came into the room and ambled to the front. The first boy was bold and defiant in the face of his lies, as though the action of the twins justified the deceit of his story. The second boy was uncomfortable and kept his eyes

54

focussed on the floor, unable to look at the twins or the magistrate. Between them, they spun a yarn that went back to the first day Jehan had encountered Kenric and had broken his forefinger. If they were to be believed, they painted a picture of a young girl who sold her body for profit and lured Kenric and his friend to their eventual undoing. Jehan, it was said, was merely waiting for the right moment to commit a murder that had been years in the planning. They pandered to the crowd and embellished the scene that many had witnessed that morning in the barn at the house of Mistress Cassiel. Their story was told to the tumultuous accompaniment of cheers and boos from the crowd. The magistrate let it string out for as long as possible before calling an end to the proceedings by way of summarising the key points of the case and announcing the verdict of guilty on all charges. He demanded that the prisoners be held in the courthouse dungeons until their penalty was carried out. The crowd erupted, chanting 'Guil-ty. Guil-ty.' The twins were forced to their feet and were about to be marched back out of the courtroom, when a lone voice carried across the clamour.

"Stop!"

Heads turned to look at the person who had disrupted their entertainment. Some people did not hear and continued to chant, others nudged each other and shushed those around them. Count Lenden stepped into view at the back of the courtroom. He had no need to repeat his order, because as soon as the people saw who it was, they quietened down. Jehanna dared to hope as the Count strode with purpose down the length of the hall to the front table where the magistrate was sitting. On seeing the Count, the magistrate stood and bowed.

"My Lord. This matter has been dealt with... if I may, I can regale you with the details as presented by our upstanding witnesses." The magistrate's eyes darted from side to side as though he was looking for someone to substantiate his case. The Count looked at the magistrate like he was a piece of muck on his boot.

"Firstly," Count Lenden said, "I have heard this complete debacle from where I have been sitting at the back of the hall. Secondly, and I have to tell you I am most displeased with you on this point, according to the by-laws of this land, a case of this severity cannot be tried by the local court; it is a matter for the district suzerain, who I might add, just happens to be in the vicinity." He made a show of looking around at the audience and preening himself, to which he received some nervous laughter and few nods of approval. "How convenient, you might say. Well, not only that, but I also have to tell you that, not least have you tried two young people without allowing anyone to speak in their defence, but you have also condemned to death two of my newest employees without so much as sending a courtesy message to the castle." There were a few gasps from the crowd.

Count Lenden fixed his gaze on the magistrate who paled and dropped his eyes to the floor. A few 'oohs' came from the crowd, as people began to prepare for another spectacle. Whispers escaped as the news was passed around that the foreigners were under the protection of Count Lenden. "Right then," the Count said. "Let us do this properly."

The crowd had calmed down, tempered enough by the Count's presence to be able to hear the twin's story with a measure of objectivity. The truth about the scale of abuse that they had encountered in Lendholm from the day they had arrived caused many listeners to turn away, shame-faced by their own behaviour or indifference. Witnesses appeared to corroborate the details of the events of that morning and Cassiel stood at the front of the room, answering questions from the Count. By the end of the day, there were only a minority of people in that hall that still held to the notion that the 'foreigners' had behaved against the laws of Tennengaul.

"I object." The magistrate's wife was one of the first to rise to her feet, her face livid. The Count turned to address her as she was now one of the few dissenting voices in the crowd.

"Mistress Altard," the Count said. "The case against the Mantars has been heard. You and your people have had your say, be seated." She stood for a moment, shadowed by a cloud of indecision, before reluctantly taking her seat.

In due course, the Count summarised the cases for and against the twins, re-iterating the severity of the accusations and peremptory penalties, before acquitting them of all charges. The relief was too much for Jehanna. The blood drained from her face, her body felt suddenly cold, then a black curtain slid across her eyes before she slumped to the floor of the courthouse.

CHAPTER EIGHT

Something cold and wet was dribbling at the corners of her mouth. She swallowed the cool droplets, then her thirst brought her back to the moment and Jehanna opened her eyes to see an anxious Cassiel dripping water into her mouth. She sat up and accepted the pitcher, slaking her thirst and not caring if half the water ended up down her front.

"Steady on, girl. There's more if you need it. You gave us all quite a fright," Cassiel said. Jehanna looked around. She was sat on her bed, in her room back at the Apothecary. Breath shortened and heart beat quickened with panic.

"Jehan," she said with a strangled cry.

"Shh, he is out there in the back room with the Count. Don't worry, he is fine. Do you remember what happened? You fainted in the courtroom," Cassiel said. Jehanna slumped back, dizzy with the exertion. "You need to get some rest and have something to eat before you start your journey."

"Journey?"

"Under the circumstances, the Count thought it best that he accompany you both to Castle Lendholm before nightfall. There is fear of reprisals and the Count won't risk letting you stay a day longer."

"Cassiel," Jehanna squeezed Cassiel's hand. "You have done so much for me; taking me in, believing in me and fetching the Count when we needed him most. We owe you our lives. We owe Count Lenden our lives. I shan't ever forget."

"Well now, don't think I shall let you off the hook that easily, my girl. I'll come and visit you at the castle and bring you supplies, as I know you like to keep your own. You helped get this business on its feet, I'll not forget that." Jehanna smiled thinking her own needs had far outweighed those of the Apothecary and that Cassiel was being modest. She felt anxious about leaving Cassiel.

"Will you promise something for me?" Jehanna said. Cassiel narrowed her eyes, but nodded all the same. "Don't be too harsh on Lugus. You have such a kind heart and he has suffered for what he did." Cassiel grimaced and declined to comment, though her pupils dilated at the mention of his name.

A few hours later, Jehanna was riding out of town on Arion, flanked on either side by the Count and his arms men with Jehan riding pillion on one of the larger warhorses. Lugus was bold enough to stop the entourage to bid goodbye to the twins. He shook hands with Jehan and bowed to Jehanna, much like their first meeting in the square years ago. Jehanna noted that he looked much cleaner and had changed his clothes. As they rode on by, she looked over her shoulder and watched Lugus walk back into town, making a direct line towards the Apothecary. She smiled to herself.

***

Castle Lendholm was a complete village in its own right. Jehanna had been preparing herself for an austere, stone fortress, cut off from people and the outside world. But it was a buzzing community within an odd collection of cottages, keeps and gatehouses. Acres of bright open space, horses, dogs, children and a constant energetic banter between staff, servants and commoners alike. They had arrived as the sun began to set and ridden through the outer circle towards the main castle building. Word of their arrival had been sent ahead by the castle watch and they were cheered and clapped and followed by an entourage of children, chickens, goats and women who threw petals over the Count. Jehanna was quite taken aback. The Count was their hero and he commanded a hero's welcome. By association, the twins were regarded as something of value; the Count had taken the trouble to ride all the way into Lendholm on their behalf, therefore his reason was just. No explanation necessary.

They were escorted through the melee of the inner circle and into the courtyard of the castle keep, where the garrison was located. Jehanna barely had time to exchange two words with her brother before he was swept away by some eager military personnel. The Count dismounted and gave his reins to the stable hands before conversing with some of the female staff in attendance. He turned, bowed briefly to Jehanna, then disappeared. She was left sitting astride Arion, amidst a crowd of strange people, wondering what she was supposed to do.

Then someone let the dogs out.

The courtyard erupted into a frenzy of excited canines, barking and growling, impatient for their feed as well as curious about the strange newcomer. Jehanna forgot all about her earlier unease and slid from Arion's back.

"Mistress," one of the stable hands said. "I would stay seated awhile, they can be a bit unpredictable with strangers. Mistress Danson will be coming for you, see?" He nodded to the other side of the courtyard where an elderly woman was skittering to and fro with her hands up in the air and dogs nipping at her heels. The stable hands were nudging each other and laughing.

Jehanna pursed her lips and let out a short, barely audible whistle, to which the dogs pricked up their ears, looked around and came bounding towards her. The smile on the faces of the stable hands dropped as they darted out of the way. Jehanna knelt down and was engulfed by a sea of furry brown heads and wagging tails all vying for attention from the strange new person. Jehanna smiled to herself; she had missed the close company of animals. She stroked their backs and tickled behind their ears as the dogs batted her with their noses, emitting a collective whine. They had lost all interest in the elderly lady.

"Well I'll be..." Mistress Danson said, now able to walk in a straight line without being harassed. The stable hands peered out from behind their hiding places and scratched their heads looking puzzled. The dog handlers arrived belatedly on the scene and for once were left to prepare the evening dog feed without having their hands shredded in the process.

61

CHAPTER NINE

Life at Castle Lendholm settled into a routine of work at the castle with precious little time for leisure. Jehanna helped out in the kitchen for a few weeks, preparing meals for the troops before being given the additional responsibility of serving the men and attending to the jobs within the garrison. In the early days, she hardly saw Jehan, as he slept in the garrison and she in the servants' quarters. Soon, as she was given more freedom of movement, she was able to get to know the soldiers more and glean snippets of news about Jehan. He had made a big impression with his peers and the military commanders, she was told. His swordsmanship, although a little unpolished, was quick and lethal compared to soldiers and knights that had undertaken years of training. Jehanna glowed with pride when she heard this and knew that it would not be long before Jehan would be moving up the ranks. On the rare occasions that they saw each other, they hugged and exchanged stories and promised to meet up and continue with their own training routine. They settled for snatched hours at the break of dawn when there was no one around to see.

Cassiel came to the castle every so often and brought supplies not only for the garrison but also for Jehanna. In time, the Count commissioned Cassiel to deal with minor injuries and ailments to keep the troops happy and healthy.

"I have told the Count that he has a perfectly good healer in residence," she said one day.

"Reluctant though I'd be to give up my only excuse to visit you both."

"You don't need an excuse to visit. Besides, I am happy enough, Mistress Cassiel," Jehanna said. "You have done far too much for me already." Though she ached to prove herself to the Count, she wanted it to be on her own merits and not through someone else playing on the Count's good nature.

"You have a rare and beautiful gift, Jehanna," Cassiel said, taking her hand between her own. Cassiel's skin felt soft and delicate, belying the strength and power that lay hidden beneath the folds of skin. "Perhaps you don't realise it now, but when you touch people, something remarkable happens." Jehanna felt a tingling sensation as she sought out Cassiel's energy stream. It was clean and bright, like the stars in the sky. "See. That is what I mean. Most people won't know or understand what you do, but they will feel warmth in your touch that will sit in their hearts and their memories. And they will like you all the more for it."

"It's a shame that people in the village didn't feel the same way."

"Oh tsk, girl. Don't you fret about their ignorance now, that is all done with." It was true that most people were quick to forget, though Jehanna had a tendency to reflect too deeply.

Time and again, she turned over Cassiel's words in her mind, trying to find a meaning and a purpose for herself in this life. She began to start reaching out to others with her aura in the same way she had always done subconsciously with Jehan to temper his fiery nature. But she had always had a unique bond with Jehan which didn't seem possible to replicate in others.

Jehanna rose early every morning, to the chirp of the sparrows outside her window. She encouraged the little birds with breadcrumbs and they duly returned at the same hour each morning. Now, she had attuned her body and mind to wake at their call, while the rest of the servants slept, impervious to the tiny chatter of conversation outside the window.

She had taken to walking around barefoot when off duty, as she liked the feel of the ground beneath her feet and it gave her the kind of stealth she needed to move around undetected. She felt less of a burden on the Count if she was virtually unseen by all when not needed. Besides, she cherished the early hours when most of the castle staff and residents were asleep and she could walk about unrestrained by the protocols of western etiquette.

The locals thought she was a bit strange; like some wild child from a far-off land, but they were friendly enough. Men admired her beauty, but never in a way that denigrated her, like Kenric used to. In time, she grew accustomed to the attention and was able to absorb or deflect it according to how she felt.

Arion waited patiently every day for his early morning ride until one day Jehanna noticed that she was getting too big for the little pack pony. Arion was getting old and needed less exercise, so she persuaded the stable hands to let her start exercising the geldings, while Arion was given free rein to wander in the back field at his leisure. As long has he had a bit of fuss from her and an apple from the kitchen, he was happy with this new arrangement. She usually had about an hour before the squires arrived to attend to their knight's horses, but there was always one who arrived late or was pulled away to attend to other matters for their master.

Jehanna slipped a bridle over the head of the large war horse, the only one left standing in the stables as all the other squires had taken their masters' steeds.

"You will do nicely for an early morning canter," she murmured, sliding onto the massive horse's back. Most ladies needed a mounting block and a side saddle, but Jehanna just hitched up her skirts and rode bare back; she found that the horses responded better, the closer contact she had with their skin. She ignored the looks of incredulity from the few squires and stable hands who were around as she cantered out into the fields beyond the inner circle. She exhilarated in the freedom of movement that riding bare back gave her and lost all thought to the wind and the power of the animal beneath her. If this was what it was like to fly, then she envied the little sparrows that danced on her windowsill every morning.

Jehanna was careful not to tire the war gelding too much, so after several turns of the circle, she took a slow trot back to the stable, by which time the bustle of the day had begun. She could sense the eyes watching her, though she chose not to acknowledge them as she dismounted, breathless with adrenalin. Then a strong and powerful presence made her spine tingle and she looked up in surprise. Count Lenden was standing on the edge of the training ground watching her, a smile framing his weathered cheeks. A short, red-faced man who was scowling at Jehanna accompanied him. He was dressed in a huntsman's outfit; heavy green tunic with long sleeves, boots and thick breeches. She looked away, wondering why his angst was directed at her. Then the Count raised a hand in a jovial way to attract her attention. Once satisfied that Jehanna had seen him, the Count sank into conversation with the man, who kept flashing an angry look in her direction. She handed the horse's reins to the stable hand who lead the animal away to be fed and watered.

"Lady Mantar," the Count said with a bow. "And how are you settling into life at Castle Lendholm?" Jehanna curtsied low, trying to hide her grubby bare feet in the long skirts of her dress. She blushed. The bold statement she had made when she first met the Count about coming from noble background somehow didn't quite fit with the wild child image she was now displaying. "May I introduce Chiefo, my chief huntsman?" Jehanna curtsied again and the huntsman reluctantly bowed.

"Hmmph. Damn slip of a girl, don't see what use she will be. Like to know who gave her permission to ride the geldings," Chiefo said. Jehanna ignored the huntsman's words and turned her attention to the Count, pushing a little warmth in the direction of Chiefo, hoping it might help him to lighten up. Chiefo shuddered as though a chill ran down his spine, then frowned to himself and continued muttering. The Count shook his head and rolled his eyes skyward.

"I am more than happy to support the decision; you can plainly see that this 'slip of a girl' rides like she was born on a horse." Chiefo looked for a moment like he was about to concede before the Count continued. "That aside, I would like to ask for your help in another matter, Lady Mantar." Jehanna smiled at his use of the noble title despite her current appearance. "Your brother tells me that you are a skilled healer. Do you heal animals?"

"Yes, I do, my Lord." Jehanna's heart started pounding. The thought of being asked to help with the animals was more than she could have hoped for. She kept calm, not wishing to corroborate Chiefo's unfounded fear of her being a silly little girl with no skill whatsoever.

"Then perhaps, I might ask you to take leave of the kitchens today to help out Chiefo?"

"But of course, my Lord," Jehanna said, glancing at Chiefo, who had no choice but to acquiesce to the Count's wishes. "I will need to collect supplies from my room."

"Good. That's settled then. Now Chiefo, what is our most pressing issue this morning?"

"Fang is in trouble again," Chiefo said. "Something wrong with his right forepaw, but he won't let anyone near it. He badly bit one of the boys who tried to see what was wrong. I'd bring a pair of thick gloves with you, Mistress." The concerned voice did not extend to Chiefo's eyes, which betrayed his amusement.

"Right...," the Count said, with a little frown. "Lady Mantar, if I could ask you to collect whatever you need, make your apologies to the cook and meet us right away at the kennels?"

"Yes, my Lord," she said with a curtsy. The two men bowed and strode off in the direction of the kennels.

Jehanna stood for a moment, watching them go, her heart pounding. When she was sure they were out of sight, she ran as fast as she could back to the castle, ignoring the odd looks she was getting from passersby, who must have thought she was engaged in a life or death mission. She stopped briefly in her shared room to collect her things, give her feet a wash and put on some shoes. Then she swept past the kitchens making her apologies to the cook and was out into the courtyard on her way to the kennels before anyone had wondered to ask what she was doing.

The dog kennels were located on the outer edge of the castle courtyard. They were designed to house more than twenty hounds at any one time in separate stalls which ran along the outer wall. Strategically placed, the kennels allowed the dogs immediate access to the meeting point at which every hunt began; the castle courtyard. Equally, the dogs had access to the fields beyond the south side of the courtyard, where they were allowed to exercise twice a day after their feed.

Jehanna raced out into the courtyard and came to a sudden halt when she saw the Count and his chief huntsman deep in conversation on the south side. She smoothed down her skirts and took a deep breath, not wanting to appear too eager, then approached. The Count looked up and smiled but the huntsman remained impassive. Well, at least his manner had improved, however slight, thought Jehanna. She followed Count Lenden and Chiefo as they walked nearly the length of the wall of stalls and stopped at the penultimate one. Most of the stall doors were open and Jehanna could see the dogs in the field chasing each other around and retrieving objects that were being hurled into the distance at regular intervals by the dog handlers. A few children had wandered over to watch, abandoning their own game of catch and chase to watch with fascination.

"There he is," Chiefo said, opening the stall door. Jehanna focused her attention on the huge grey wolfhound that lay on his side panting, clearly in pain. "He hasn't eaten anything for over a day. If he carries on like this, I'll recommend him for the chop." He glanced at Jehanna who frowned when he said the word 'chop', then he shrugged. Jehanna dropped to her knees beside the dog and reached for his injured paw. Fang's lips curled menacingly up over his canines and he started to snarl.

"You can stop that nonsense," Jehanna said as she began to feel the paw up and down, gently pressing the bones beneath the grey tufts of fur. Fang subsided, his ears folded down and his tail gave a little wag. Jehanna looked at the Count and Chiefo who stared, mouths open. Fang lay still, allowing Jehanna to assess his injury. "It's not broken," she said finally. "But it is a bad sprain. He'll be out of action for a few weeks." She reached for her bag of supplies and pulled out some bandages and liniment. There was a look of curious bewilderment on the face of the huntsman as she proceeded to treat the wolfhound's paw. Fang remained stoical and calm throughout the entire procedure and the Count watched her with a look of amusement and awe on his face. "There," she said, tying off the bandage. "He'll probably pull this off in a few days, but it should have done its job by then." Jehanna patted Fang as he tried to lick her hand. He reminded her of Lobo. She had felt worse about leaving Lobo than she had her adopted parents. She stroked Fang's head and he let out a soft whine and for the first time since arriving at Castle Lendholm, she felt at home.

"So...," said the Count.

"Was there anything else?" Jehanna said, slinging her bag over her shoulder and rising to her feet. Fang lifted his head, alert to her sudden movement. "No, you stay here and recover, silly dog. I'll be back to see you later." He dropped his enormous head to his paws with a disgruntled sigh.

"Urrmm...," Chiefo said, unable to take his eyes off Jehanna. "Well..., there's Lil."

"One of our best hunting bitches, going through a difficult first litter. She's no better then?" The Count said. Chiefo shook his head.

Count Lenden and Chiefo took Jehanna to Lil's stall which was slightly bigger than the rest to accommodate the litter when it arrived and filled with blankets and her own supply of food and water. Lil was lying down and panting heavily. Jehanna sat down in the stall and started to gently feel the dog's distended stomach. Lil looked at her with soulful eyes.

"She is well overdue. When was the last time she ate or drank?" Jehanna said. Chiefo looked as though someone had just delivered him a death sentence. He shook his head.

"She hasn't eaten or drank anything for a day or so."

"Good," Jehanna said. The huntsman looked startled. "It should happen tonight or tomorrow, I would think. Come and get me when she goes into labour." Jehanna stroked Lil's head and ran her hand once again over her stomach. She didn't know so much about delivering pups, but had once or twice attended a labour with Cassiel. "I would say you can expect at least six pups from this litter."

As predicted, Jehanna barely had time to finish her chores in the castle that evening before word was sent from the chief Huntsman to release her from her duties. When she arrived at the kennels, Lil was restlessly pacing up and down the stall. She had begun to rip pieces out of the blankets and arrange her bedding with clumps of straw, making a nest for her whelps. Jehanna's presence began to calm her a little, but still she got up and sat down at regular intervals. Jehanna stayed up all night with Lil, nursing her through the labour contractions and delivering six beautiful puppies; five female, one male, all healthy. She helped Lil to clean the pups, then cleaned and replaced her bedding, before returning each pup to Lil. Exhausted, Lil lay on her side and allowed the pups to suckle, while Jehanna gave her a mixture of milk and soggy bread, which she lapped up greedily. The pups latched onto Lil instinctively and only when she was satisfied that all six were feeding, did Jehanna leave the little family in the care of the dog handlers. On her way back to the castle she passed Chiefo, who was hurrying out towards the stalls. She curtsied when he stopped to address her.

"Any news?" he said.

"All six well and safely delivered, Sire," she said. The creases of worry on Chiefo's face smoothed out and for the first time since she had met him, he offered her a genuine smile. He took her hand and shook it vigorously.

"Remarkable," he said. "This is the first full litter this year to survive. My thanks to you, Mistress... Lady Mantar." He bowed deeply and rushed off to admire the new additions to his family. Jehanna smiled to herself, yawned, then made for her own bed stopping only to inform the cook that she would be out of action for the remainder of the day by special dispensation from the Count.

CHAPTER TEN

Jehanna settled into a routine that split her time between the kitchens, the garrison and the kennels. Every morning, during her free time, she kept up with her riding and squeezed in a precious hour of practice with Jehan in a shaded patch of grass within the woodland on the outer circle of the castle grounds.

It was a drizzly day and the dew clung to her bare feet. Soggy footprints marked the area as she squared up to Jehan in readiness for his attack. The wolfhound, Fang, had accompanied her to the edge of the woods. Ever since she had treated his paw he followed her around like a shadow. The other servants who shared her sleeping quarters had a heart stopping moment when they woke one morning to find Fang sitting in the doorway casting a watchful eye over Jehanna as she slept. The cook had banned him from the kitchens, so he sat outside in the courtyard waiting for Jehanna to finish her kitchen duties, then padded after her as she went to attend to her duties in the garrison. At first, she had tried to take him back to his stall, but he developed a cunning way of unlocking the bolt on the door and escaping, which to that day, Jehanna had no idea how. One day, she had spent more time taking Fang back to his stall than actually doing her work, so decided it was just as well to let him be.

He sat upright, on the edge of the clearing, staring at Jehan.

"Would you tell that mutt to mind its own," Jehan said. Fang flattened his ears and began a low growl in the back of his throat. Jehanna turned and glared at the dog.

"Fang, be still," Jehanna said. The dog let out a soft whine and dropped onto his front paws to watch.

"It's Lobo all over again, isn't it?" Jehan sighed.

"It needn't be, you just have to trust him, that's all," Jehanna said. She gave a short, sharp whistle and the dog jumped up and trotted over to her. "Grab that branch over there," she said. Jehan picked up a short, thick piece of branch that had been splintered from a rotten dead tree trunk. "Hold it up between your hands extended in front of you and call his name." Jehan frowned at his sister but did as she said.

"Fang..." he said uncertainly. The dog looked from Jehanna to Jehan and back again, wagging his tail.

"Fang," Jehanna said, with a bit more authority. The dog leapt up and clamped its teeth around the branch, splintering it into pieces and sending Jehan reeling back onto the wet grass. The look on Jehan's face was awe-inspired as Fang gnawed through the branch and looked set on starting on Jehan's face. "Enough," Jehanna said. Fang dropped back to her side and sat looking at Jehan as though he were breakfast, waiting to be served.

"That animal...," Jehan said, sitting up, "should be locked up."

"Don't be like that," Jehanna said, wrapping her arms around the dog and squeezing him. Fang let out a sigh of contentment and nuzzled her with his huge, long nose. "He can be your friend too, look." Jehanna jumped up and found another tree branch. She held it up in front of her face with two hands as Jehan had done. "Now you command him, but this time speak to him like he is one of your troops." Jehan sighed but played along.

"Fang, here." The dog looked at Jehanna first, who nodded, then he ran to Jehan's side and sat attentively, wagging his tail in anticipation of this new game. Jehan pointed to Jehanna, holding the branch at arm's length. "Fang," he said. The dog leapt and sunk his teeth into the branch, knocking Jehanna backwards in the process. As Jehanna fell backwards, she heard Jehan scream "Enough," though Fang had other ideas and proceeded to lick her face with an apologetic whine. Jehanna giggled and pushed Fang away.

"Oh that's great, he nearly rips my face off and you just get licked to death," Jehan said. Despite his words, Jehanna could tell that he was pleased that the dog had responded to his command.

Once they had run out of dead branches, Fang had to be satisfied with sitting down and watching the twins as they ran through their routines. Although it must have seemed confusing at first for the dog, Jehanna saw that before too long, the instinctive pack mentality began to kick in and Fang was starting to understand the nature of the bond between them.

They walked back across the vast space of green land towards the middle circle, where they could just see the squires attending to the geldings; a few were mounted and taking a turn around the grounds, others were outside the stables brushing coats and polishing saddles and bridles. It was early still, so few people noticed the twins emerge from the woods, barefoot with a sheen of perspiration masking their faces and a large grey wolfhound trotting along beside them.

"I can't stay here for much longer," Jehan said, turning to face Jehanna. A knot of anxiety twisted in her stomach. Just when she was getting used to the castle and its strange ways. She looked down at Fang, who returned her gaze.

"I thought you were doing well. They gave you a promotion," she said hopefully.

"Yes, but I will never be able to progress any further. Junior Marshal is about as high a rank as I will ever go. I am not from a noble house."

"But, you said…"

"Shh. I know, I know. But we are still strangers here. We don't belong and we don't have a noble house to our name. Look at you. They may call you Lady Mantar, but you are still doing servant's duties." Jehanna thought about this and realised that it had been rankling her, though she had paid it little heed until now. "I can never be a squire, so I can never progress to knighthood. I'll never be able to lead an army from Castle Lendholm. That is the way it works here."

Jehanna was crushed, as though her world was once again about to fold and crash in on her.

"I can't go back on the road, Jehan, I can't. I'm so tired of moving around. Can't we just stay here?" She could sense that Jehan was not finding this easy but at the same time he was not considering her situation. He took her hand in his and squeezed it. She looked up into his face and there was a furtive look in his eyes. Then she smiled. "You have a plan, don't you?" He nodded, put a finger to his lips then tapped the side of his head. Good grief. She sighed.

"Don't worry," he said, turning to resume their walk. "We're not leaving straight away. But there is something that I want you to do in preparation." Jehanna folded her arms and raised an eyebrow. She hoped that this was not some crackpot idea that was going to take her away from Castle Lendholm and on some journey to who knew where. "And we won't be going too far, either," he said, reading her thoughts.

"Why the secrecy?"

"There are a lot of jealous soldiers in the garrison. People who have been there for years before I came along and was promoted ahead of them. It especially irks them, the fact that I am not even from Tennengaul." Jehanna nodded. It made sense. "If you don't know too much it will make our preparations so much more natural."

"What do you want me to do?"

"Just keep on doing what you are doing, but try to get more hours in the garrison, helping with the day to day running, that kind of thing. Absorb as much information as you can." Jehanna smiled to herself. She thought she had an inkling of what Jehan was up to, but kept her silence. She nodded and they walked together back to the garrison.

Before they parted at the courtyard, Jehan knelt down and extended an open hand towards Fang. The dog lifted his paw and placed it in Jehan's hand. Jehanna giggled and Jehan looked up at her. "You taught him to shake paws?" He looked back to Fang and held his gaze. "Now, you look after my sister for me while I'm working. Good dog, Fang," he said patting the great shaggy head. He hugged Jehanna before disappearing to the garrison.

Jehanna walked around to the kennels with a mind to try putting Fang back in his stall before presenting herself for duties at the kitchens. As she rounded the corner she saw Count Lenden in the animal park deep in conversation with Chiefo, watching the dogs being exercised. It was Chiefo who saw her first, as he looked up and waved. When the Count saw her he beckoned her to join them. She hurried to where they were standing, glancing with concern behind her at Fang who was loping along behind her.

"I'm sorry Count, he follows me everywhere. I can't stop him," she said looking to Fang as he sat at a respectable distance, watching. "He should be back in training soon. I should think he makes a wonderful hunting dog with his size and strength."

"You would think so, wouldn't you, my Lady?" Chiefo said. "But the truth is, he isn't; he is too strong and self-willed. In fact he is useless in a hunt because he dominates the pack and takes them off wherever he feels like regardless of the prey we are following." Jehanna suddenly understood. She gave a little flick with her hand and Fang was instantly at her side. To the astonishment of the Count and Chiefo, he lay down beside her and rested his big head on her feet, with a blissful sigh.

"He just needs a stronger pack leader, otherwise he will always dominate," she said, kneeling down to rub his ears.

"Well, that's as may be, but the pack is what it is and quite frankly I don't know what I'm going to do with him," Chiefo said.

"I'm afraid that is all too true and he is very expensive to keep," the Count said. "If he's no use to us, then there is only one solution." Jehanna leapt up, tears smarting her eyes.

"No. You can't. You simply cannot put him down," she said. The Count gave her a quizzical look.

"Actually, I was thinking of giving him to you. If you want him, give me a couple of hours, then come up to the castle for his papers." The Count shook hands with Chiefo, who was grinning, then bowed to Jehanna and left the animal park. Jehanna stared after him in disbelief. Chiefo nodded, before bowing to take his leave. She was left in the middle of the green with a big grey wolfhound stuck to her feet. As far as Fang was concerned, he was happy to follow wherever his goddess would lead him.

CHAPTER ELEVEN

Carentan

Jabir ed-Din steepled his fingertips, dipping his chin to meet Gereinte's gaze. He broke eye contact, glanced back down at the papers on the oak table in front of him, then looked back to Gereinte.

"They are not going to like it, you know." He fingered the gold earring in his left ear, then stroked a palm across his hairless head. Gereinte was bursting with the impulse to jump up and shake him, but held back, having learnt that Jabir would not be rushed.

Since his ascension to the throne of Carentan, Gereinte could no longer afford the emotional outbursts that as a boy, had landed him in trouble. Trouble that drove his mother, the late Queen Regent, to hide him away on a Coustiller ship under the pretense of being kidnapped into slavery. He shuddered with the memory of waking up on that ship with the sick realisation of what had happened to him. Despite Jabir having been part of that conspiracy, Gereinte had forged a lasting relationship with the dark easterner who had been instrumental in his psychological survival at sea and his education of world politics. Enigmatic as ever, Jabir turned the document over once more and pushed it across the table to Gereinte. "We shall see," he said.

A sharp knock on the door announced the arrival of the King's closest cabinet of advisers. Kemal ed-Din took a seat next to his kinsman, Jabir. Kemal, quite different from his cousin, was a fierce warrior prince and master swordsman who had trained Gereinte. Kemal nodded; a man of few words, though Gereinte noted a twitch of a smile at the corner of his mouth which made his facial scar shift ever so slightly. The only time he had ever seen the warrior smile openly was when he quite happily slaughtered a group of Klaganstill bandits who were making a nuisance of themselves in Tennengaul. Even then, coupled with his scarred face, it merely served to make him look more vicious. Gereinte returned Kemal's nod.

"Well," Alliane said, breezing into the room. "Will this take long? I have a training session with Fulk." Gereinte smiled at his sister. She was dressed in forest green and brown. The only man who could ever have had a chance at winning her affection was a giant of a northerner, deadly in battle, but with all the social skills of a mouse. It just so happened that Fulk was also captain of the King's Guard. His sister was certainly in safe hands.

"Sit down, Ally, Fulk will understand. Besides, you know how I value your opinion and this," he said tapping the document on the table, "is going to affect everyone."

His cabinet was completed by warmaster Alaric Beothys, info-meister Etienne Martan and Chancellor Rupert Lorquin. For the first time, Chanac Issoire was invited to join the select group. Baron Issoire was his brother-in-law; very recently married to his elder sister, Roda. Gereinte had also asked two distinguished counsels to attend for their advice on legal and constitutional issues. He felt a twist of anxiety in his stomach as he rose to address his advisors.

"This," he said, picking up the document, "is a draft proposal for a new Citizen's Charter." He made eye contact around the table and saw that he had piqued a level of interest and curiosity. For some weeks now, he had separated himself from all but Jabir's company and taken advice only from the man who had helped to shape his ideologies. The anxiety faded as he took confidence in his audience's attention. "These are the firm principles to be embedded in the final Charter, which will take Carentan towards a future that my father had envisioned but sadly could not see through to its natural conclusion." There were empathetic nods from those around the table who remembered the King. "There are, no doubt, many constitutional issues that need to be addressed in this draft, which is partly why I have asked you here today. But also, there is one aspect of the Charter that I feel duty bound to act upon without delay."

By the time Gereinte had finished outlining his plans for the Kingdom, he noted that an uneasy fidgeting had commenced around the table. Baron Issoire was smiling, Alaric was nodding appreciatively but Alliane sat with her mouth open in disbelief. The others mumbled amongst themselves but no one dared to state their opinion, other than Alaric.

"About time those bloody-handed priests were introduced into the real world," he said. There were a few nods of agreement around the table and although the sentiment was largely shared, it was the audacity with which the plan was to be executed that most appeared concerned with.

"Morda has been allowed run amok in Malvas as we all know. We cannot afford to let that happen in Carentan. I for one back this decision to the hilt." Baron Issoire said, surprising all present by breaking his customary silence. Gereinte nodded his thanks to Issoire.

"I will need some help from the rangers, Alliane. Perhaps we can both go and talk to Sir Fulk."

"I... this is all very sudden. I mean, have you thought this through?" Alliane said.

"How much trouble can Morda cause?" Gereinte said. "He has just a tentative foothold in Carentan now but if we let him loose for much longer, that may change. We all know how Borsa was able to stir up the Barony in my absence once the Queen had taken to her sickbed. No, Ally, it must be done without delay." Alliane nodded, though it was evident she didn't like it. Kemal slowly rose to his feet. "While I am gone, Jabir will take you through the Charter so that any further queries can be smoothed out. Etienne, I will need use of your networks to get the word out about the Charter." Etienne smiled at Gereinte with a glint in his eye, clearly enjoying every moment. Chancellor Lorquin, on the other hand, was visibly fuming.

"Religious tolerance is something your mother took very seriously," Lorquin said, his eyes narrowing.

"As did my father," Gereinte said. "Which is why I am taking a stand against Morda."

"Tolerance," Lorquin said, "is a two-way track. You cannot advocate religious tolerance on the one hand and outlaw the belief systems of an entire religious order on the other. Your mother understood that."

Gereinte put both hands on the table and leaned across to address the Chancellor. "Your loyalty towards the late Queen is admirable. However, there comes a time when a decision has to be made for the greater good. And this, Chancellor, is one of those moments." Their eyes met and for a brief instant, Gereinte wanted to wilt under Lorquin's gaze, the man who had seen him grow from a boy to a young man, had coveted his mother's attention and comforted her in her final days. But he held fast, knowing that this was one man's approval he needed more than all those around that table. Lorquin steadied his gaze, and then gave an almost imperceptible nod. Gereinte let the corners of his mouth curl in a boyish smile, to which Lorquin shook his head as though Gereinte were still only ten years old.

Without further delay or opportunity for protest, Gereinte stood up, glanced at both Alliane and Kemal before leaving the room. His intentions were clear and he had no need to look over his shoulder to know that his sister and the warrior sword master were close behind.

***

Abiel Morda's Church of the One God stood on the edge of the main thoroughfare leading into the village of Canrac, which lay west of the mighty river Caren. The building was a large sized converted gatehouse, detached from the manor of a local lord, who had generously donated to the

Church's coffers. By the same token of generosity, the lord had readily offered the names of local sinners to be submitted to Questioning by the Church's Inquisitors. Morda had been mildly disappointed when at first the Carentans had been far too ready to convert their unholy belief in polytheism to the One God without even the whiff of a torture rack. However, he was pleased with the progress made so far, though his influence reached only as far as the peasants that flocked to his church in search of redemption from the godlessness that had come to reign in Carentan.

The nobility were another matter. The only way to root out the rampant heresy in Carentan would be to build a bigger network and that meant negotiation with some of the lesser church leaders. Though the common people were all too enthusiastic to hear his sermons, the local lords kept their distance, maintaining a pretence of tolerance; an implicit custom in Carentan that was infuriating for outsiders.

Morda sighed as he looked out over the parapet of his stone walls and into the courtyard below where white-clad figures milled about, attending to duties and maintaining the upkeep of the Church. Every so often, he would catch the wail of sinners on the breeze, as the dungeons directly below opened up shop for the work of the Church's Inquisitors.

He had anticipated a different outcome when he first witnessed the events after the death of the Queen Regent. Caitlin Andolen, though it pained him to admit it, had given him the foothold he had needed to launch his campaign in Carentan. Once the boy had challenged Baron Borsa to a duel, Morda would have bet his future on a Borsa victory. Swiftly resulting in a free reign to fully establish his dreams of a unified Holy Church Authority, capable one day of challenging the hereditary monarchy that had ironically secured his future in Carentan.

Then, something remarkable had happened. The boy had become a man. One of his Immaculate Knights was close enough to the action to catch a spatter of blood on his robes. Scarlet drops on pure white; an indication of how very far this monarchy was prepared to go to retain power. He shuddered at the memory and the ease with which the young prince had dispatched one of the most feared warriors in the Barony of Carentan.

Morda had no great love for the nobility, but all the same feared for their eternal souls. If he could only get them to see the wisdom of the One God; how the old ways would reunite the Western Isles. And if it weren't enough to preach from the scriptures, then his Inquisitors would set some examples for others to follow. Surviving the Questioning guaranteed the loss of material desire and helped to keep the people in abeyance of sin in accordance with the Church's rules and regulations.

Abiel Morda closed his eyes and listened to the sounds of success filter up from the depths of the Church's dungeons.

Silence.

Success either way. If they survived, they would tell the story to others who were in danger of falling away from the old ways. If they died, they became a martyr to the cause; so great was the sin that death only would deliver redemption for the sinner. He relished this moment; the time to read the verdict of the trial, which depended largely on how quickly the person had submitted to the Questioning. Those who were grounded in their own belief system tended to last a bit longer, clinging on to the hope that their own god would somehow save them. Poor deluded souls. Those were the wretches that became the Church's martyrs; no point in wasted work. So far, it had been slow going, but his expansion into Carentan had guaranteed a foothold in the south which he had every intention of exploiting.

Morda was just about to turn and make his way down to the dungeons when a plume of dust on the horizon caught his attention. He stared for a moment before the dust cleared and he could recognise the purple banners of the King's Guard making their way steadily away from the town and towards his church. A shiver of prescience snaked down his spine. It was too late now to stop the Inquisitors, even if he wanted to. He could only hope that whatever business the King's Guard had with the Church, they would not linger long or too close to the good work going on in the bowels of dungeons.

CHAPTER TWELVE

Time seemed to roll by without a care for anyone. Jehanna had almost forgotten about Jehan's plans and continued to work in the garrison, absorbing information in keeping with her inquisitive nature. Everyone was accustomed to her asking questions and it just seemed like the best way to get a job done efficiently.

Jehan had reached the rank of Junior Marshall at the young age of seventeen and they both knew in their hearts that the time to leave Castle Lenholm was long overdue.

Jehanna woke late one morning to receive a message from one of the castle maids that her company was requested at a special breakfast in the Count's private dining room. She stretched and yawned, surprised that even the sparrows' early morning chatter had not been enough to wake her at the usual hour. Fang, who was lying at the foot of the bed, lifted his head, sensing her movement.

She had been up for most of the night looking after one of the Count's favourite geldings after it had sustained a leg injury in training, which had become infected. It had been touch and go, but the animal would pull through and make a good recovery. The invitation to breakfast was no doubt in thanks for her hard work. She washed and dressed quickly, not wanting to keep the Count waiting and remembered at the last minute to put on some shoes before descending the stone staircase and crossing over to the Count's private chambers. Fang padded alongside her.

As she passed the Count's private kitchen, she noticed that there was a remarkable amount of activity for the time of day. The main castle kitchens that served the garrison would have had breakfast under regimented control by that late hour and they routinely had to serve upward of a hundred hungry mouths. Oh well. Perhaps the private staff were not used to dealing with last minute requests from the Count. She put her head down, ignoring the disarray, and passed through to the corridor that served the dining room. There was an armed soldier standing guard who bowed briefly as though expecting her and opened the door. Fang emitted a low growl and flattened his ears as the soldier wavered over his decision to let the dog pass.

"The dog is fine, as you well know by now," the Count shouted from behind the door. The soldier opened the door wide enough to let both Jehanna and Fang pass, then snatched his hand back from the door handle, keeping a wary distance from Fang. The Count's beaming face met Jehanna and she was surprised to see Jehan seated opposite him. "Good grief, I thought the staff around here were used to the sight of that mutt following you everywhere." Count Lenden and Jehan both rose from their seats as Jehanna sat down beside Jehan, then reseated themselves while Fang settled himself at her feet.

The dining room was small but lavish. The windows were part covered with drapes coloured in the Count's distinctive insignia of sky blue and buttercup. The sun cast a dazzling hue across the table and the dust motes danced in its beam.

"I wanted to thank you for your hard work, but I invited your brother because there was something else I wanted to talk to you both about." Jehanna frowned at Jehan who raised a quizzical eyebrow. She shook her head in response; no, she had not been talking to the Count about their plans. "You must be thinking, young man, about where you can go from here, no doubt?" The Count turned his gaze upon Jehan. "Don't look at me like that, do you think I haven't noticed how quickly you have risen to Junior Marshall? You know as well as I that in Tennengaul, the traditions of leadership acquisition are restricted to the noble classes; at least within the formal armed forces. Had you wound up in Tordre or even Carentan, things might have been very different."

The door swung open and one of the man servants entered the room with three silver platters on a tray. "Hello," Count Lenden said, "you're new here. Where's Vanno?" Jehanna thought the man looked more like a street thug than a servant and she glanced at Jehan whose jaw was clamped shut, muscles twitching. Jehanna clenched and relaxed her fist and was reassured by Jehan's mirrored response.

"He's not well m'lud," the man servant said. "Stomach upset, nothing serious. Name's Bant and I'm just stepping in to help out." He moved around to Jehan's left and placed a silver platter in front of him. Jehanna looked to the Count, whose eyes had widened. He had noted that the new servant failed to observe protocol; the Count should always be served first, followed by any ladies present. Bant seemed unaware of his mistake and continued around the table to place a platter in front of Jehanna. She wondered if the Count was embarrassed by the shortcomings of his serving staff or whether he too had serious misgivings about the authenticity of this particular one.

"Anyway...," the Count said with one eye on the servant. "There may be something I can do to help you."

Bant moved behind Jehanna's chair and as he passed, Fang emitted a low rumbling growl. He placed the final platter on the table, then swung behind the Count, looped his brawny left hand around the Count's neck and held a dagger to his throat. At the same time, the door burst open and the soldier outside along with two ragged looking thugs came rushing in brandishing knives. The soldier ran behind the twins while the other two moved towards the Count who was being held by Bant.

"Be very still, be very quiet," Bant said, gripping the Count with shaking hands. His breath rasped in and out, then he coughed and smiled. "If you co-operate, I might even spare the dog."

"Heh, heh... spare the dog," the soldier said behind Jehanna. His words enabled her to frame a picture in her mind of his exact position without turning her head.

"I wouldn't do that if I were you," Jehan said. Never let it be said that her brother did not at least attempt a peaceful solution.

There was a pause. For the briefest of moments, the knife in Bant's hand relaxed. Jehanna grabbed a meat knife from the table, whirled around and buried it deep into the neck of the soldier holding

91

guard behind them. He gasped with shock, his hands flying to his neck as a red fountain of blood spurted, bubbled then ran down his front. He toppled and fell, the blood pooling around his body. Jehan leapt across the table towards the Count, platters and knives flying in all directions. A look of disbelief solidified on Bant's face, just as Jehan's foot connected with his jaw sending him flying away from the Count, his knife clattering to the table. Jehan withdrew his own dagger and slit the thug's throat. Jehanna shouted "Fang," and the dog hurdled the table and launched himself at one of the remaining men, who shielded his face with his arm when he saw the dog coming. There was a sickening crunch as Fang sunk his teeth into the man's arm. The man fell onto his back with a terrified shriek as the dog ripped into his face. As the final man turned to run from the room, Jehan threw his dagger at the fleeing man. The knife made a thud as it hit him in the back and then sent him sprawling face down onto the floor.

Jehan walked over to the man and retrieved his knife, then said to Fang, "Enough." The dog released his prey. The faceless assassin had stopped screaming, but Jehan finished the job with a knife in his throat. The Count rose to his feet, shaking and wide-eyed.

"By all the gods in heaven," he said. "I've never seen such speed. You are the most lethal pair..." He looked at Jehanna as though seeing her for the first time. "N... needless to say, I am deeply grateful."

"You saved our lives in Lendholm," Jehanna said, as the twins set about covering the bodies and setting things back on the table.

"We won't ever forget what you have done for us," Jehan said, wiping the blood from his knife and sheathing it. "But you are quite right. I can't stay here if I want to progress. I have some ideas myself and I'd be interested to hear your thoughts, my Lord."

"Indeed... yes. Well... let us meet later today when this... mess has been cleared." The Count cast his eye around the room. "I have a mind to know where these assassins came from and will follow a few enquiries of my own before the day is out."

**

It was late evening before the twins were summoned back to the dining room. This time the table had been laid with a late supper of bread and meats, accompanying pickles and a pitcher of wine.

"This will calm the nerves," Count Lenden said pouring Jehanna a cup of wine and placing it in front of her. She picked it up, sniffed at it, then took a small sip. It was strong and fruity and warmed her insides as it went down. "Not that either of you two have any problems with nerves." He chuckled to himself and shook his head. "Where did you learn all of that?" The Count waved his arm about, imitating the movements of the twins. Jehan took a sip of the wine and helped himself to meat and bread, then shrugged.

"Here and there," he said. The Count looked blankly at him. "We've been practising a long time together."

"Yes, I can see that," the Count said. He looked at Jehanna, smiled, then looked at Fang. "Perhaps you can teach our dog trainers a few things too. I never thought I'd be so glad to see the sight of that mutt at your feet." Jehanna smiled and ruffled Fang's ears. The dog laid his head on her feet.

"You mentioned this morning that you might be able to help us, my Lord," Jehanna said, feeling brave enough to help herself to some meats and take another sip of wine. The Count paused, tore off a chunk of bread from the loaf in the middle of the table and speared a chunk of yellow cheese.

"Perhaps," he said, taking a mouthful. He chewed thoughtfully before continuing. "But your display this morning has lead me to some other enquiries. I have a proposition for you both." Jehanna looked up at Jehan. He caught her eye and smiled briefly before focusing his attention back on the Count. "The men that attacked me this morning belonged to a group of mercenaries in Dern. This particular group of professional misfits will take any job if the price is right. It seems that one of our wealthier nobles in Dern has a personal vendetta against me for refusing to take on his lazy, good-for-nothing nephew. I now have two choices; I can sit it out and wait for the next assassination attempt which will come as surely as the sun will rise, or I can take control of the situation."

A flutter of excitement settled in Jehanna's stomach as she looked from the Count to Jehan and back again. A flicker of a smile twitched at Jehan's lips and she knew that he was feeling the same way, as they both speculated internally about the possibilities.

"So, I choose to take control," the Count said. "This group of mercenaries has a sadistic and brutal leader named Brazzano. He rules by violence and intimidation. Fortunately for us, they still cling to their archaic values that state if the leader is challenged and defeated, the winner assumes leadership." Jehan was silent, but thoughtful, absorbing the Count's words. When the Count was met with silence, he continued as though afraid to linger too long without the sound of conversation. "It just so happens, that I might need to commission the work of such a group of mercenaries. Under suitable leadership, you understand."

"If it is protection you need, why not just use your own soldiers?" Jehan said. The Count smiled and nodded his head.

"That is a good question, indeed. It is partly to do with protection, but that would be merely treating the symptoms of this little ailment without addressing the actual cause. This is a blight, which if allowed to proliferate, will eat into the very heart of our community. It must be stamped out quickly and decisively."

Jehanna knew that her brother had already been out searching for a possible way to progress, but now it looked like an opportunity had found them. Jehan looked over at his sister. It was going to be a long hard job to bring about change to such a band of misfits, but neither of them was shy of a challenge.

CHAPTER THIRTEEN

What was that smell? Gereinte wrinkled his nose and coughed into his hand. Morda appeared not to notice the rancid stench wafting across on the breeze. Even the white robed priests that ambled about their business appeared oblivious. He glanced over his shoulder at the three squads of his best rangers lined up behind him. Despite their martial training, even they were having a tough time maintaining a neutral expression. Morda was glowering in front of him in the courtyard of his converted gatehouse, like the weasel he was.

"To what do we owe this unexpected pleasure?" Morda said, through clenched teeth. "Perhaps I can offer you a tour of our prayer rooms, your Majesty." He was attempting to steer Gereinte in the opposite direction and away from the dark hole at the back of the courtyard from which Gereinte was almost certain he could now hear a low, desperate wail. He dismounted and signalled for his closest guards to follow. Fulk, his Captain of the Guard, dismounted and was right behind him, casting a shadow mightier than the church's makeshift spire that topped the building and threatened the skyline of Canrac. The priests made way for the King, who strode towards the sounds and smells emanating from the entrance to a dark stairway at the back of the courtyard. "Your Majesty," Morda raised his voice, perhaps in some vain hope to hide the screaming that had intensified on Gereinte's approach. "There are far more scenic parts of the building to explore."

Indeed. He had no desire to see what was going on in the depths of this so-called holy place, but he knew that it must be seen. Whatever lay down there, justified his presence in this gods forsaken place. "Your Majesty, please, I implore you – this is not of your concern." Morda was starting to sound desperate, but Gereinte was no longer listening as he carefully stepped down into the darkness of the dungeons.

The pitch black of the stairwell blinded him, so he had to feel the edge of each step with his leading foot so as not to fall down. Fulk followed behind him along with two rangers. As they descended, his eyes became accustomed to the dark, but the stench worsened when they reached the bottom. Gereinte turned his head away, only just managing to prevent losing his breakfast.

He braced himself and within seconds had his bow nocked and an arrow loosed. There was a grunt and a thud as a white figure hit the stone floor, a steel poker clattering beside him and the arrow shaft protruding from his arm. The priest wailed in pain. Beside him a man was hanging by his arms, which were twisted at an impossible angle behind him. The expression on his face was excruciating as he lifted his head to plead with his eyes. His face and body were covered with dirt, faeces and blood and though he sobbed, each time his chest moved he cried out in pain at the mere effort. Gereinte swept to his side and took hold of his legs to ease the pain in his arms and chest while Fulk took a knife to the ropes that held him hanging.

"What is this? How dare you interfere with God's work." Morda was screeching as he pushed into the room. The rangers had their bows trained on Morda and his accompanying priests.

Gereinte lowered the man to the ground and left Fulk to tend to him. He strode up to Morda and brought his face up close to his, invading his personal space. The man still had the audacity to look defiant in the face of his King and in front of such evil Gereinte had not before witnessed in his young life. Gereinte's eyes narrowed and his voice came out in a low growl.

"This is no work of any god in Carentan." He held Morda's gaze for a moment before breaking away, not trusting himself to handle the situation further without impunity. "Get that man some water and medical attention, if you value your freedom," Gereinte said to Morda's assistants who sprang into action to aid Fulk. "You," he said, suppressing the urge to spit on Morda. "I will you see in the courtyard now." He pushed past the flabbergasted fanatic and took the steps two at a time, holding his breath until he burst out into the outside air of the courtyard.

The rangers had already taken control of the gatehouse and the priests had been herded into a group in the centre of the open space. The entire building was surrounded now, with rangers holding the walls on each side, bows at the ready for any ill-thought attempts to flee. Gereinte's head was pounding with anger, giving rise to a rush of blood that only exacerbated his mood. He took a few deep breaths, but all he wanted to do at that moment was to rip someone's head off. And right in the middle of all this, there was a group of people who would do quite nicely. How many more people had suffered or died at the hands of these barbaric practices in the name of religion?

"It stops here. Today." Gereinte pointed his finger at the astonished crowd of Morda's followers. Suddenly, it was very clear to him what he must do. There was a mumble amongst the crowd as they absorbed his words. Then a hesitancy as Gereinte noted without turning that Morda had entered the courtyard behind him. The incongruous expressions of the faces of the priests were testament to the levels of indoctrination to which they had been exposed. Morda's presence alone was enough.

Gereinte did not acknowledge the demagogue's appearance. "As of today, under the rules of a new Citizen's Charter which is, as I speak, being ratified, religious tolerance in Carentan is guaranteed." He could feel the confusion rampant amongst Morda's followers. Did this mean that they were free to go? Surely by this standard, the Church of the One God was guaranteed its existence. He could feel the exultation of their leader before he even heard the laugh behind his back. This was really too much.

Gereinte swung around to face Morda, whose expression changed quickly from glee to mild surprise. "You, on the other hand," he said punctuating his words by pointing his finger at the priest. "Will take your dirty habits and leave this land within three days, or you will be hunted down and brought to justice at the King's Court." There was a gasp from the crowd. "And I personally guarantee you as fair a trial as you have offered my people. Forthwith, Abiel Morda, you are banned by the King's decree from the land of Carentan."

Morda's face had paled and his eyes darted to his followers beseeching their support. Got you, thought Gereinte as he looked from the confused melee of supporters to their leader, now fallen from grace in the eyes of the King and Crown.

"Of course," continued Gereinte addressing the crowd. "You may follow your leader into disgrace and banishment, or you can serve your country in a noble and just cause." He allowed his words to sink in and watched their faces change, with hope in the eyes of some and despair in the eyes of others. "As it happens, I am putting together a new corps of shock troops to defend Carentan and will be conscripting every able-bodied male here present to be trained. So. You may serve your country, or face banishment and disgrace."

Without allowing the priests time to reconcile their relations with Abiel Morda, Gereinte had them marched out of the gatehouse and back to Castle Helmstedt, where they would be given time to come to terms with their situation. Morda was left alone, save for a few servant women, to ponder his own predicament and plan his flight from favour.

CHAPTER FOURTEEN

Count Lenden's offer was simple. He would support the twins with their move to Dern. And until such a time when the mercenary outfit became self-sufficient, he would also fund its training and development. In return, Jehanna and Jehan would provide the castle with additional men in the Count's private quarters and keep him informed of any intelligence from Dern on the activities of his would-be assassin.

The move to Dern was not as traumatic as Jehanna had initially imagined. Dern was a crowded place, with its trading market and close proximity to the Royal Palace. It had a very close-knit community feel; something perhaps to do with the fact that the entire city was walled off from the outside world and protected by a royal guard. They had modest accommodation above a popular tavern in the heart of the city. It provided them with a good central point from which to start their enquiries and enabled them to lie low for a while to get a feel for the city before making a play for the mercenary group.

It was a city where you could easily slip away from prying eyes and suited the twins' desire for anonymity. The tavern was frequented by locals and foreigners alike, being within a day's ride from the port of Sternhelm. It pleased Jehanna that she no longer felt out of place in a roomful of people with every shade of skin colour under the sun. That kind of detail didn't seem to bother Jehan in the least.

In the meantime, Jehanna had found an herbalist who had plenty of work for her making tonics and treating minor ailments. Jehan was too busy staking out the mercenary outfit to find any additional work, but spent a large part of his day drawing up plans and mapping out the perimeters of the camp. They met each evening in the tavern lounge to eat and share ideas. It was two weeks after their departure from Castle Lendholm and Jehanna was beginning to worry that they were keeping the Count waiting too long.

"Don't worry," Jehan said, poring over his plans in the tavern one evening. "He'll wait." Jehanna felt a growing impatience with her brother. He had a habit of brushing aside her thoughts without addressing her anxiety. He was always so sure of his inner vision, that sometimes he forgot or didn't think it necessary to share his reasoning. Jehanna sighed and poured another cup of ale for her brother in the hope that it might loosen his tongue.

"It's all very well for you to say, don't worry, but I can't help it and if you don't give me a good reason not to, then I shall continue to bother you about it." Jehan put down his sheets of paper and looked up at his sister.

"You worry too much. The Count will wait because he knows he is getting a good deal. If it all goes according to plan, he'll have another army at his disposal."

"Huh. From what you've told me, he might have to wait some time before they're in any fit state to call an army," Jehanna said. She took a slug of ale and broke off a chunk of bread from the loaf on the table. With a furtive glance around the room, she dropped the bread onto the floor where it disappeared. The steady swish of a dog's tail sticking out from the other end of the table kept prying eyes at bay. Jehan raised an eyebrow.

"Are you sure they don't mind Fang being down here? I thought he was scaring away the customers."

"It's all right, as long he is out of sight. Besides, he helped break up a fight the other night, so the landlord is okay about him being down here now."

"Oh?"

"When you were out on one of your scouting missions, Fang jumped up between two drunks who were about to knock each other out and pushed one of them over with his front paws," Jehanna said. "You should have seen the look on their faces. They ran out the door like they were being chased by a pack of hungry wolves. Since then, he has been okay about Fang being down here as long as he keeps out of the way." Jehan laughed and returned to his paperwork.

"I think," he said after a while, "we are almost ready to do this. The forces are depleted at the moment, as there is some jostling for position going on at the Palace. I believe that the Prince, Rupert Darron, has fallen ill and his daughter, Jessamine is too young to rule in his stead, so a Regency Council is being set up."

"Prince Darron is dead?"

"No. Not yet, but as usual, all the schemers and the ambitious barons suddenly crawl out of the woodwork when there is a position of power to be had. Jessamine is next in line for the crown. Who wouldn't want to be her closest advisor at a time like this?"

"So the mercenaries are keeping the peace at the Palace?"

"If that's what you like to call it," Jehan said. "Depends entirely on how much money they are being paid and by whom as to whether they are actually keeping peace or creating a climate conducive to civil uproar."

"That will have to stop," Jehanna said.

"As soon as," Jehan agreed.

"How about tomorrow then?"

"Tomorrow is as good a time as any, especially with half the forces preoccupied at the Palace."

"Good. What about this leader?" Jehanna said.

"Brazzano? He is at the camp. He deems himself far too important to sully his hands with such menial work at the Palace. His second in command, Pauli is much the same and is also at the camp," Jehan said.

"Good. Two birds with one stone, I like it."

Jehan looked appraisingly at his sister. "For all your healing empathy, you can be a hard bitch when you want."

Jehanna smiled. "It's all a question of values, dear Brother."

"Money is the only thing these people value, you'd better get used to that," Jehan said. But Jehanna had her own ideas about her part to play in organising this mercenary outfit. By the time they had finished with them, money, she thought, would be the least of their concerns.

CHAPTER FIFTEEN

The next morning, the twins presented themselves to the guards at the mercenary camp gates. The camp was a sprawling array of mismatched huts, tents and wagons that looked like they had been driven as far as their battered wheels could carry them, and then abandoned. Some of them didn't even have wheels at all and were being propped up by anything from tree stumps to tea chests. In the heart of the ground, just visible above the mismatched rooftops was a large tent that flew a red flag with a crude painting of a boar's head.

That was probably where Brazzano was and that was the direction the twins headed. The perimeter of the ground was fenced off with crude wooden slats, hardly capable of keeping people either out or in, but promoted a message to those who cared to venture close enough; enter at your own peril. Since the only way in was through the front entrance and the two men on guard appeared less than interested in the twins' presence, they continued their path through the gated perimeter.

"Not so fast," the guard said, stepping in front of them. He was dressed in ragged clothes like the assassins at Castle Lendholm. Either the pay wasn't so great or the money earned from ventures such as assassinating the nearest influential noble, went to fund things other than training clothes or weaponry. The guard on the other side of the path stepped across to join his companion and the two of them barred access to the twins, lowering their spears across the entrance.

Jehan stopped and looked at the spears with curiosity. The weapons were fashioned from wooden shafts, with steel heads that looked like they had been hastily forged at a less than professional blacksmith's establishment. Well the funds certainly didn't stretch to weaponry, that much was evident. Jehan raised a finger in a gesture that to the guards might have looked defensive, but to Jehanna indicated which one she was to deal with if this encounter turned sour. She fixed her gaze on the guard to her left. When he noticed her looking, his spear arm relaxed and almost wavered away from Jehan. She smiled and the guard could not take his eyes off her. To disarm him would be like taking milk from a baby.

"We've come to sign up," Jehan said brightly and the other guard almost dropped his spear. Jehan's words began to dawn on the two guards who were not the brightest pair of soldiers Jehanna had ever met. They began to laugh. Then their laughter slowed and died as they took in the serious expression on Jehan's face and they realised that neither of the twins shared the funny side of the situation.

"Right then," said the guard nearest to Jehan with an uneasy tension.

"You'd better follow me."

He took them across the camp grounds, weaving in and out of wagons and tents that were populated with soldiers and the occasional woman, attempting to keep house in the most basic of accommodation. One or two children lingered around, playing with sticks or staring at the strangers being marched across the ground. Jehanna was surprised to see a couple of women who in all appearances were soldiers, cleaning weapons or sharpening knives. It had not occurred to her that there might be women who wanted to be warriors. Where else would they be allowed to practise their trade?

The large central tent came into view, flying its aggressive boar-head flag as a warning to any who dared venture closer. The guard stopped outside the entrance.

"You sure you want to do this?" he said, glancing uneasily at Jehanna. Jehan nodded. The guard shook his head, tutting to himself, then drew back the tent flap.

Inside, it became evident where most of the funds from the activities of the mercenaries had been spent. In the centre of the tent was an ornate throne-like chair on a raised dais. The man who sat there was a brute of a fellow with long dark tangled hair bunched up beneath a hat which would have sat well upon the head of a sea pirate. His jacket was clearly more expensive than the entire wardrobe of every mercenary soldier they had so far encountered. He looked like a king in a pauper's show.

This was Brazzano.

Another man stepped into view from behind the dais; expensively, though equally distastefully, dressed. Pauli, Jehanna guessed. Around the dais was an arena that was empty, save for a few hopeful pigeons pecking at the dust. The perimeter of the arena held benches, presumably for spectators. Perhaps this was their training ground, or maybe they just liked to bring along a few enemies for sport once in a while.

"This is where our leader presides over disputes, hears requests and complaints. That sort of thing," the guard said, reading Jehanna's thoughts.

"You have a lot of disputes within the organisation?" she said. The guard looked askance at her and shrugged.

"Brazzano is not easy to get along with." That said it all, really.

Brazzano was lounging on his throne as the twins were marched forward by the guard. His eyes swept lazily over them and then he slowly leant forward in order to get a better view.

"Well, well. What is this? Such a pretty looking pair. What do you want?" Brazzano said.

Jehanna was aware that Pauli had slipped away and out of the back of the tent. She nudged Jehan and whispered.

"Don't make it too quick, Jay, we could have an audience before long." Jehan didn't look at his sister; he was staring ahead at Brazzano, but she saw his face in profile and noted the corners of his mouth curl up in a smile.

"My name is Jehan Mantar and we've come to join up," he said. Brazzano looked from one twin to the other, and then back again at Jehan before creasing up with laughter.

"Have you indeed? Well I hope the girl is readily available," he said almost barking in Jehanna's direction. The implication made her skin crawl. "I wouldn't want to have to kill you for her." Ignoring Brazzano's crude wit, Jehan drew his sword.

"Why prolong the inevitable? I am challenging you to the leadership of this group. Come down here and fight, if you dare," Jehan said.

Jehanna moved away from Jehan and took up a position on the outside of the arena. The guard followed her example and drawing to one side, whispered excitedly.

"Is he mad? He doesn't stand a chance with Brazzano."

"Go and get some back up," Jehanna said.

"Back up? No one is likely to want to face Brazzano when he is angry," the guard said.

"I meant, for Brazzano. Better still, round up as many spectators as possible to witness your new leader in action," Jehanna said with a sly smile. The guard frowned, then raced out of the tent flap. It was not long before a steady stream of onlookers started filtering into the arena and watching with curiosity from the benches.

"Why, you puking little brat." Brazzano was on his feet waving a fist at Jehan. "I'm gonna cut you slowly into small pieces and feed you to the pigeons."

Jehan moved into the centre of the combat area and began to taunt the big man, shrugging his shoulders as if to say, 'so what?' Then he beckoned Brazzano with a 'come on then' signal. The growing crowd of onlookers started to make 'ooooh' noises and someone from the back shouted, "Are you gonna let him get away with that?"

Brazzano's face had turned scarlet with rage. He drew his sword, a massive hand-and-a-half blade, as he charged down from the dais and into the arena. The sword swung down in a murderous arc that should have cut Jehan in half had he not nimbly sidestepped the blow. He might be a good fighter, this Brazzano, and he certainly had the advantage when it came to strength and size, but speed gave Jehan the upper hand. Jehanna watched her brother dance about the arena, neatly circumventing a number of serious attempts to slice him in two. His movement was effortless and merely served to outrage his opponent even more, making Brazzano clumsy in his attacks.

The spectators cheered with gusto at every blow attempted by Brazzano, then made 'ahh' noises of disappointment each time his attempts were thwarted by the antics of the lithe dark stranger. Jehan dropped his guard tauntingly and as predicted, Brazzano drove forward with another great swing of his sword arm. At the last second before contact, Jehan stepped into Brazzano's swing, cutting his distance down and riposted with a lightening thrust which he pulled short at the last moment, pinking Brazzano's cheek without doing any serious harm. Brazzano's hand shot up to his cheek and came away bloody. He looked from the blood on his hand to Jehan in disbelief. A heavy silence hung over the arena. The spectators, who had been growing restless at Brazzano's inability to give them a good show, had suddenly quietened down and there was a renewed buzz of excitement in the crowds as they realised that the balance of power had shifted.

Brazzano roared his defiance and swung his sword high over his head before bringing it neatly down towards Jehan. But before the sword even levelled, Jehan was no longer there. This time, he stepped on the outside of the swing and neatly sliced open Brazzano's other cheek. The deadly ease with which Jehan responded to Brazzano gave rise to a cheer from the audience. Loyalty was apparently a fickle bedfellow, Jehanna noted.

She observed the onlookers, standing in astonished silence. Slowly, as reality dawned on their faces, some of them began to cheer and holler for Jehan. It was obvious to most who witnessed this extraordinary event that despite the fact that Brazzano was fast for such a big man, his sword skills were poor; he had all too often relied on brute force and intimidation. The gulf in fighting skills between the two warriors became embarrassingly clear to all who looked on in amazement. Jehanna whispered under her breath "Finish it, Jehan."

One last despairing thrust from Brazzano was enough for Jehan to parry with ease before running his sword straight through the big warrior's heart. Brazzano looked down at his chest, then up at Jehan and smiled, as trickle of blood ran down his chin. He fell to his knees, then dropped head first to the ground with a thump. It seemed like minutes but was probably just seconds before the silence in the tent was broken by Pauli's strangled cry.

"No! You can't be the chief." He ran screaming into the combat area. Jehan had no time to retrieve his sword from the semi-prone corpse of Brazzano before Pauli was charging him with a broadsword. Onlookers only saw a quick flick of Jehan's wrist as a dagger sailed through the space between them. It found its target with a sickening thud and Pauli's charge came to an abrupt halt, the dagger protruding from his neck. In a defiant final stand, the second-in-command reached up and withdrew the weapon, throwing it desperately to the ground. A fountain of blood spewed from the open wound and Pauli dropped to his knees, eventually toppling over sideways to join Brazanno. Silent disbelief hung in the air for what seemed an eternity before Jehan spoke.

"Well, my good people. Who are the senior Marshalls around here?" Four men reluctantly raised their hands, their expressions vacant and faces ashen. "Good. Perhaps you would be so kind as to show my sister and me to some accommodation and we can make a start on reorganising this outfit."

Jehanna turned to look at the guard who had just returned to her side, staring at the battle ground with his mouth open. "Would you mind taking care of that?" she said indicating the mess of corpses on the ground. The guard looked at her, then back at Jehan and nodded, perhaps a little too enthusiastically.

"Y... yes, errm... my Lady."

"Thank you," Jehanna said, and stepped over the bench to follow her brother. This was perhaps going to be easier than she had initially hoped.

Jehan had always maintained that despite Count Lenden referring to the mercenaries as a 'sorry bunch of misfits' all they needed was good leadership. Jehanna was beginning to see the wisdom of his words. The first thing they did was establish a clear set of boundaries and guidelines, based on the eastern ideologies of the sheikdoms which operated as co-operatives with a structure that fostered a sense of collaboration and community interaction. The dust had barely settled on the battleground before Jehan ordered Brazzano's arena tent to be brought down and his golden throne to be dismantled and sold off in various parts to the highest bidders. The funds made through this little venture were then distributed equally amongst the soldiers and their families, including those who had recently returned from assignment at the Royal Palace.

Jehan took charge of training the troops, while Jehanna took care of administering to the needs of their families and organising a garrison of sorts. She returned briefly to the tavern to pick up their supplies and collect Fang, who had successfully ingratiated himself with the landlord and now was released from guard dog duties with some measure of reluctance. Fang, himself, was more than willing to follow his mistress to the camp and partake in whatever new and exciting adventures were on offer, so long as he was within barking distance of Jehanna. The rest of the inhabitants of the camp watched this new addition to the 'family' with the measure of respect deserved by both; the sight of a dog and a woman practising fighting moves had at first unnerved the soldiers but it soon became a familiar sight. Jehanna had even had approaches herself to teach some of the younger ones a few moves to practise while their elders were getting down to the business of tactics with Jehan.

The Count saw to it that there were enough funds available to build a new camp with a properly equipped training ground, a secure perimeter fence and decent uniforms for the mercenaries. Very soon, the Count enjoyed a return on his investment as an elite corps of soldiers was dispatched to Castle Lendholm to take care of the Count's most immediate needs. Before long, the mercenaries were building a reputation for themselves as a reliable and effective means of dealing with local problems and were bringing in enough income to be independent from the Count's funds. The Count was never left lacking protection and it became a custom that would always remain; to protect the interests of the local Lord who helped found the new group.

A food hall was set up and staff were recruited from the mercenary's families to cook, clean and serve the garrison; their work well rewarded with both money and better living conditions. There were some who preferred to remain in their ramshackle wagons on the outskirts of the camp, which was their preference. But even they, due to increasing income from the work of the mercenaries were beginning to improve the conditions of their private homes. Before long, the wagons were being decorated with colour and fixed up with superior windows, steps and new wheels. The mercenary camp soon became known as the Caravanserai of Dern with the idealists from the East, where visitors were welcomed and people came to either sign up or experience the group of soldiers for hire known as Mantar's Mercenaries.

CHAPTER SIXTEEN

Mercadier de Taroudant, the Chevalier Supreme, looked out of the large oval window of his chamber in the Southern Lands of Arrontierre. In the distance, he could almost make out the coastline of Vermondie on the horizon. He sighed and wrapped his cloak tightly around his shoulders in response to the bitter chill wind that was battering the bay. Not the best place to build a city, granted, but he had inherited it along with the name of Taroudant, from a long line of noble forefathers. It was a bright and gaudily decorated castle, built on the top of a mount, which had evolved into a city in its own right. It was his destiny to rule the northern coast of Arrontierre from this impenetrable promontory, ever teased by the potential spoils of the Western Isles.

Born into nobility, Mercadier had fought alongside the former Emperor of Arrontierre and earned his title of Chevalier the hard way, unlike some of the young upstarts who managed to progress purely on the strength of their birth right. It seemed all too common an occurrence to find young chevaliers riding through the towns and cities of Arrontierre, having freshly graduated from the military academy, with not a single battle to their name. Their arrogance was almost justified by the manner in which they were given strongholds across the country by the new Emperor; like giving candy to children. The new Emperor was churning out chevaliers as if there were some shortage of armies, with no strategic overview of how the country might accommodate such a vast number of military men in its hierarchy.

Too many chevaliers and not enough foot soldiers. If the country ever did go to war, Mercadier didn't doubt that they would win through sheer numbers alone. But he did not envy the warmeister who would have to coordinate the reporting lines. And the new Emperor was certainly not without his own partiality. How many times in the years gone by had Mercadier been overlooked for promotion because of some younger noble who had come to the attention of the Emperor through his social circles? Perhaps the time really had come to realise his dream.

"And what, my dear Chevalier, do you dream of tonight?" He turned at the sound of his wife, Adaliz, who had slipped into the room while his thoughts were elsewhere. She sidled up behind him and stood to his side, following his gaze out to sea. "You have waited too long," she said in a whisper, adjusting his cloak around his shoulders. Her soft claret gown clung to her figure and when he turned to look at her, his body burned with a passion that could not be ignored.

It was true to say that he was not a particularly handsome man and for Mercadier to have turned the head of a woman like the Lady Adaliz, many remarked that it was not his own ambition he stoked at Castle Taroudant. This, he realised to be true very early on in their relationship. And yet, somehow it made not one iota of difference to how he felt about her. "You have the Emperor's blessing and an army to boot. What could possibly hold you back now?"

Her voice held a subtle but nonetheless accusatory tone.

"Strategy," Mercadier said. "You cannot rush a thing like this. Numbers alone might easily quash some of the northern barbarians. But the southerners are a little more accomplished in their civilisation and structure."

"I hear the southern countries are divided. That they have been warring amongst themselves for many years," she said. "I also hear that Carentan has a new King and he is only seventeen." She smiled at him and raised an eyebrow as though she knew what affect this observation would have. He seethed inside, but resisted the temptation to voice his angst. May the One God preserve him from nepotistic young kings and emperors who knew nothing of strategy and only wanted to further their own interests. Adaliz's eyes sparkled. He knew she had got him and that it was just a question, then, of reeling him in. "Strategy, you say. Hmm, what a good idea," she said. "You could send a trade delegation."

A rush of pride engulfed him. Yes. A trade delegation. That would give them enough time to gather the necessary political intelligence from within the country itself. It was perfect. He turned and kissed his wife and she returned his passion with her undivided attention.

"Of course," he said, pulling away and looking into her dark eyes. "A visiting dignitary would need to have his wife by his side." She smiled mischievously and nodded her head in acknowledgement.

117

"What a marvellous idea. You are such a clever man."

Mercadier pulled his wife back into his embrace and they both looked out of the oval window of Castle Taroudant at the distant outline of Vermondie.

***

"A trade delegation?" Gereinte stared at Etienne Martan. They came to a slow halt just outside the large training ground in the middle ward of Castle Helmstedt. Gereinte was dressed in a thickset green tunic and breeches with his sword sheathed in its battered scabbard on his belt. He had come out to watch the training of the priests and to find out how his new corps was coming along, when Etienne had caught up with him to give him this rather surprising news.

The two men stood side-by-side, unaware of the attention that followed in their wake, as two of the most eligible bachelors in Carentan. Etienne had a knowing smile on his face, which infuriated Gereinte. But the women found this irresistible, coupled with his sandy hair and boyish dimples. Gereinte had no time for flirting, despite the effect his presence appeared to have. He had inherited his father's dark tousled hair and emerald eyes, which shone with clarity of purpose unusual in someone so young. Two ladies of the court walked past, casting their eyes downward and with a demure curtsy in their direction, giggled behind their hands. Etienne nodded politely in their direction, but Gereinte deliberately ignored them. "Why would the

Chevaliers of Arrontiere send a trade delegation to Vermondie?"

"Well I hardly think it is to trade. Arrontierre is rich enough without the need to import goods from the Western Isles. Besides, Vermondie barely produces enough to keep themselves sustained," Etienne said.

"A smokescreen, then. That doesn't bode too well." Gereinte looked out across the training ground. The Chevaliers were an elite class of knights, trained to defend the Southern Lands in war and educated to run the country in times of peace. He knew something of their ambitions from his eastern allies, Kemal and Jabir. They were a race that liked a challenge. They had already made attempts in the past to infiltrate Vermondie and Tordre. Perhaps the Chevaliers thought they still had claims on the Western Isles. Or perhaps they came to finish what they started, though Vermondie and Tordre had been independent for hundreds of years.

He looked at Etienne who was frowning into the distance. A group of unlikely looking soldiers had appeared on the training ground and were waving practice swords around, like oversized toothpicks. The marshal in charge of training the soldiers was trying to show them how to properly hold a sword and yet, even the squires were making light work of these soldiers in the sparring ring. Good grief.

"Is that the best you can do?" Etienne said. "Whose idea was it to train up the priests anyway?"

Gereinte shook his head, a hand over his face in despair.

"You bring me news that the Chevaliers of Arrontierre have taken a sudden interest in our meek little Isle, then you mock my attempts to muster a fighting force. I'm truly hurt," Gereinte said, a little smile hovering on his lips.

"Believe me," Etienne said. "You're going to need a lot more than that poor excuse for an army if the Chevaliers do decide to wage war on the Western Isles."

One of the priests was systematically being battered by one of the larger squires with the flat side of a practice sword. Without warning, the priest dropped his sword and ran in the opposite direction. The squire took off after him and chased him, making several circuits of the area before the marshal got fed up with the farce and ordered them both out of the training ground.

Gereinte paled and turned to look at Etienne who was clutching his sides trying desperately not to laugh.

"Perhaps you have a point. I think I need to find Jabir," Gereinte said, giving him a withering look.

Gereinte found the easterner Jabir ed-Din in the library, poring over the scrolls that were to make up the draft of the new Civil Charter for Carentan. The library was like a shrine of peace to Gereinte, who often spent time there when he needed space to reflect. Its oak panelled walls gave way to a vast array of shelves with books, ancient and new, classified according to subject. The stone floor was covered in rugs and large tubular receptacles for storing scrolls. Jabir stood at a circular table in the middle of the room with several scrolls unrolled in front of him. He frowned and began propping the scrolls open with a small flat stone at each corner. He favoured a long flowing dark robe because he said it was closest to the kind of clothes he might wear in his home country. Gereinte thought it made him look like one of the priests of the ancient gods and gave him an air of mystery. He looked up when he noticed Gereinte enter the library, though he didn't seem at all surprised to see him.

"And what do your gods have to tell you today?" Jabir teased him. Without looking up from his scroll, he picked up a small round stone.

"I don't speak to the gods, as you well know," Gereinte said approaching the table and looking over Jabir's shoulder.

"Oh, and why might that be, I wonder?" They often had theological debates which could sometimes go on for hours, but Gereinte was in no mood to discuss the merits or otherwise of differing religious beliefs.

"Because they don't talk back to me, for one thing. Otherwise, I might have been forewarned of our impending visit from the Chevaliers of Arrontierre." Jabir dropped the stone to the table, which made a loud clunk. He looked up at Gereinte.

"Now that, I wasn't expecting so soon."

"So soon?"

Gereinte had always puzzled over the two easterners, Jabir and Kemal ed-Din. He knew they had pledged their help to his mother and father to educate him in politics and strategic warfare, training him in the fighting arts and preparing him for his ascension to the throne of Carentan. Their presence had been undeniably crucial in ways he could not have foreseen and their company more than welcome. But why were they still there? He had just assumed that they chose to make his court their home and that he was honoured by having such distinguished and knowledgeable members of his cabinet. That was, until Jabir just made that comment. So soon.

CHAPTER SEVENTEEN

"How many and when?" Alaric said. Gereinte glanced around the table at his advisers. Jabir's reaction to the news of the imminent arrival in Vermondie of a trade delegation from Arrontierre had deeply concerned Gereinte. So he had called a special meeting to discuss the matter further. In addition to Warmaster Alaric were his trusted cabinet, Etienne Martan looking pleased with himself, Chancellor Lorquin who had the air of an elderly uncle, Chanac Issoire with his heir Darien, his sister Alliane, Jabir and Kemal.

"Ten, we think," Etienne said. "Including the wife of a man named Taroudant, the Chevalier Supreme." The Warmaster looked baffled for a moment.

"Hardly a threat to Carentan, I think," he said. He sounded almost disappointed that they had not declared an all-out war on the Western Isles.

"Think about it," Gereinte said. "What possible reason could they have to negotiate trade with Vermondie?"

"True enough, Vermondie has nothing much to trade. But in order to get produce to the coast from other locations in the Western Isles, they would have to negotiate trade routes *through* Vermondie." There were several nods around the table. Gereinte felt suddenly deflated, like a little boy again, seated at his father's great war table listening to words he did not understand and feeling the weight of the world on his shoulders. He looked to Jabir who merely smiled in his enigmatic way.

How could he tell these trusted and seasoned warriors that his instinct warned him the Chevaliers had more pressing concerns than the movement of goods from one part of the world to another? His father had always relied on his instinct. Look where that got him; both his father and mother had spent more time planning how Gereinte would succeed than watching their own backs. He pushed aside a stab of melancholy and thanked the gods that his parents had the foresight to leave him in the company of the people around that table with whom he now shared this burden of rule.

"Why, then, would the Chevalier Supreme bring his wife to such a negotiation?" Alliane said. Gereinte smiled to himself at his sister's astute observation and looked to the Warmaster for his reaction. Alaric paused for a moment to collect his thoughts, opened his mouth to say something then promptly closed it and shook his head. Alaric had obviously not been as exposed as Gereinte had been to the internal logic of women.

"Evidently," Chancellor Lorquin said, "she has come to support her husband in his negotiations." There were a few nods around the table.

"Evidently," Alliane said, not in the least bit put off by the Chancellor's avuncular tone, "she has come to view her new home." Some of the men around the table frowned. Alliane was wearing a gown of crimson velvet, trimmed with ermine and topped with a jewel-encrusted headdress. She looked every bit the princess she was and Gereinte sat silent, smiling at her observation. A balanced perspective was every bit as necessary as a strategic plan.

"Perhaps," Jabir said, "I can throw some light on the situation." At last, Gereinte breathed an inward sigh. He was wondering when the wily old scholar was going to rescue him. "About fifteen years ago, myself and my kinsman, Kemal," he nodded at the eastern sword master who remained impassive, "were sent on a journey to the northern coast of Arrontierre. We were dispatched from our Sheikdom with the express wishes of the ruling Sheik, Mamman ed-Farik, to return his two young children to him, who were kidnapped and set ashore in Arrontierre by an ambitious noble family, hoping to put an end to the heirs of the ruling blood line." Alliane gasped.

"That is appalling," she said.

"As you well know, Ally," Gereinte said. "Kidnapping is not unheard of, even in the Western Isles." Alliane paled, as the memory of their own missing brother washed over her. "Why did they set them ashore? Why not just kill them?" Gereinte said.

"Why indeed, you may ask. Well, that might have solved the problem, but we are not an aggressive race and we believe even children should be given a chance at survival. It became common practice to abandon unwanted children in another land where they might survive and grow, but never be able to stake any claim to Eastern rule. They were too young to remember who they were or even where they came from."

"What does all this have to do with the trade delegation?" Alaric said with growing impatience.

"Peace, Alaric, I will come to that in good time," Jabir said. Gereinte smiled to himself, empathising with the Alaric's frustration.

Jabir continued. "We spent a year searching the Northern parts of Arrontierre to no avail. The local people were particularly aggressive at seeing foreigners on their soil and we quickly learnt that if two eastern children had appeared on the shores of the Southern Lands that it would not have gone unnoticed for so long. So we headed down south and continued to ask questions and turned up blank responses until eventually we came to the attention of the Emperor. Or should I say that we became very well acquainted with the Emperor's Chevaliers and in turn with the inside of his dungeons." Gereinte could not imagine Kemal allowing himself to be captured and slung in a dungeon unless he had some ulterior motive. "And it was there we learnt of a plot to invade and overthrow the Western Isles." A heavy silence hung in the air around the room. Despite the heat of the midday sun, it suddenly felt very cold. Alliane shivered. Chanac Issoire looked deeply troubled, but remained silent. Darien frowned at Gereinte, then looked at Jabir.

"But..., that was, what... thirteen years ago?" Darien said looking around the table. He caught Gereinte's eye and challenged anyone to deny the distant connection between Jabir's experiences and what was happening today. "Isn't there a new Emperor in Arrontierre?"

Gereinte folded his arms across his chest and sat back; he had a feeling he knew where this was going.

126

"Indeed," Jabir said rubbing his chin, appearing in no hurry to elaborate. "There was an attempt to invade Tordre around that time. King Reiner himself rallied his troops and marched in alliance with what little martial forces were available at the time in Tordre and Vermondie. Had Kemal and myself not been able to escape the clutches of the Chevaliers and travel to warn the leaders in the Western Isles of this threat, most of us would not now be sitting around this table today."

The silence in the room was stifling as they all absorbed this information. Gereinte had a vague recollection of stories being told of this attempted invasion, but along with most of the people around that table, he needed to be convinced of the connection between an old plot and today's intelligence regarding the trade delegation.

"Tell us what you know about the Chevaliers," Gereinte said. Jabir leaned behind his chair and plucked a large scroll from one of the holders. He carefully unrolled it, the paper crackling with the weight of age. Alaric sat up straight as the familiar sight of King Reiner's battle map unfolded before them. Jabir secured it at each corner with a small stone, then took out a small wooden bamboo stick and tapped the map on the South coast of Vermondie. The map was faded with age and covered in pencil marks and annotations, sometimes just squiggly or dotted lines, sometimes words. Gereinte peered closely at the section Jabir was pointing to and noticed a scribbled note followed by a dotted line, which lead from the coast through Vermondie and into Tordre.

"This is where the original attempt at invasion began. Of course, I say original, the natives of the Southern Lands were some of the first settlers in the Western Isles. Indeed, the population of Vermondie and Tordre share many of their characteristics to this day. Some of the more rural areas still speak a local version of Langan. So you can see how the Chevaliers assume that these lands rightfully belong to Arrontierre."

"How bloody dare they?" Chancellor Lorquin said. "Those lands have been independent for centuries. Trumped up, arrogant Southerners." He grumbled to himself amongst a few murmurs of agreement.

"Yes, well...," Jabir said, looking a little uneasy. "Whoever or whatever they seem to be, it appears that they have built up a substantial military force over the last five years since the new Emperor came to rule. Whether this is a significant part of their strategy to expand westward, or merely a result of being driven back at Tordre all those years ago is largely irrelevant. The fact that their forces are considerably stronger and they now appear to be taking more than a passing interest in these isles is indeed cause for concern. I personally think they are jumping too soon, if indeed that is the intention. They are not ready yet, but within two to three years they will have a fighting force that no one in the West without help will stand to overcome. So it is to our advantage that they make a move now. However, just because they are sending a trade delegation now doesn't mean they will make an invasion attempt so soon. It could be now, tomorrow, next year or the year after. The only certainty is that they will come." There was a shiver of anticipation around the room.

"Upon our return to the East, Kemal and I discussed the volatile situation with our own leaders and it was agreed that we should join King Reiner as advisers to militate against any further threat from Arrontierre." Jabir looked at Kemal, seeking reassurance. Kemal gave the briefest of nods before lowering his eyes to the map on the table. Jabir continued. "You may know that the various Sheikdoms in the Eastern Congress exist in an uneasy state of armed neutrality, but one issue on which they are all united is that the plans Arrontierre have for the conquest of the Western Isles does not bode well for the future of the East. Quite simply, we are here to help the Isles remain independent of the Southern Lands. Anything we can do to further this end must be good for both our countries." There was silence around the table as the implication of Jabir's words was absorbed. So. It was not just luck that he happened to meet Jabir on that Coustiller ship. Any more than it was luck that brought his kinsman, Kemal, to his court to teach him how to fight.

"So," Jabir said, tapping the map and waking those around the table from their sombre musings. "It is likely that when they choose their moment, the forces will be initially deployed here... and here." Everyone around the table leaned in to see the points at which Jabir was indicating with his stick.

"How many are we looking at?" Gereinte was not in the mood to tip toe around the reality of the situation, however futile things looked at present.

"I don't believe that we are sitting here discussing war strategy over the arrival of ten foreigners in Vermondie who are negotiating trade routes," Alaric said; his gnarled fist opened and closed in frustration, fighting the urge to bang it on the table. He leaned forward to look at the map. "How can we hope to fight off an invasion with the poor excuse we have for an army in Carentan?" Gereinte grimaced as an image of Morda's renegade priests in training sprang to mind.

"Well...," Gereinte said. "We don't. But if we plan ahead, we have time. Time to raise an army from the length and breadth of the Western Isles that could easily match any threat from Arrontierre." Alaric's mouth opened as if to say something, but nothing came out. He looked around the table at the faces of the others, slowly absorbing Gereinte's words. Gereinte had said it so casually that even some of the others present had not fully comprehended his intent. The Chancellor was frowning, Kemal remained impassive as though he cared not one way or the other, the Issoires were nodding their approval, while Etienne merely smiled as though he already knew the answer. Gereinte caught Jabir's eye and the old man nodded, like it were a done deal.

"I guess," Chancellor Lorquin said, breaking the silence at last, "there is no need to ask who will be leading this great army?"

Gereinte paused, considering the Chancellor's question.

"That rather remains to be seen," he said. But there was no mistaking his tone. He looked to his closest friends, Darien and Etienne who were exchanging a disparaging look. Gereinte shrugged. "Any better ideas?"

"I suppose a consort for the King is out of the question?" Darien said, rewarded only by a few stifled smirks around the table. Darien shrugged. "Well... it might keep him out of trouble long enough for the Chevaliers to get bored and go home."

***

The sun began to go down, as the war cabinet continued to discuss strategy, both short and long term. Servants came with platters of fruit, bread and cheese and a pitcher of ale. As the light began to wane and the conversation reached its natural conclusion, the meeting chamber began to empty of its occupants.

While most of the group were taking their leave, Alliane sat still in her seat, staring at Jabir. By the way she kept frowning, Gereinte could see that something had been niggling her. However she kept her peace whilst the discussion had crossed from the northern most reaches of the Western Isles down to the Southern coast of Vermondie. Perhaps she was hoping for some elaboration that never really arrived. Now, with proceedings called to a halt, she looked ready to burst with curiosity.

"But what happened to the abandoned children?" she said. Jabir looked startled for a moment, suddenly remembering where the discussion had begun. Kemal stirred as though the subject of the children had never really left his preserve.

"That, your Highness, is as much of a mystery today as it was thirteen years ago," Jabir said.

132

CHAPTER EIGHTEEN

Mercadier de Taroudant was resplendent in his military attire, as Chevalier Supreme of Arrontierre. He turned to his wife, Adaliz, and offered his arm before the door attendant announced their names to the gathering in the Great Hall at the Royal Palace in Verton, the capital city of Vermondie.

The journey from the northern coast of Arrontierre had been swift and uneventful and the short crossing over the sea had only served to remind Mercadier of how close they were in distance to the Western Isles, albeit far removed in culture. The grim walls of the city did little to invite trade and negotiation from overseas. The arrival of his own delegation had been received with a measure of scepticism that could only be described as abject suspicion. Still, that would all change before long. Once the Chevaliers had established control, he would be able to convert this grey little corner of the Isles into a thriving port, welcoming visitors and settlers alike from the Southern Lands.

He shuddered to think that these barbarians had once descended from his own fair people. Their streets were choked with filth and their buildings designed by some crude architect with no concept of aesthetics. The guards at the palace gates had been as surly as the lowest of the Emperor's Order and the Palace itself as austere as its occupants. Except perhaps the Prince and Princess. They were almost certainly his biggest problem. The country had made a fundamental shift of late, owing to the recent death of its King, who, from what he could glean from his sources of intelligence, had not been well liked. This could be problematic only if that shift were allowed enough time to establish a foundation. It would appear that he and his Chevaliers had arrived just in time.

Mercadier swept a discerning eye over the assembled nobility before his gaze came to rest on the current ruler of Vermondie; Prince Rann, soon to be crowned King and his sister, Princess Lirra. Rann was striking leader, with ash-blond hair and a ruddy, out-doors look to him. Not a great start; he was just the sort of role model a nation like this would look up to. His sister, Lirra, had a Patrician look to her, coupled with a lively, intelligent manner that would irritate Adaliz no end. To make any progress at all, these two would have to be displaced.

"Mercadier de Taroudant, at your service," he said, bowing low before the royal twins. "May I introduce my wife, the Lady Adaliz." He spoke in a heavily cultured form of Langan, with the assumption that they would understand his words. Rann and Lirra exchanged glances. Adaliz nudged him in the ribs. "Oh, I do apologise. I forget that our language has moved on somewhat over the years." Mercadier adjusted his accent to reflect the more familiar local dialect. Still, the Prince and Princess appeared to exchange a silent appraisal before smiling and introducing themselves.

The evening progressed in much the same manner; Mercadier trying and failing to make minor social adjustments, while the Vermondiens remained impassive and non-committal in their conversations. They seemed reluctant to get to the root of the Chevaliers' visit, those inexplicable trade negotiations, and happy to accept their visitors on face value. The first of their many mistakes. Adaliz had engaged Princess Lirra in conversation and was comparing fashion trends as well as explaining the hierarchical structure of the Southern Lands. By and large, Mercadier deemed it to be a successful first introduction and as non-threatening to the future of Vermondie as he could possibly have made it.

"My Dearest Chevalier," Adaliz said in a thick Langan accent that left no danger of being understood by anyone in the near vicinity. "How dull and crude these people are. I hope you will make it swift enough that I can enjoy the spoils of this war without having to endure such company for too long."

"My Lady, do not fret," Mercadier said in a hushed voice looking around the room. His concern was premature, however, as everyone present seemed to be adequately engaged and not paying them the slightest bit of attention. Except for the white robed holy man, who kept looking in his direction and nodding sagely, as though he knew something that the Chevalier did not. "We will be long gone before the fighting starts and when we return, it will be a different reception you will receive as the new Queen of Vermondie. That much I can assure you." This seemed to satisfy Adaliz, who returned to her conversation with Princess Lirra with a renewed sense of purpose.

The priest was suddenly on his feet and making a direct line for the Chevalier. Mercadier himself had every respect for the religious orders in the Southern Lands, which promoted worship of the One God and ensured the control and subjugation of

135

the masses; fear is a very motivating factor. He had heard rumours of widespread religious tolerance in the Western Isles, which of course was something that could not fit with his own and the Emperor's beliefs.

"May I introduce myself?" The priest bowed with respect and Mercadier nodded in acquiescence. "Abiel Morda, Archbishop of the Church of the One God, at your service." Mercadier smiled to himself. This could be one of his more fruitful conversations of the evening.

Morda's accent was tricky to follow, but his enthusiasm for the arrival of the Chevaliers could not be denied. They discussed the recent overthrow of Marcus Dassan, a Lord and personal adviser to the late King Haveritas. He learnt that the royal twins had seized control of the Palace against the express wishes of the old King on his deathbed, who had appointed Lord Dassan as his Regent. Dassan was now incarcerated in the Palace dungeons, awaiting trial for treason. Prince Rann may well be the people's choice, but according to local law, he was not yet of an age to assume control and there had not yet been a coronation. Mercadier listened to the priest with increasing optimism. Indeed he had arrived at the best possible moment in time and this plan could not wait for a time when the royal twins had established control of this little backwater country. The moment was ripe for exploitation.

In time, their discussion lead to Carentan and the recent ascension to the throne of a young man only just turned eighteen years, Gereinte Andolin. It was clear to Mercadier that the priest had an underlying animosity towards the young King for reasons he did not disclose. It was also clear that Morda had ambitions beyond helping the Chevaliers re-take Vermondie and establish a stake on the rest of the Western Isles. Certainly, for the first part, he would be a useful ally; not least in securing the release of Lord Dassan and the displacement of the royal twins. Indeed, might the Chevalier Supreme even set his own sights a little higher?

"How hard can it be to overthrow an eighteen-year-old boy?" Mercadier said. He watched Morda's complexion pale as the priest gulped a few times and took a large draft of ale from his cup. How curious. Carentan definitely warranted further investigation.

CHAPTER NINETEEN

Gereinte took a turn around the training ground with one of his senior military advisers, Count Barra. The Count was a distinguished military man, now retired from action but still with huge knowledge and experience. He had served under Gereinte's father and in more recent years acted as second to Warmaster Alaric.

"The plan is an ambitious one, I'll say that much." Barra raised an eyebrow at Gereinte and looked around at the current fighting force in training. Gereinte had a sinking feeling that Barra was weighing up their chances of surviving an all-out assault from Arrontierre based on the army showing off their newly acquired martial prowess. Granted, they weren't the most fearsome warriors to be seen in the Western Isles, but they were a darn sight better than they were some months ago. Barra looked back to Gereinte with an appraising look. "If I hadn't seen you with my own eyes defeat Borsa just under a year ago..."

They looked out across the dusty ground and Gereinte was suddenly relieved that their soldiers were starting to look like soldiers and their knights were engaged in developing the next generation of squires and future knights. It was a far cry from the painfully inept re-deployed priests of the One God. The remnants of Morda's army had been put to use within the castle and those who had shown just a spark of martial talent had undergone a gruelling few weeks under the guidance of the Warmaster himself. Yet... he knew that it was still not going to be enough.

138

"I'll be blunt with you, Barra. If we are to succeed, we shall need a full-time professional fighting force. I fear that the freeholder levy my father relied on in the past will not cover us. The freeholders will have to return to their holdings at sowing and harvest time. And if we do not allow this, the country could suffer serious food shortages. Carentan is too populous to be served entirely by imports." Count Barra nodded his agreement and they continued walking in silence for a while.

As they skirted the perimeter of the grounds, Gereinte watched his sister, Alliane, in the distance, practising her sword skills with Sir Fulk. As a young girl, all she had wanted was to play outdoors with the boys and it had caused such ructions in the royal suites that eventually she had been banned from being outdoors at certain periods and given extra lessons in deportment. Now that she had been given the freedom to train, hunt and ride as she saw fit, she had become the very princess that she had originally railed against. And it suited her surprisingly well. Of course, it helped that they all knew she was never far from Fulk, who had doted on her since the day he had set eyes on her. It was almost comical to see the gentle giant daintily sidestepping his sister's fearless thrusts; it looked like a tiny doll attacking a grizzly bear with a toothpick. Though anyone foolish enough to get in the way of Alliane's sword arm was in for a very nasty surprise.

"There is, of course, another possibility your Majesty," Barra said. Gereinte looked away from his sister and concentrated on the Count. "I have heard good reports from Dern about a mercenary outfit." Barra paused and Gereinte shook his head. They had considered employing mercenaries in the past, but Alaric had been quick to point out that they could never be trusted; more likely than not to change sides if the price were right. But Count Barra would not be deterred. "Prince Rupert himself has employed this group and I believe that their initial set up was in fact funded by Count Lenden, a very well-respected nobleman in Tennengaul, who owns the garrison at Castle Lendholm and still commissions their services."

"Oh?" Gereinte was intrigued. It was almost unheard of for a group of mercenaries to have backing from nobility in addition to being recommended by a royal prince.

"It is run by a young man named Jehan Mantar, who used to work for Count Lenden. Their reputation is quite outstanding... if to be believed." Gereinte stopped walking for a moment and gazed into the distance. It could work. But only if Barra's reports were true. He would certainly not dismiss it out of hand without further investigation. The frustration of the past few weeks was suddenly washed away by his vision of a complete and utterly competent armed force, drawn from Carentan, Tennengaul, Malvas, Sarlat and Tordre. Five nations he was certain he could bring around to his idealistic creation of a defence league for the Western Isles.

Vermondie was already under attack and there was little he could do there, save for offering asylum to Rann and Lirra if it came to that. He had for a long time wrestled with the idea of approaching Klagenstill for help, but decided against it given that they were largely wild and barbaric. To all intents and purposes, they appeared to have a loose confederation of semi-autonomous clans with little formal structure or hierarchy, which to Gereinte, seemed a recipe for disaster.

He turned to address Barra, eyes sparkling with the excitement of new possibilities and connections.

"Barra. Would you return to Tennengaul? Speak again to Prince Rupert and seek out this Jehan Mantar. Watch the mercenaries in training and in action. I am planning a trip very soon to Dern in order to begin negotiations with Prince Rupert, but I am sending my sister Alliane ahead of me, as she has become very good friends with the Princess Jessamine since my last trip to Dern. I am hoping that Alliane can pave the way for my arrival in the spring. If what you find out about this mercenary group rings true, I would like you set up a meeting for me upon my arrival with this Jehan Mantar." Count Barra looked taken aback and slightly bemused by Gereinte's sudden and complete confidence in this solution to their problem. Over the years, people closest to him had grown used to the way his mind worked, which in some ways was a blessing because often he just could not explain why he knew when something was right. He just threw all his energy into making sure that his visions were realised.

CHAPTER TWENTY

The twins were invited to the Royal Palace in Dern to look at the security set up and discuss with Prince Rupert Darron a strategy for improving it. Jehanna could sense her brother silently assessing everything from the ease with which they had gained entry into the Palace grounds, to the number of guards on duty and their strategic deployment. Jehan always made decisions that were calculated, based on information available and knowledge of prior systems and procedures. Jehanna smiled to herself. In Jehan's mind, the Prince had already commissioned them and they were merely meeting today to seal the agreement. They were accompanied by two of their senior officers and they all wore their distinctive black and gold livery that had been adopted by Mantar's Mercenaries and set them apart from other local sovereign regalia.

On arrival, they were ushered into a receiving room with large oblong windows and velvet green curtains trimmed with gold. As they were waiting for the Prince, Jehanna ran her hand down the fabric and parted the curtain to look out into the palace garden. A young woman, about her own age or maybe younger, was hiding behind a tall mulberry tree. Delicate fair ringlets of hair held gently away from her face by a small jewel encrusted tiara framed her slim, fragile looking face. Her dress was long and flowing, though she held her skirts above her anklebone to enable movement amongst the bushes and trees of the orchard. There was a mischievous look in her eye, which sparkled with understated wit and charm. Jehanna wanted to get to know her better. The woman turned her head as though sensing she was being watched and sure enough saw Jehanna looking out of the window. She smiled at Jehanna, then lifted a finger to her lips beseeching complicit silence. An older man with colourful and regal robes strode through the orchard, completely missing the young woman who on seeing him, darted off in the opposite direction.

Jehanna's attention was drawn back into the room, as the doors were flung open wide and attendants escorted a thin looking gentleman into the room. Prince Rupert, she assumed. A tall, middle-aged man with striking looks and all the grace of nobility followed him up in the rear. He didn't look like a Gaullian. His stance was solid and his eyes carried the weight of experience few of the nobles in Tennengaul could boast.

Prince Rupert was helped to a seat, while his attendants withdrew. Another servant laid a small round table with jugs of wine, ale and snacks of bread, cheese and cold meats. The Prince looked pale and withered, but unmistakably the father of the young woman in the garden.

"My daughter will not be joining us today," the Prince said, breath rattling from his lungs. "She is busy setting challenging tasks for her new regent." He smiled wanly and Jehanna nodded; she could imagine the princess being challenging if the mood took her. "As you can see, my health is fast deteriorating. Things need to be set in place for her succession." The Prince sounded weary, which was understandable given the condition of his health. However, Jehanna thought she detected a subtle undertone to his words; something about the Princess's situation that was left unsaid.

"Your Highness," Jehan stepped forward. "We would like to make a proposal that would serve your most immediate needs and look after the interests of your daughter when the time comes." The Prince glanced to the stranger beside him, who was smiling broadly at the twins.

"I'd like to introduce you to an emissary from Carentan, Count Barra. The Count is here upon the wishes of a very good friend and ally of Tennengaul."

The man named Barra stepped forward and firmly shook Jehan's hand. He turned towards Jehanna and she curtsied to his bow. He emanated a feeling of warmth and humility, which was unusual, particularly for a noble and especially in a situation where they knew so little about each other.

"Count Barra is very close to the new King of Carentan, to whom I have pledged my allegiance." Jehanna had heard stories during her stay at Castle Lendholm of a group of nobles from Carentan who had rescued the Princess from a band of Klagenstill slavers. A memory came unbidden into her mind, of many years before when they had first travelled across Tennengaul. It was the face of a little girl in the back of a wagon staring at her in despair, hands gripping the bars that denied her freedom. She shuddered. Then she looked up into the eyes of the Carentan noble and felt herself warm to his presence. She glanced at Jehan who had a fleeting smile on his lips. He too had picked up on the subtle relationship between these representatives of the two nations.

"I've heard a lot about your mercenary outfit," Barra said. "If you have no objection, I should like to observe your methods and take a tour of your camp. It is not often that a band of mercenaries are given due attention and I have heard first hand from Count Lenden reports of your successes." Jehan looked impassive, but Jehanna could sense the pride warming his aura.

"It would be my pleasure to have you accompany me," Jehan said. "With permission from Prince Rupert, I would like to take a tour of the palace to assess security needs. Perhaps you would join me?" Barra looked to the Prince, who sighed.

"Yes, yes, go," Prince Rupert glanced at Jehanna. "It would please me far more to share a cup of wine and a few gentle words with this young lady than to huff and puff around this rattling old building talking protocol." Barra and Jehan took their leave of the Prince and left him with Jehanna.

They sat for some time in comfortable silence. Prince Rupert poured two cups of wine and encouraged Jehanna to take a bite to eat. When he declined to eat anything himself, Jehanna gently took his hand and squeezed. The Prince sat for a while longer with a contented smile on his face, then eventually took some cheese and a piece of ham.

"You have remarkable presence," he said.

"I wish that it were enough." As she held his hand, she could feel his life all but slipping away; the remaining spark tugged gently at the flow of energy, willing it to stay for a while longer. The best she could do was to give him some comfort and release from the constant battle going on inside. For that short moment it seemed enough.

"The best you can do for me now, is to help my daughter," Prince Rupert said. "There is a Regency Council in place, but I fear that it is corrupt from within. Seth D'Alban, my Chancellor, is too close to her. His influence is seen to be not entirely impartial by the other members of the Regency Council but I am too tired and too ill to fight that battle. I have asked you both here on the pretext of taking care of the palace security. But, I have another request of you, which is above and beyond the security contract." Jehanna raised an eyebrow and Prince Rupert continued. "I have heard that you have a talent for... shall we say, internal relations?"

Was he hoping that she might be able exert some influence over his daughter?

"The King of Carentan will arrive in the spring to begin negotiations over a treaty," he said. "Whatever happens to me in the meantime, that treaty must go ahead. At the moment, the Regency cannot displace D'Alban. At least, not whilst I am still here." He paused for a moment's reflection. "For some years now, Princess Jessamine has been a firm friend of the sister of Gereinte Andolin, the King of Carentan. Princess Alliane is due to arrive any day now to remain with Jessamine until the King arrives." Jehanna frowned. "Yes, I know, get to the point Rupert. Well, I have been given some information that leads me to believe that there will be an attempt to remove Princess Alliane from the company of my daughter where she cannot have any influence over the coming months."

After witnessing first-hand at Castle Lendholm, what some of the local nobles were capable of, Jehanna was not in the least bit surprised that they thought they might get away with kidnapping a Royal Princess to further their own ambitions. Undeterred by Jehanna's silence, Prince Rupert continued. "Your reputation in these parts is well known, so I am hoping that your presence at the Palace might be enough, along with your brother's enhanced security measures, to dissuade certain conspirators from attempting such a measure. However... should an attempt be made, I have it on good authority that you are more than capable of dealing with it." Prince Rupert smiled grimly at Jehanna.

She understood him perfectly. It was not just the kidnapping or assassination attempt that he was concerned about. She recalled that twinkle of mischief in Princess Jessamine's eye as she darted amongst the trees in the orchard. Perhaps one or even both of the Princesses were the biggest challenge in this assignment.

"I should like to meet with your daughter first, if I may," she said.

"Of course," Prince Rupert said. He waved at one of his attendants who left the room.

"And there is one other condition attached to my stay at the Palace," Jehanna said.

"Ah. I'm guessing that would be the infamous wolfhound," Prince Rupert said.

"He can be useful..."

"So I've heard. I'm sure Jessamine will be delighted." He smiled to himself and the doors to

147

the receiving room swung open. Princess Jessamine swept in and strode towards Prince Rupert.

"Delighted about what?" she said, smiling demurely at her father, but at the same time managing a sly wink at Jehanna.

"May I introduce…"

"Jehanna Mantar," Jessamine said, taking a low curtsy. Jehanna returned the gesture. "I have heard so much about you. Will you teach me how to be a warrior princess?"

"Well, I…," Jehanna glanced nervously at Prince Rupert.

"Good grief, child, is there no end to your continual desire for adventure? When are you going to grow up and accept that a princess has responsibilities?" Prince Rupert said.

"May I remind you, Father, that Alliane is being taught how to handle a sword, ride a horse and forage like a ranger by the leader of the Carentan King's own Guard."

"Who also happens to be her future husband," Prince Rupert said.

"And she looks no less a princess for it. Come to think of it, Lady Mantar looks no less a princess than either of us," Jessamine said.

Jehanna was caught off guard by this last comment. She certainly didn't feel or dress like a princess. Her functional, no-nonsense attire had become a comfortable and an occupational necessity in recent months.

"I am sure there are many things that we can learn from each other during my stay here at the palace," Jehanna said, trying to be as non-committal as possible.

"Good. That's agreed then," Prince Rupert said. "Jessamine, may I introduce your new companion and... shall we say, dance teacher?"

Jehanna sighed. This was going to be a tough assignment and for all the wrong reasons. But the Princess Jessamine was clapping her hands and dancing from one foot to the other in apparent glee.

CHAPTER TWENTY-ONE

It had been several weeks since Jehanna's initial deployment at the Palace of Dern. Under the pretext of teaching the Princess how to dance, she had managed to show her, the very first of the fighting routines she had learnt from Jehan. Although Jessamine was a fast and agile learner, she feared that they were fooling no one. It became increasingly difficult to extract her from the ears and eyes of her Regency Council, who followed her around almost as obsessively as Fang followed Jehanna. It was mostly Seth D'Alban who was hiding behind every balustrade, spying on her every step. Although he was the one person Prince Rupert wanted Jessamine to take advice from, it was plain to see that Seth was merely doing the bidding of the rest of the Regency Council like a child's hand puppet.

Princess Alliane had duly arrived, flanked on either side by Carentan officials, who insisted on checking out the Palace security. Jehan was more than pleased to acquiesce and took a certain pride in showing them around. The Carentans were impressed.

Jehanna could see why Princess Alliane had become a firm friend of Jessamine's. They were alike in many ways, although Jessamine was a little flightier and more unpredictable than Alliane, who was more grounded and practical. Jessamine had a beauty that radiated despite her attempts to downplay it with dowdy dresses. She had worryingly taken to wearing breeches, shirt and a jerkin, almost in parody of Jehanna's habit of dressing down to blend in with the environment. Alliane by comparison was not particularly fair looking, but had an inner beauty that shone through despite what she wore. Some days she would wear brown breeches and a forest green tunic and other days she looked utterly regal in a velvet gown and headdress.

To dissuade Jessamine's critics from thinking that Jehanna was an unwelcome influence, she had taken to dressing again in long skirts that could be hitched up at the waist should the need arise for freedom of movement. At least it served to confuse those people who poked their noses into the business of the princesses. The sight of Jehanna's dark barefoot figure followed by her four-legged shadow served to remind everyone of the legends that had followed her from Lendholm to Dern. Most were wise to keep their distance.

Alliane too, had proved to be a quick learner. Both princesses were unusually adept at fighting techniques and their confidence grew when they heard stories of women fighting amongst the mercenaries.

"I was taught that it was wrong for a woman to fight," Alliane said as they stopped for breath whilst a group of courtiers passed them by in the palace gardens. To all outside eyes, it looked like they were learning to dance; even the dog, panting with exertion, was collecting a useful pile of loose sticks and branches which the princesses launched into the air for him to chase at regular intervals. The fact that they never saw the resulting splinters that were faithfully returned to its mistress did not in any way ruin the idyllic image.

151

"It is only since my brother became king that he allowed me to train."

"Did I tell you about the time King Gereinte rescued me from the Klagenstill slavers?" Jessamine said.

"Yes." Alliane and Jehanna said in unison. Jehanna had heard the story so many times, she was starting to wonder if it were real or imagined. The Prince of Carentan and his blue sword, overcoming the biggest and meanest slave traders in the North. As the story went, he and his travelling companions descended upon the Klagenstill camp, destroying them one by one and delivering Jess back to the hands of her eternally grateful father. It was enough to cement a long-term friendship between the two nations, but not enough unfortunately to temper Jessamine's taste for adventure. Jess always embellished the part that she played in whole scenario.

"Let's borrow some horses and ride out to the mercenary camp. I'd like to see the colourful wagons and watch the warrior women in training. Perhaps we could even sneak in amongst them. We could end up going out on assignment." Jessamine was talking whilst she moved through the first five combinations of the routine.

"That would be..." Alliane said.

"Out of the question, your Highnesses," Jehanna said. The look of disappointment on the princesses' faces was priceless, but it was more than her reputation was worth to fail to keep those two inside the palace walls and out of trouble until the king arrived, which would be any day. Jehanna had been on high alert since Alliane arrived and could not afford to let her concentration slip for one moment. Although, she had to admit that it seemed unlikely that any attempt might now be made to abduct the princess, given that her brother's arrival was imminent.

As the light began to wane in the gardens, Jehanna encouraged the princesses to bring their practice to a close. Fang was running to and fro between Alliane and Jessamine as though gently warning them to follow his mistress's instructions. He nudged Alliane with his nose.

"Fang, you are incorrigible," Alliane said, laughing. Jehanna smiled to herself, then turned to walk away, confident that the girls would soon follow her lead. "Lady Mantar. Will you be joining us for dinner?" Jehanna turned and looked at the beseeching faces of the two girls, giggling and dodging the antics of the wolfhound. She turned and curtsied, wondering only if she would be able to find something suitable to wear to the royal table. Fang made little warning barks, so Jehanna continued towards the palace listening to the princesses, shrieking with laughter as they followed in her wake.

Jehanna had a small room opposite Jessamine's chamber and Alliane had the guest room next door. The walls were thick stone, so it was rare to hear any noise from either side; however, before too long she could hear the princesses tumble into Jess's room. A few moments later, she heard Alliane come out of Jessamine's room and shut the door to her own chamber. Shortly afterwards, a quiet scratching at the door took her away from preparing herself for dinner. She opened the door and let Fang into the room, who slumped down beside the outer door to keep watch while his lady washed and dressed. Not ten minutes after Fang had got back, Jehanna heard a thump, followed by a door banging, then the princesses' unmistakeable squeals. Fang began to paw at the door and started to whine. Thinking that maybe Alliane and Jess were exchanging their wayward tales again, she decided to check out the disturbance to be on the safe side.

Jehanna emerged from her room, wearing a long flowing skirt of cherry velvet with underskirts of white cotton, topped with a close-fitting black bodice and white long sleeves. She swept up her hair into a black beaded net, which let it run down her back in a river of dark curls. Black velvet slippers completed the outfit, which still allowed her a certain freedom of movement.

It was quiet in the corridor outside, so she gently knocked on Jessamine's door. The door swung open and Jess stood there wide-eyed and curious, dressed in a long flowing robe of silver fabric with sequinned trim. Her fair, light hair was tied up in a bundle on top of her head, kept in check by her bejewelled tiara. Her face lit up at the sight of Jehanna.

"You look... incredible. You'll have all the courtiers eating out of your hand." Jehanna regretted this whole business of attending the evening dinner, as the thought of attracting unwanted attention from men was the last thing she either wanted or needed. Not to worry, no one was likely to get very close to her with Fang hanging around. She swung around, realising that the dog was not at her side and saw him across the corridor sniffing at Alliane's door.

"Fang. It is very bad manners to disturb a princess when she is getting ready for dinner," she said. But Fang did not acknowledge her words and instead of coming to heel, he continued to sniff, then started to scratch and whine. She turned to look at Jessamine and saw her own concern mirrored in the princess's eyes. "Your Highness... were you out here, not ten minutes ago with Alliane? I was sure I heard your voices." Jessamine shook her head.

Fang was becoming insistent now, pacing in front of the door and looking at his mistress. Jehanna and Jessamine ran to the door and without bothering to knock, flung it open. Fang bounded into the room growling from the back of his throat. Jehanna followed, indicating for Jessamine to remain back and the princess stayed in the frame of the door with a worried look on her face. Jehanna searched the room, looking in the closets and bathing area, even beneath the bed, not quite knowing what she might find. On the bed lay a beautiful gown of fennel green velvet, trimmed with white fur. Evidently, Alliane had been disturbed before she had been able to dress for dinner. There was no sign of any struggle, so it was hard to tell if anything untoward had happened or if Alliane had just gone off to request more water or bathing cloths. Fang was behaving in a very unusual manner; he had sniffed out just about every corner of the room and was starting to grow impatient to get out and follow his nose.

"She's not here, but I don't like this," Jehanna said, moving aside just in time before Fang shot out of the door. She started after him, then turned to Jessamine who looked unnerved and unsure what to do. "Go and find Jehan, your Highness. Tell him I think that Alliane has been abducted. Fang and I will follow their trail." Jessamine nodded and sped off in the opposite direction.

CHAPTER TWENTY-TWO

Gereinte had been assured by Count Barra that the security at the Palace of Dern was second to none. However, when he arrived with a small entourage, expecting a welcome reception, chaos was the only word to describe what he saw. There were guards running this way and that and orders being issued by a young man who appeared to enjoy the respect and authority deserved of an officer of rank, but looked barely of age to command such a position.

He had ridden hard in order to get to Dern before nightfall to see his sister and Princess Jessamine. His travel worn clothes and dusty hair were hardly representative of a king on a royal visit. The forest rangers he brought for security blended with the countryside in their green and browns, bow and arrows slung over their shoulders and looking like they were born on horseback. His personal advisers would have much preferred to send the King's Guard in their purple regalia carrying the House Andolin standard, but given the unstable political climate in Tennengaul, Gereinte was insistent on making as inconspicuous an entrance as possible. The Royal Guard at the Palace of Dern could be forgiven, therefore, for thinking that he was just some visiting noble from the lower echelons of Gaullian society.

It wasn't long, however, before some of the staff recognised him and he was hastily ushered in to a receiving room. There he was met by Count Barra, the Princess Jessamine and the young dark man he had seen issuing orders.

"Your Majesty," Barra said, bowing low. "May I introduce Jehan Mantar?" The young man bowed low, but seemed agitated. Princess Jessamine curtsied in a hurried fashion, but her face betrayed the anxiety of someone with bad news.

"Is it your father, Jess? Am I too late?" Jessamine shook her head and looked nervously to Jehan.

"Your Majesty," Jehan Mantar said. "Please forgive me, but I must go at once. We believe the Princess Alliane may be in trouble."

"Trouble?" Gereinte's adrenaline surged and he scanned the faces of Barra, Jessamine and the Mantar boy.

"My sister thinks she may have been abducted from her room only moments ago. She is currently in pursuit, but I must go," Jehan said, making a quick bow and turning towards the door.

"Wait. I'm coming with you," Gereinte said. Jehan Mantar turned and nodded.

"But, Your Majesty, it is all in good hands," Barra said. But his plea was not heard as Gereinte followed Jehan out into the corridors of the Palace.

"I know the Palace plans inside out," Jehan said. "And if someone were going to try and sneak another person out of here, there is only one place they could go unnoticed." Gereinte jogged alongside him. Jehan took them through a small door that lead into an inconspicuous narrow corridor running between the outer wall and what appeared to be the kitchens and utility rooms along the back wall of the palace. Gereinte knew the palace fairly well himself but he had no idea that this secret passage existed. If he was correct in thinking, they were heading for the goods entrance. "The back entrance behind the storage rooms is the only place someone might come and go undetected. Don't worry, your Majesty. We have been expecting something like this to happen for weeks."

"Weeks?" Gereinte stopped and grasped Jehan's arm. "Why the gods wasn't I informed?" Jehan had a curious look on his face as he scrutinised Gereinte, but he was reassuringly unfazed by Gereinte's sudden and demanding tone.

"I can't answer that, your Majesty, but I can assure you that we have that exit covered and Jehanna is most likely already there with Fang."

"Fang?"

"You'll see." Gereinte released Jehan, uncomfortable with the fact that this possibility was kept from him. He let the young man lead him on. "They're not very clever these Gaullian nobles," Jehan said as they hurried down the passage. "It can only have been an inside job, as I've had all entrances and exits covered for weeks now." Jehan took them out of a virtually invisible exit door leading into the back of the courtyard to the goods entrance. There was a small wagon waiting at the far end near the gate, with two horses prepped and ready to make a quick exit. The man sitting behind the horses was wearing a big floppy hat and overcoat. In the distance, Gereinte saw Alliane being manhandled by a brute of a man. She was putting up a heck of a fight, stamping on the big man's feet and kicking him in the shins. The big man managed to subdue her by slapping her across the face. Gereinte's blood was boiling and he launched forward into a sprint.

159

Then something bizarre and almost magical unfolded before his eyes. One minute he was running at full pelt towards the man holding Alliane, his throwing knives at the ready, his blue sword humming at his side. Then a shadow appeared across his path, several yards ahead of him. No, make that two shadows. A female figure and an animal of some description. Gereinte stopped in his tracks and watched the dark, sleek woman launch a blistering attack on the man holding Alliane. At the same moment, she shouted a command to the animal, which he could see clearly was a wolfhound. It leapt up into the air with astonishing speed and alacrity, then clamped its teeth firmly onto the forearm of the wagon's driver. The driver started to shriek, his forearm firmly held by the animal which appeared to be standing over the wretched man and growling from the back of its throat.

Meanwhile, the woman, who he could see was little more than a young girl, had impossibly kicked the man in the head from a distance of barely a yard. Her foot had appeared from beneath her skirts, found its target and returned to the floor so fast, it was a blurr. She followed it up with several well-aimed attacks to vital points on his body, before he slumped unconscious to the ground. To top it all, Alliane kicked him squarely in the groin for good measure and had Gereinte not been so astonished by this spectacle, he might have laughed at his sister's belated retribution. Another man appeared out of the shadows and roughly grasped the young dark woman from behind, pinning her arms to her sides in a vice-like grip. At that point, Gereinte had seen enough and was just taking aim with his throwing dagger, when the woman shifted her hips to one side and struck a blow with her open hand to man's groin. As the man bent double, she dropped her weight and toppled him over her shoulder and onto the ground, at which point Alliane stamped on his head.

Two men unconscious, the other subdued by a large wolfhound, which looked as though it were begging for an excuse to tear the man's face off.

"G... get it off me," the man wailed. Then, the wagon was swarmed with palace security guards, dressed in the same uniform as Jehan.

"Enough, Fang," the young woman said and the dog relinquished its hold to the mercy of Jehan's soldiers. The woman turned and looked Gereinte straight in the eye. It felt like she was reaching inside his soul. He could not take his eyes off her, still not quite believing what he had just witnessed. Huge, almond shaped eyes assessed his gaze with an uneasy tremor and her chest rose and fell in time with his own laboured breath. For a moment, he completely forgot why he was there, frozen to the spot.

"Ger!" The enormity of what had just happened came crashing back to him as Alliane launched herself into his arms. Someone, here within the Palace of Dern had attempted to abduct his sister. Had it not been for the foresight and planning of Jehan and his sister, it might have been a very different reception he had encountered at the start of his visit. He looked over Alliane's shoulder. Jehan was attending to the captives and his sister was petting that enormous wolfhound. She looked up, caught him staring and looked away. Did he detect a flash of anger in her eyes?

"Come, come... I want you to meet someone," Alliane said, dragging him over to the Mantars.

"I've already met Jehan and yes, I am impressed," he said.

"No," Alliane said. "I want you to meet Jehanna Mantar." Alliane looked pleased with herself as she made the introduction. Gereinte felt his cheeks flush and mentally berated himself for being so socially inept. He bowed low, hoping to hide his embarrassment. But he needn't have worried. She wasn't even looking at him as she curtsied and stayed down low, avoiding his eyes altogether.

"Your Majesty," she said. "Please excuse me." Then she was gone, her four-legged shadow following in her wake. He didn't know why, but despite her respectful manner, he felt rebuffed.

"Oh, don't worry," Alliane said. "She is difficult to get to know at first, but you'll warm to her." Difficult, indeed, thought Gereinte as he stared at the empty spot she had occupied moments before. He looked up and saw Jehan watching his sister's departing figure with a curious expression on his face.

"Come Ally," Gereinte said staring into the distance, a frown creasing his brow. "There is a lot of work to be done here." He urged his sister to accompany him back into the palace, leaving Jehan and his men to their captives.

CHAPTER TWENTY-THREE

Jehanna closed the chamber door behind her and let out a breath she'd been holding ever since the King of Carentan had fixed her with his emerald gaze. She had met many nobles, royalty even, men in uniform, men-at-arms, some even quite good looking. She lifted her hand, which trembled as she studied it, turning it slowly. That had never happened before.

Fang padded over to the outer door and slumped down in his preferred spot with canine sigh. Jehanna looked at her dishevelled dress and decided that it could probably be rescued in time for dinner if she changed her underskirts, which had ripped a little through her exertion. She took some bathing cloths, dowsed them in water and cleaned her skin. Her fingers and toes tingled and she couldn't get those damned emerald eyes out of her mind. Fang was watching her with interest.

"What?" she said. "I'm not so stupid enough to let some foreign king get to me like that." Fang lifted his head as though mocking her words, so she wrapped the cloth into a ball and flung it at him. It landed square on top of his head, the corners flopping over his ears like a serving girl's cap. The dog sat there for a moment, before shaking his head and dislodging the cloth, which dropped to the floor. She laughed despite herself and went over to sit by Fang, caressing his ears. "I shall just not go to dinner, how about that?" No. She couldn't do that. She had promised Jess that she would join them and now more than ever, she would be expected. "I'm afraid, Fang, that you'll have to stay here, as Prince

163

Rupert doesn't like animals in the dining room." Fang sighed again and settled his head down on his front paws. "I'll have the kitchen keep you some scraps."

Jehanna finished washing, changed her skirts and re-set her hair so she didn't look quite as if she had just been dragged through the forest backwards. Then finally, she made her way to Prince Rupert's private dining room, where a small and select gathering were buzzing with the excitement of the evening's events.

"Jehanna." Alliane stood from her seat on the far side of the table and waved her over. She was dressed in the green gown that had lain on her bed and looked the very picture of royalty. Her brother, the King, sat smouldering next to her. Jehanna took a deep breath and made her way across the room, cursing the fact that she was unable to make an inconspicuous entrance. Several courtiers looked up, nodded and smiled. Prince Rupert was beaming at her the whole time and Jess could hardly keep her backside still in her seat as Jehanna joined her and Alliane. On the opposite side of Alliane sat King Gereinte, who studiously ignored her and talked in a low voice to Jehan.

"I'm just so annoyed that I missed all the action," Jess said. "Ally has filled me in on the details. Tell us your version, Jehanna. How did you know where to go? Were they real brutes? Did you have to hit them very hard?"

"I...err," Jehanna glanced at Jay, whose eyes flickered towards her without diminishing his concentration on the King's conversation. A flicker of a smile lingered at the corners of his mouth. She grimaced. "I really don't think..."

"They were huge, Jess," said Alliane. "I had to kick them again while they were down just to make sure they wouldn't get up again." This time, King Gereinte turned his head towards his sister and frowned. Alliane just shrugged and the conversation dissolved while the serving staff busied themselves with laying the table with joints of meat, platters of vegetables and jugs of wine. From across the table, Prince Rupert caught her eye. He smiled, placed his hands together in prayer – as was the custom in the Eastern Lands – and bowed his head to her. She smiled and returned the gesture. Despite not having been brought up in the East, it somehow made her feel whole.

She was uncomfortably aware of several sets of eyes on her as they ate their meal; mostly male and all with an eagerness that made her skin crawl. Each time she looked up and caught the gaze of a courtier, she looked away hoping she had not attracted further attention. Even with Alliane wedged firmly between the King and herself, she could feel the warmth of his aura spilling into the empty spaces between them. It made her feel both excited and angry, but more than anything; confused.

"My brother has offered a contract to Mantar's Mercenaries," Alliane said in a hushed tone.

"And now that my overly vocal sister has given away my plans," Gereinte said, turning to blast Jehanna with his gaze. "I would like to extend my invitation to you, as a key leader of the group, to join us." Her breath caught and her fingers and toes tingled. She felt very exposed as though the King could read her every thought. She looked down at her plate, wishing that the ground would open up and swallow her. This was ridiculous. Was she not a grown woman? She took a deep breath, smoothed her face into a neutral expression and looked back at the King. His eyes danced with a curious mischief and he had a quirky, almost cheeky smile.

"I believe," she said cautiously. "That my brother and I shall discuss the offer at length and give you an honest and informed decision." The King held her gaze, his eyes flicking from one pupil to the other, then to her mouth, her forehead, her chin. His smile wavered, then broadened. Jehanna was usually a very good judge of character and adept at reading emotions, particularly in men. But at that moment, she could safely say that she had absolutely no idea what this man was thinking. And that was unnerving.

As the evening drew on, the conversation around the table faded along with the sunlight. The candles in the sconces were lit and soon enough, the guests began to retire to their chambers. Jehanna remained for as long as she felt necessary, so as not to appear too eager to leave. She made her excuses, knowing that Fang would be waiting for his scraps and a run around the orchard before settling for the night. She glanced once again at King Gereinte, but he was deep in conversation with Jehan.

Fang was virtually hopping from one paw to the other by the time Jehanna arrived. But he still managed to find a moment to devour the scraps that had been provided by the kitchen. Before long, Jehanna was in the cool evening air of the Palace orchards, walking at a leisurely pace while Fang bounded around the trees. She suddenly felt exhausted; emotionally and physically drained.

She was about to call Fang and return to her room, when she sensed movement behind her in amongst the fruit trees; someone was out there with her. Her heart began to beat a steady pace, adrenaline rushing to her blood stream and eliminating her fatigue in an instant. She stood stock-still. Nothing moved in the orchard. The only sound of movement was the dog in the distance; too busy sniffing around the juniper bushes to catch the scent of someone new. She held her breath for what seemed an interminable length of time. Slowly she turned her head, so that her face was in profile, yet she could see behind her out of the corner of her eye.

There it was - a flash of cloth. Someone was moving from one tree to the next, following in her wake. She took a deep breath and slowly edged her way forward, pretending she had not noticed. Sure enough, she sensed a presence following her. She stopped casually, to seemingly adjust her skirts and slowly slid a throwing knife out of her garter. She felt her stalker pause, then resume walking the moment she stood upright. As she moved forward, reducing her pace to narrow the gap between them, she gripped the knife and steadied her nerve. The crunch of her pursuer's foot on a dead branch gave away the exact location as she turned swiftly and was about to release the blade, when she saw the King of Carentan standing before her. He swiftly moved his body to one side in reaction to the knife, then returned with composure when he realised she had not thrown it.

"Is that how you treat your guests in the Eastern Lands?" he said, brushing a stray twig from his tunic. Jehanna was furious; partly for allowing someone to creep up on her like that and partly for the fact that he was following her at all. She didn't know what to do; bow, curtsy, apologise, beg for mercy? Instead, she did the thing that both she and the King were least expecting and slapped him around the face.

The King looked stunned as he held his palm to his cheek. A cloud of anger rolled across his face, then he grabbed both of her wrists as though afraid of what he might do with his fists. She dropped the knife and twisted her wrists against the weak point of his grip and pulled upwards and out, escaping easily from his restraint. She tried to turn on her heel to run, but he was faster than her and held her fast, gripping her upper arms. She resisted the temptation to struggle and was about to knee him in the groin when the King did something that she definitely was not expecting.

He kissed her.

Her last memory of being kissed was of Kenric, pushing greedily and lustfully with his tongue in a hateful and punishing manner. This was an altogether different experience and presented an altogether different kind of danger. His lips brushed softly against hers and her spine tingled from the base right to the top of her head. The warmth of his aura enveloped her in a blanket of security and every touch left an imprint on her skin, like being scorched by invisible fire. He pulled her closer and wrapped his arms around her slim waist, gentle yet firm. His lips pressed closer to hers. Eventually, he pulled away and cupped her face in his hands looking into her eyes.

"Come back with me to Carentan," he said. Jehanna was stunned. Her head was whirling with a cocktail of emotion, desire and exhaustion. The King of Carentan was asking her to go away with him. But they had barely just met. What did he mean, come back to Carentan? Did he have a harem of women that he collected from various parts of the Isles and kept in his castle to meet his desires at the appropriate time? Her experience of men was limited to those that wanted to bed her and those that wanted to fight her. Excepting Jehan, of course, she had never had a male friend who didn't fall into either of these categories. Even those that claimed not to want either, eventually succumbed to one or the other. Besides, she didn't like the way he had said it. Sounded more like a command than a question or an invitation. Here was a man who was too used to getting everything he wanted.

Her momentary lapse of control had nearly led her straight into the arms of the enemy. She tried to pull away, but his arms held her fast and he smiled. It looked like a playful smile, like he was daring her to fight against him. Or was it a smile of victory, a triumph of acquisition? Her heart beat fast in erratic waves and then it was the face of Kenric she saw leering at her. Immobilised by panic as she had been on that day in Lendholm, she struggled against his grip, all her martial skill eluding her. How was it that she could not read this man? She could not trust a man she could not read; she could not allow herself to be taken in like this again.

In the background, rising above the noise of her thoughts and her panic, she heard a soft and menacing growl. The King let her go and she fell onto her backside, the grass softening her landing. Tears streaked down her face and her breathing came in shallow, short bursts. Fang was standing at her shoulder now, his ears flattened to his skull, baring his teeth at the King, who now had a worried expression on his face.

"Jehanna," the King said, drawing his sword. "I'm sorry if I have offended you, but can you please call off your dog." At first, the sight of his sword, glinting with intent in the moonlight, caused her panic to escalate and Fang reacted in kind by growling louder and snapping his jaws. She slowed her breathing, took control over her emotions and realised that he was holding the sword in a protective position, not an attacking stance.

"Fang," she said, drained of energy. "Enough." Fang stopped growling and dropped to the ground beside Jehanna, licking her hand. She kept her eyes focused on the King, who lifted the sword to sheath it in the battered old scabbard strapped to his side. The bluish hue that emanated from the sword slowly dissolved into grey as the blade disappeared. Without another word, the King of Carentan, bowed formally to her, as though they had just met in passing at Court, then turned on his heel and strode smartly out of the orchard and back towards the Palace. Jehanna sat on the grass, staring after him, trying to recover some composure and wondering what the hell had just happened there.

CHAPTER TWENTY-FOUR

"Do you have any idea what it all means?" Jehanna said, fixing her brother with the steeliest gaze she could muster.

"I don't know why you are being so contrary," he said, batting aside her question as though the bigger picture had no significance in their situation. "You are usually the one who seeks the most harmonious approach to our decisions." Jehanna glared at Jehan and started to bunch her fists, more out of frustration than any desire to hit something. She knew where this was leading and she didn't like it.

"If you join forces with Carentan, you will just become the King's puppet."

"Chief of Staff, actually," Jehan said.

"What's in a name? You will still answer to him and lose your complete control over the mercenaries, which is something we have fought so hard to maintain." Jehan narrowed his eyes at her.

"Do you have something against the King of Carentan?"

"What? No." Jehanna looked away, knowing that it was not possible to fool her twin. Jehan grinned.

"I knew it. There is something going on between you two."

"No, there is not and there never will be," she said. "I am just trying to get you to look at the long-term implications of this union." Jehan stopped grinning and turned away from Jehanna.

"In the short term, it means more funding to expand. To run the garrison at Castle Helmstedt, recruit and train more soldiers whilst maintaining our base in Dern." He turned around to look at Jehanna. "In the longer term, it means the probability of taking our army into a war from which there may be no guarantee of victory."

"War?" It was far worse than she had initially thought.

"There is a plot to invade the Western Isles," Jehan said. "Arrontierre have invaded once before, thirteen years ago. Now they plan another attack. They have already established some kind of presence in Vermondie to the South and plan to use that as a springboard for conquering the rest of the Isles. And they have forces to outnumber ours, even with this union."

Jehanna's mouth dropped open. Her resistance against going to Carentan seemed petty and small-minded in context. Of course they would go to Carentan and of course, they would join forces with the rest of the Western Isles. Despite where they might have come from, this was their home, these were their people and she knew they would fight together to protect the land that had grown dear to them both, the land that had shaped them into who they were.

"So when do we leave?"

"I will be leaving with the King in two days' time," Jehan said, not in the least bit surprised at his sister's sudden change of direction. "But I need you to stay in Dern for a while, just to keep things running at the camp until I have things set up in Castle Helmstedt. You will need to train one of the Senior Marshalls to take over when you leave. I'm not taking all the troops to Carentan; just enough to get by for now. There is still work to be done here."

Jehanna's heart shuddered with relief. Two days and she would not have to worry about seeing the King. She would miss Jehan, of course, but before long she would join him in Carentan, by which time the Western Isles would be so embroiled in preparation for this war that no-one would have the time of day to pay her the slightest bit of attention; least of all the King of Carentan.

***

Gereinte sat alone in his guest chambers in the Royal Palace at Dern. The room was in virtual darkness, but for a small candle stub that was burning on borrowed time.

He couldn't sleep.

He couldn't get Jehanna out of his mind. Her solemn and sad eyes haunted his memory every time he closed his eyes, like her face was imprinted on the back of his eyelids. The lingering warmth of her lips and her body made him shudder, then at once feel guilty. When he opened his eyes she was still there, looking at him as though he were some kind of monster, her expression reflecting stark panic.

He stood up. Paced back and forth. Sat down for a moment, then stood again and resumed pacing. His mother always said that he had inherited the habit from his father, who used to think while he was pacing. But now he couldn't think at all. He was stifled by a gamut of conflicting emotions that were rippling through his chest, making him feel quite nauseous. Why did he have to be so stupid to kiss her like that? He cursed his own ineptitude with women and wished, rather belatedly, that he had taken more notice of Darien Issoire, who would have been cringing if he could see Gereinte now. Darien always seemed at ease with women. A sudden pang of jealousy stabbed his gut, as he thought of Jehanna in Carentan with Darien Issoire on the loose.

No. This way of thinking would not do. He had more pressing things to concern his thoughts right now. He would return to Carentan after commencing negotiations with Prince Rupert, then forget about Jehanna Mantar. She clearly did not reciprocate his feelings, that much was obvious. The look of disgust on her face when he had suggested she come with him to Carentan put paid to any thoughts of a future with her. It had been a moment of utter madness that had made him even ask. When he had held her in his arms, it seemed almost as if they fitted together in perfect unison. For that one instant, he could almost have believed that there could be no future without her.

And then she had changed. He held onto his anger and hurt; after all, she very nearly skewered him with a throwing knife, then she slapped him in the face and as if that were not enough, she set her mad dog on him. No. Jehanna Mantar was not a woman to be trifled with. He should have listened to the rumours of her reputation and kept his distance. Well, he wouldn't be making that mistake twice. Besides, with the unstable political situation brewing in various nations of the Western Isles, coupled with the ongoing threat from Arrontierre, it

174

would not be too hard to redirect his attention. And she would be far too busy with the mercenaries. He hoped.

175

CHAPTER TWENTY-FIVE

Two days later, Gereinte left Dern with his advisers and his new Chief of Staff plus half the mercenary troops from the Caravanserai. Jehanna agreed to stay in Dern to train the remaining senior Marshalls in the running of the mercenary camp and to help recruit new soldiers to replace those that Jehan had taken with him to Carentan. Gereinte had not had occasion to see or speak to Jehanna, which left him with a dull ache inside and a feeling that there was too much left unsaid between them. The fact that she had remained aloof, not seeking his company or attention only served to strengthen his resolve to cast aside all his thoughts about her and concentrate on the difficult situation ahead. Which theoretically should not be too tough, if it weren't for the reality that she kept appearing in his thoughts with alarming regularity.

He slowed his mount to enable Jehan to ride alongside him, then glanced warily at his new Chief of Staff. He was going to have to get used to seeing Jehanna's face reflected in Jehan's every time he cast his mind to business. He sighed.

"Tell me more about the training regime you have in place for your troops," he said. Jehan looked at Gereinte with a faintly amused expression. For a moment, Gereinte thought Jehan knew what was going through his mind, as though there were some kind of link between he and his sister. He understood about sibling links. He sometimes felt flashes of unexplained angst when his own sisters were in trouble. And they all felt a deep and sad longing for their baby brother, Josselin, who was missing, presumed dead. So he had no doubt that Jehan knew something of what his twin might be going through. He fought to maintain a neutral expression while Jehan began to explain the system of recruitment and training he had set up for the mercenaries. Occasionally he would refer to Jehanna's involvement and it seemed almost as if he were searching Gereinte's face for signs of distraction. But Gereinte was practiced at maintaining an impassive look as they discussed business.

After several days hard riding, with regular breaks to make camp, rest the mounts and feed the troops, Gereinte and his entourage made a spectacular entrance into Carentan. They rode the length of the main thoroughfare and were met by the King's Guard flying the sovereign colours; a show of patriotic solidarity. The public needed to always have faith in their monarch and it did more good than harm to let them see how their defences were growing. He needed people to see where the extra troops were coming from; the fact that other nations in the Western Isles were supporting their growth was an important consideration.

It wasn't long before the streets were lined with peasants and nobles. All it took were a few cheers from the back of his entourage to encourage the people to follow suit and start a ripple effect through the streets. The King is back with his army. Long live the King. Never mind the fact that he doubted anyone really noticed that he'd gone in the first place. It was also good for Jehan. A taste of the kind of glory that lay ahead if his reputation lived up to its expectations.

Children ran in and out of the crowds, throwing flowers at the passing troops. A mixture of dirty-faced street urchins and well-fed nobles, curiosity transcending social status. Gereinte did not distinguish between those who owned land and could afford to buy and import goods and those who lived off the land. He was happy to dismount and talk to anyone who sought audience with the King. The new Citizen's Charter was on the lips of many, as were predictable suspicions surrounding the appearance of Chevaliers in Vermondie.

His eyes were drawn to a woman in the crowd, holding a young boy, who squirmed and struggled to break free and run with the other children. She was staring at Gereinte. She held that boy with such a vice-like grip, Gereinte could almost believe that he was being held against his will, but for the expression of devotion the boy held for her. Then she relented and set him down. Gereinte held the woman's gaze for a moment, while the boy made a direct line towards Jehan. Pieces of the puzzle fell into place then, as Jehan lifted the smiling little boy onto the back of his horse and allowed him a few precious moments to live out his dreams of becoming a soldier. The woman smiled then. A little nervously, thought Gereinte, but he understood her reluctance. A soldier's life was not one that every mother wished for her son. She followed the entourage, allowing the boy his moment of happiness. They eventually passed through the main street and as they turned to make their way towards Castle Helmstedt, Gereinte nodded in passing as Jehan handed back the little boy, who was now squealing with a passion at having to return to his mother.

***

A feast was prepared in honour of Jehan and his newly appointed troops. Gereinte sat at the top table in the Great Hall at Castle Helmstedt, surrounded by those closest to him; his elder sister Roda, with her husband, Chanac Issoire. His closest friends, Darien Issoire and Etienne Martan. Jehan sat to his left, next to Jabir and Kemal, who spent most of the evening chattering in their native tongue of Hassian. It did not escape Gereinte's attention that the two Easterners were clearly taken aback at the sudden appearance of Jehan and even more surprised at his inability to speak Hassian with enough skill to be able to converse with them. Jehan looked uncomfortable and frustrated at being sat next to two of his countrymen but being unable to understand their conversation.

Gereinte recounted the story of Alliane's attempted abduction to disapproving glances from Roda and blushing modesty from Jehan as his part in the whole affair was honoured. Gereinte described how Jehanna had appeared out of the blue with her hound in tow and Roda snorted with derision as Gereinte recounted Alliane booting the thug whilst he was down. Roda, along with Alliane's twin sister, Nerys, had always disapproved of Alliane's propensity for boyish behaviour and ever since she was young had supported their mother's attempts to thwart every action of Alliane's to take up activities unbecoming

179

of a Princess. Roda's cause had been somewhat diluted since the death of the Queen Regent and the fact that Alliane's twin sister, Nerys who often kept her in check, was now married to the King of Tordre and many miles away, running her own affairs as Queen of Tordre. Gereinte knew that Roda disapproved, but he also knew that Ally was better off with the freedom to live her own life.

"Perhaps," Roda said, fixing Gereinte with a stern look. "If you had not allowed Alliane to go rampaging off to Dern, learning goodness knows what from this mercenary woman, she might not have been placed in such a dangerous predicament."

"I hardly think that going to stay with her dearest friend, Princess Jessamine, is going on a rampage," Gereinte said, smiling playfully at his sister.

"Huh. Well we all know what a sensible young girl Princess Jessamine is." The irony was not lost on company present, as a few people chuckled at Roda's words.

"This 'mercenary woman' has a name, Roda, and I'll thank you not to be so rude, considering the proximity of her twin brother," Gereinte said nodding at Jehan. Roda flushed crimson and made a quick apology to Jehan, who nodded respectfully. He didn't seem in the least bit offended. Jabir and Kemal, however, had stopped chattering and were now looking at Jehan with more than a little curiosity.

"As you well know, Roda," Gereinte said. "By giving Ally the space to grow up in her own way, she has more than adequately developed into the Princess you and mother so longed her to be." Roda tutted under her breath but made no further comment in her defence. Gereinte smiled to himself.

"If you'll forgive me," Jabir said, addressing Jehan. "How is it that you and your sister came to the Western Isles? It is certainly very generous of your Sheikh to allow you such time abroad. The Congress of the East can be quite restricting, especially in the case of young talent such as yourself." Jehan looked momentarily startled. "I'm so sorry. Of course... it is none of our business," Jabir said. "Please, forgive my rudeness." He put his two palms together in a traditional prayer sign and bowed his head.

"Err... I guess, it is okay," Jehan said, glancing nervously at Gereinte. "I mean... we don't really have a home in the East. We were raised here by a small family in a fishing village called Villan, just south of Sternhelm. The name Mantar is the Gaullian name of our adoptive parents." Gereinte's curiosity was piqued.

"At what age were you adopted?" he said, trying to sound casual but failing. Jehan was starting to look uncomfortable. All eyes and ears were alert around the table as everyone present found this story particularly interesting.

"I... err... about four, I think," Jehan said, frowning to himself as he noted the surreptitious glances being exchanged. "Is there something I should know?"

"It is nothing," Jabir said. "Just an old Eastern fable that I will tell you one day when we have the time and we are not likely to bore everyone rigid in the telling." The atmosphere lifted at Jabir's words and several people broke off and began conversations of their own. Gereinte let out a long breath and continued to eat. Roda was looking at Jehan curiously.

"So, how do you find our little country?" Roda said. Jehan looked at Gereinte, then back to Roda and smiled.

"The reception in the town was astounding and everyone here has been most welcoming," he said.

"Yes...the people can get a bit carried away by the spectacle of troops riding by," she said, glancing at Gereinte. "Don't let my brother mislead you. The people can just as soon turn nasty if things don't go their way."

"I think it is important to involve your people in such activities. It gives the young ones a sense of pride and ambition. After all, they are the next generation. I have already found your next chief of staff," Jehan said. Gereinte remembered the little boy dodging his mother's restraints in order to ride up front with Jehan and shook his head with a smile.

CHAPTER TWENTY-SIX

Over the next few weeks, Jehanna threw herself into re-structuring the hierarchy of Mantar's Mercenaries at the camp in Dern. She and Jehan had agreed on a structure before he left, which enabled a meritocracy to flourish and secured a stable future for the group, whether either Jehan or Jehanna were present or not. They had agreed with King Gereinte not to commit the entire force to aid Carentan, but that a substantial army would remain in Dern to protect the interests of Tennengaul in the coming troubles. All troops would remain under the overall leadership of Jehan and be ready at a moment's notice to deploy their strength. As it turned out, their help was needed rather sooner than anyone had expected. Not three weeks after Jehan had left for Carentan, Prince Rupert took a turn for the worse.

Jehanna was sitting on the steps of her painted wagon, idly throwing a ball for Fang to chase around the clearing. She had recently taken to staying in the Caravanserai, preferring the company of the many travellers that came and went and the few permanent residents, who made the community spirit so strong and welcoming. Small children ran about, chasing the dog, which was almost twice their size, shrieking with laughter when he hunkered down and challenged them to a game of throw and catch.

She wondered what Jehan was doing. And when she thought of Jehan, she thought of Gereinte and a pang of longing fed her restlessness. She would eventually have to see him again and she would eventually have to face up to her awful behaviour in the orchard on the day he had followed her. Worst of all, was the feeling that she had now ruined any possibility she might have had with a man who had made her feel for just one instant, utterly whole. It was her own fear that had created this wedge between them. She sighed and consoled herself that he would probably have turned out like all the others anyway. But that didn't quell the unremitting ache she felt inside whenever she thought of him.

In the distance, beyond the wagons, she saw a flash of green on ivory, which denoted the Prince's livery. A messenger was heading through the camp entrance and making a direct line for the Caravanserai. He was on foot, having dismounted at the entrance and was now picking his way in and out of the wagons, while people pointed and directed him towards Jehanna. She watched him approach and as soon as he saw her, he went down on one knee and when assured of her undivided attention, began his message.

"My Lady, with great regret the Regency Council of Tennengaul have to inform you that Prince Rupert Darron, may the gods protect his soul, died yesterday morning with his fair daughter at his side. Princess Jessamine Darron, being not yet of age, will defer leadership of our fine country to her Regency Council, pending her coronation on reaching eighteen years of age."

Jehanna rose to her feet, a wave of sadness for Prince Rupert preventing her from acknowledging the words the messenger was delivering. There were some shocked gasps from onlookers, who were hanging around to catch the latest news. A ripple of

184

whispers, spread across the camp as word was passed on.

"The Regency Council have asked on behalf of Princess Jessamine," the messenger continued, "that the Palace be left to mourn their loss as is fitting for the passing of their monarch. It is also requested that your troops be withdrawn from the security staff at the Palace as a mark of respect during these difficult times."

Poor Jessamine. Jehanna had no doubt that the Regency Council had taken this opportunity to tighten Jess's leash and start dictating to her what they felt was *in the best interests of the country*. Jehan had warned her of the corruption that ran rife within the Council. Damned Gaullian nobles. And where in all this was Seth D'Alban? Jehanna sensed that the messenger was impatient to leave and was waiting for some kind of acknowledgment.

"Thank you," she said. Just as the messenger rose to leave, Jehanna added, "but tell me… if the Prince died yesterday morning, why has it taken the Council a full day before sending a message?" The messenger paled under her gaze and looked around him at the assembled populous of the camp; a mixture of women and children, interspersed with mercenaries, hands wavering towards their weapons.

"I… I cannot answer that, my Lady," he said nervously. Jehanna stepped towards the messenger and Fang appeared at her side.

"Where is Seth D'Alban?" Jehanna said, knowing that however much Jessamine had attempted to wriggle away from D'Alban's avuncular scrutiny, he had been the one person in

185

that Council who would always have the best interests of the Princess and the country at heart. The messenger was starting to sweat profusely under the heavy green and ivory army coat.

"I... I... think. I don't know, but it has been said..."

"What has been said?" Jehanna said. Fang flattened his ears and emitted a soft growl. The messenger looked around at the other mercenaries who were moving in tighter.

"Seth D'Alban has been dismissed and placed in protective custody at the Palace," he said as though the act of speaking fast would negate the fact that he had said more than he should.

"Thank you. You may go," Jehanna said. The messenger all but ran from the compound and Jehanna called for her Marshalls and instructed their own staff to carry a message to Jehan in Carentan.

Despite being asked to stay away, Jehanna rode to the Palace and requested an audience with Princess Jessamine. Her immediate thoughts were how she might be feeling, having lost her father and her most closest adviser in one day. Then, as she neared the Palace walls it became apparent that access to the Princess might not be as straightforward as she first had envisaged. She met a troop of mercenaries returning from duty, only to discover that they had been dismissed on the request of the new Regency Council. Two of the senior leaders stayed with her to accompany her to the Palace, while the remainder reluctantly made their way back to the camp.

As they reached the perimeter of the walls, there was a large group of merchants wearing the

186

various colours of their guilds, gathering in numbers outside the gates. The Palace guards looked smug and determined, as though they had been given their orders and nothing short of an earthquake would persuade them to relent. Jehanna walked her mount up to the gates, cutting a path through the onlooking crowd.

"I wish to speak to the Princess," she said. The guard on duty took a long look at her, then shook his head.

"The Regency Council have given express orders that the Princess Jessamine is not to be disturbed. If you have come to relieve the Palace security staff, then I am obliged to tell you that they have already been dismissed." The guard's eyes flickered towards the two men that flanked Jehanna on either side. His eyes narrowed in suspicion.

"Then I wish to see Seth D'Alban," Jehanna said.

"Yes," the guard said, raising his hand. "I was warned that you might ask that." A small troop of guards appeared above the wall, levelling crossbows on Jehanna and her men. The group of merchants gasped and a few began to shuffle back. Jehanna remained still and looked impassively at the guard. She held his gaze for long enough to see his eyes waver with uncertainty, then turned her horse around and beckoned for her men to follow. The group of merchants parted to let her through and she caught the whispers of discontent in her wake.

"Did you see that? All she did was ask to see the Chancellor."

"They can't get away with this. First it's the taxes they raise, then it'll be conscription for all our workers. You wait and see. Where else will they get the troops now the mercenaries are gone?"

"I'm not paying no extra tax – Prince Rupert would never have allowed this. And only a day since he passed on."

"Shameful."

"Outrageous. Who will buy our wares if we have to put up prices to pay the extra? Like as not, people will go further afield."

"We'll be out of business come winter."

"Shameful."

"Shameful."

Jehanna rode into Dern and the discontent grew louder and more fervent where the population became denser. The first decree to come from the new Regency Council had been a raise in the taxes on sales of goods in Tennengaul. The justification being that it would go towards improving security and defences. She would have laughed had it not hit so close to home.

People had just about got used to the fact that they now had additional security in the shape of Mantar's Mercenaries, whom they could trust for the first time in history. Now that the Regency had dismissed the mercenaries, the working public were expected to pay for a new set up? Most people were cynical enough to see through the thin veil of deceit to the corruption beneath. And poor Jessamine was trapped at the heart of it like a ship without a sail. It would be two days at least before Jehanna's message reached Jehan and then two or more days for him to mobilise an army to come and rescue them.

People were out on the streets, buzzing with conversation, frowning with disapproval. Jehanna walked her horse down the main thoroughfare, which was lined with market stalls and heaving with merchants and customers alike. A few familiar faces waved in her direction, casting anxious glances at the two mercenaries, which flanked her on either side. Marla, the herbalist, flagged her down and she brought the horses to a standstill, dismounting to greet her.

"Jehanna. So good to see you, let me give you some extra supplies for your bags." Marla thrust a packet towards Jehanna, who was gracious in accepting anything that the aging herbalist was willing to part with. Marla brushed a few grey hairs from her face, her skin wrinkling as she grimaced. "Oh, but it is all despair in town today. I suppose you have heard? I don't know how I will cope now. Might have to move out of Tennengaul altogether, though I don't know where I will go."

"Don't fret, Marla," Jehanna said. She grasped the old lady by the shoulders and leaned in close as though to greet her with hug. In a low voice, she said, "Let everyone know that a message has been sent to Jehan in Carentan. There is hope. In four days' time, an army will march down this street. If unopposed, they intend to put an end to this Regency rule and re-instate Princess Jessamine with all the powers to rule in the memory of Prince Rupert." Marla's eyes widened.

"But who? How? Are we to be invaded before we can sleep soundly in our beds?"

"Believe me when I say that the man behind this strategy is our best hope for a peaceful future.

Let the people know, that the King of Carentan is coming to liberate them." Marla stared at Jehanna for a moment, then scurried away. No sooner had the words left Jehanna's lips, than the whispers began. She re-mounted and walked idly out of town back to the Caravanserai, smiling to herself as she left.

CHAPTER TWENTY-SEVEN

Two days later, Gereinte led a small but powerful force of mercenaries to Dern. They embarked on a fleet of specially hired Coustiller carrier ships from Kallanin and sailed to Sternhelm.

By some kind of perverse reckoning, Gereinte felt motivated by the news that trouble had erupted in Tennengaul. Had he not been so close to Prince Rupert and his daughter, he might even have welcomed the distraction. The news of Prince Rupert's death had not surprised him. Etienne had his ears and eyes ensconced within the Palace despite the Regency Council's attempts to isolate Jessamine from all outside influence.

The mercenaries met with little or no resistance from locals at the port of Sternhelm and once their horses had found their land-legs, had marched en masse towards Dern, even picking up a few local stragglers along the way. The closer they came to the capital, the more apparent it became that the Gaullians had become discontented with the corrupt and incompetent rule of the Regency Council, despite having only held office for little more than a week.

A massive cheer erupted as they marched unopposed down the centre of the main thoroughfare in Dern. Evidently, they had been expected and Gereinte wondered whether Jehanna had been responsible for that. As they continued through the streets and onward towards the Palace, their numbers grew with every step. Gereinte looked around him and could see a mixture of merchants, nobles and mercenaries picking up the rhythm of their movement as they snaked their way towards their final destination. Mantar's Mercenaries merged with the Carentan army to boost their number and present a formidable force of resistance to the Regency rule in Tennengaul.

They reached the Palace gates, which were uncommonly open and inviting, save for a few brave guards who were cowering behind the ramparts. Gereinte raised a hand and his army began to slow its pace and came to a gradual standstill.

His adrenaline surged when he saw Jehanna mounted bareback at the head of a smattering of mercenaries, waiting to greet them. Her hair was pulled back from her face and she wore a long-sleeved white shirt, black breeches and gold and black jerkin; the colours of the mercenaries. She looked more stunning than he could have imagined, with an elegant poise and regal bearing, staring ahead with anticipation. She walked her horse forward and as he moved alone to intercept her greeting, he tried to keep his beating heart still and his face impassive. As they neared, her face lit up with excitement and her eyes darted from side to side. She was looking for something; someone. Then her face dropped and Gereinte's heart crashed back in on itself when he realised that the delight in her face had been for her brother, not for him.

"Your Majesty," she said, bowing her head.

"Lady Mantar," he said, swallowing his pride. "Your brother sends his greetings." She looked up, then returned her gaze to the ground. "He sends apologies for not being here in person, but hopes that once the events of today have been concluded, that you may return with us to Carentan." Gereinte had hoped to get some reaction from her about that, but she just kept looking at the ground. Then she nodded, almost imperceptibly and moved her horse to one side.

"The future of Tennengaul lies in your hands," she said. And with those words, Gereinte began to move his army forwards.

CHAPTER TWENTY-EIGHT

Mercadier de Taroudant returned his wife, Adaliz, to their Castle home in the Southern Lands. He remained in Vermondie as a guest of Abiel Morda, Archbishop of the Church of the One God. Initially, he had planned to return to Arrontierre and let his Chevaliers overthrow Vermondie, sweeping in to clean up and take control when the fighting was done. However, events had taken an interesting turn in the direction of Carentan. He listened to Morda's story with utter disbelief. How such a young upstart of a king could have the disrespect and audacity to interfere with the work of God was unimaginable. In Arrontierre, he may well have been hung for heresy.

"I hear that the King of Carentan has almost doubled his troops in the last few weeks," Morda said, frowning at Mercadier over breakfast. Mercadier chewed over this news as he chewed on his bread. He took his time with responding to Morda, never allowing the Archbishop to see too clearly into his thoughts or to let him think his influence was too great. It was true, Mercadier needed the cleric in order set his plans in place; plans that had grown in the few days since he and his Chevaliers had arrived in Vermondie. He swallowed and took a long draft of ale.

"You forget, Seigneur. If Carentan had even four thousand, it would not match the Chevaliers of Arrontierre," Mercadier said. The Archbishop bristled at being addressed in the style of a Southern Lord. "I doubt they have even four hundred at present," he added with a grunt. Morda narrowed his eyes. Mercadier wondered not for the first time in the last few days what it was that the Archbishop hoped to gain from this collusion. Some control in Vermondie? A foothold in Carentan, once the Chevaliers had flattened the incumbent king and his cobbled together army? Morda leaned forward in conspiratorial way.

"My Lord Chevalier," he said, watching Mercadier flinch at the crude use of Langan in his address. "Do not underestimate the guile of your enemies. The King of Carentan is well known for his insidious deception." Mercadier nodded and smiled, then tore off a chunk of bread. The cheese and meat were certainly of fine quality, it was just a shame that the ale tasted more of dirty water than anything else. He grimaced at the contents of the mug before swallowing a mouthful.

"If you ever have occasion to visit Arrontierre, I must introduce you to some fine wines that make breakfast the best meal of the day," Mercadier said. Morda's eyes lit up, but Mercadier couldn't be sure if it were the thought of fine wines or the thinly veiled invitation to visit Arrontierre that so excited the priest.

"I have an idea," Morda said, idly sweeping breadcrumbs into a small pile beside his plate, "that might take the focus away from Vermondie just at the most opportune moment." Mercadier's interest was piqued.

"Oh?" he said.

CHAPTER TWENTY-NINE

Gereinte sat in the council chamber in the Palace of Dern. Seth D'Alban and Princess Jessamine sat in front of him on the opposite side of the round table that filled most of the room. All the other council seats were empty.

Only hours ago, Gereinte and his soldiers had swept into that same chamber, much to the startled and enraged defiance of the seven council members who had begun to run Tennengaul into the ground within the space of barely a week. To protect their own interests, they had dismissed Seth D'Alban and several other of Jessamine's personal friends and servants, including the mercenary security staff and anyone who had any slight connection to Jehanna Mantar.

Seth D'Alban sat looking at Gereinte with a mixture of relief and anticipation on his face. Seth was the country's most long-standing chancellor and a friend and ally to both Prince Rupert and his daughter. The tactics of the corrupt Regency had clearly been implemented in order to isolate Jessamine from any influence other than their own. Gereinte's first action had been to put the entire council into custody pending an investigation into their activities and to appoint Seth D'Alban as sole Regent to Jessamine. Beneath the relief and his loyalty towards Jessamine, there were questions in Seth's eyes; questions that related to the future of Tennengaul and the price they would have to pay for their freedom.

Jessamine's eyes sparkled almost as brightly as the sequins on her gown. She looked at her Regent, a measure of pride in her gaze, and then looked back at Gereinte with the same questions in her eyes.

"I know what you both must be thinking," Gereinte said. "And there is indeed a price to be paid for the freedom of Tennengaul. Your father, Jess, was aware of this; in fact we had already begun negotiations along these lines. His death, may the gods protect him, has merely brought this issue to a faster resolution." Jessamine and Seth D'Alban exchanged glances. "I want to reassure you both that what I am proposing has only the best interests of Tennengaul and the future of the Western Isles at heart." Gereinte produced two documents and laid them out on the table in front of them. Both Jessamine and Seth D'Alban looked down at the documents in front of them, then at each other. The Chancellor reached out to briefly lift the cover of the larger of the two.

"That one is an agreement between our two nations," Gereinte said. Seth flicked the pages forward, while Jess leaned in to scrutinise words. "It includes the treaty that we were working on with Prince Rupert." Jess looked up at Gereinte and he could see that she was struggling to maintain composure as her eyes filled with tears. "I can see you both need time to think and reflect. I know it hasn't been easy for you over the last few days."

"Please," Seth said. "We are in your debt, but tell me straight what we are looking at here and I guarantee you will have our decision in the next two days." Gereinte nodded.

"Two days is very generous, I can give you longer if needs be. I realise this is not a decision to

197

be taken lightly. This document has two other important provisos. One is a clause committing the signatory to incorporate this," he placed his hand on the second document on the table, "into your constitution, which is our Citizens' Charter. The other feature is that you must personally swear allegiance to myself or my heirs in Carentan." Jessamine looked at Seth, who placed his hand on her shoulder. "I do not seek to undermine your rule in Tennengaul. That is one thing that your father and I were very clear about, Jess. You and your Regent will have complete authority and autonomy. What it means is that we are bound by this agreement to look after the interests of each other and work as a united force for the greater good." Jessamine's smile quivered. But Gereinte was reassured by Seth's silence. The Chancellor knew how the treaty had been formed and understood the threats that both their nations faced from outside invaders. He had been a party to the rationale behind the forming of such a document. "I think you'll find the Citizens' Charter a very reasonable stipulation." He paused to allow his words to sink in. "In fact, your father, Jess, even helped me to form a large part of the Charter."

"We shall let you have our decision in two days," Jess said. She placed the documents into the hands of Seth D'Alban, who nodded and took his leave, bowing to Gereinte on his way out.

Jessamine watched Seth leave the room, then sat in silence and stared at the empty space between them, fighting back her tears.

"Oh, Jess, I'm so sorry," Gereinte stood up and moved to her side. He took her in his arms and held her close while she buried her face into his shoulder. As her sobs subsided, Gereinte produced a handkerchief and she laughed despite herself as he wiped her face.

"You know, they wouldn't even let me see Jehanna," Jess said. Gereinte stiffened at the mention of Jehanna and Jess looked at him curiously. "What is it with you two? She goes all funny when I talk about you as well."

"We, err... had a bit of a misunderstanding last time I was here."

"Well you should sort it out then because you two are meant for each other."

Blood rushed to his cheeks. "Never mind about me," he said. "How are you coping?"

"That's it, change the subject. You are just like her." Jess laughed and playfully batted Gereinte on the arm. Obviously, he hadn't done such a good job on hiding his feelings. Jess took his arm. "Come, walk with me awhile. Let's remember the good times we had, instead of talking about all this political stuff." She led Gereinte through a large set of double doors and into the serenity of the Palace gardens. He thought perhaps it was just as well that it was Seth who was scrutinising the treaty documents.

"Seth will do the best for you, Jess. You will be wise to listen to him." She shrugged and took a deep lungful of air.

"I do love to be outdoors," she said, gripping tighter to Gereinte's arm.

CHAPTER THIRTY

Jehanna was in a foul mood. She was packed up, ready to go and throwing orders around the camp like it was her last chance to make a first impression. The mercenaries gave her a wide berth and cast surreptitious glances at each other, which did not help her mood in the slightest. Two days ago, they had witnessed the historical overthrow of the Regency council and now, the word had come down from the Palace that they were to make ready to leave. The treaty was in place, signed and sealed by the true Regent, Seth D'Alban and the heir to the throne Princess Jessamine. Jehanna had made her farewells to a tearful Jess and promised to come back to Dern as soon as her work with the troops permitted. At least, for the time being, she was able to get away from the King who she understood was staying in Dern to oversee Prince Rupert's burial. And of course, she desperately wanted to see Jehan.

The camp was buzzing with excitement as the Carentan troops were enjoying a reunion with their friends and families. The Dern troops had massed together in order to support the Carentan army with the siege on the Palace and there was now a true sense of solidarity in the camp. Not that Carentan had needed it, since most of Dern had rolled over and allowed the King to march in unopposed. She smiled grimly. She didn't suppose that he even appreciated the part she herself had played in making it so easy for him. When he had ridden up to meet her, her heart had filled with joy at the sight of him, then his face – so passive and remote – had quashed those feelings on the spot. It was then that she noticed Jehan was not with him. Her face had dropped as the King of Carentan stared at her. Hateful man. Why couldn't he have just left her alone?

She would be travelling back to Carentan with the troops and was due to leave within the hour. The commotion at the entrance to the camp did not turn her head since there had been so much coming and going in the last day, she cared not who had now turned up on their doorstep. She busied herself with tidying up the wagon that had been her home for so long and did not pay attention to the heightened sense of excitement in the Caravanserai. She stepped outside to check on the rugs hung up to air and several children ran past her as they usually did when they got wind of a group of travelling performers or some such entertaining visitor.

"I came to say goodbye. For now."

Jehanna swung around, startled at the sound of his voice. One minute, he had been in her thoughts and the next, there he stood. The only defence she had against the sick feeling in the pit of her stomach was to look at the ground, look away, look at anything but those emerald eyes. He must think her such a rude and uncaring person. She forced herself to look up and meet his gaze. To her surprise he was smiling. "Can we start again?" he said. "When you rode towards me outside the palace only two days ago, if I hadn't been on horseback, my legs would have collapsed beneath me. You are stunning. Beautiful."

Her mouth fell open. Then she snapped it shut in case he thought she was some idiot catching flies. Did she dare to hope?

"I was happy to see you. I thought that you didn't share my feelings," she said.

"I'm sorry. I've become too used to hiding my thoughts and feelings behind this regal mask. Something I learnt from my mother."

He looked somehow different. All the airs and graces of a king came tumbling down before her and he looked just like a boy. A lost and lonely boy, with scruffy brown hair and shining eyes. He scuffed the ground at his feet with his boots, shy and uncomfortable.

"I think I should be the one to apologise," she said. "I behaved atrociously in the orchard that evening."

He looked up and said, "No. I mean... well, I can't say that I relish the idea of being stabbed, slapped and nearly mauled to death by a ferocious beast..." She paled at his words, then noticed the teasing glint in his eye. "But... it wasn't very clever of me to sneak up on you like that and I wasn't very tactful in my choice of words." He paused and looked hopefully at her. "My close friend Darien would have been horrified if he had seen how I behaved." He grimaced and looked at the ground, then looked up, locking her eyes with his gaze. "Would it be too much to ask if we could start again?"

Jehanna's heart was thumping inside her chest. Her cheeks flushed crimson and she was only now becoming aware of the people that had gathered around to see the king. Their time was short as the King's attendants waited patiently for him to conclude his business. That fleeting glimpse of the boy-king he had revealed started to change back into the self-assured monarch that he had become. Before any onlookers got the impression that they had stumbled upon a very personal encounter, King Gereinte assumed his authority and stepped forward towards Jehanna. He bowed formally, took her hand in his and kissed it gently, as any courtier would in bidding goodbye to a lady. A rush of energy steeled through her veins and she gasped. Gereinte looked up, a tiny smile tugging at the corner of his mouth and a mischievous glint in his eye. She smiled curiously at him and curtsied without taking her eyes from his face.

"No," she said. He wrinkled his brow at her. "It would not be too much to ask." He looked faintly relieved.

"Then I wish you a safe journey, my Lady." The King turned on his heel and strode off towards the exit without a backward glance. Jehanna stood still on the spot, unable to move, watching until the signs of his ever being there had disappeared beyond the walls of the camp. With an uncertain smile, she rubbed the back of her hand where he had kissed her.

***

Gereinte could feel Jehanna's eyes boring into his back as he left the Caravanserai. It took all the self-control he possessed not to look back at her. He wanted to reassure himself of the warm invitation that had danced in her eyes. But with so many people around him, he could not afford to appear distracted, so he kept on walking and kept his eyes ahead and his heart - he left in her hands.

Four days later, after the public ceremonies in remembrance of Prince Rupert came to a close, Gereinte was summoned to the receiving room in the Palace. He was irked by the distraction, anxious as he was to finish packing up his affairs to precipitate his return to Carentan. He longed to see Jehanna again and make sure she was safe and he had not imagined their last encounter. He couldn't dismiss the gnawing worry that she had somehow changed her mind or it had all been some cruel joke played on his naivety. He visualised that scene in the Palace gardens over and over, trying to see it all from her point of view. He had just about reconciled his rejection with his own abrupt and ill-conceived behaviour. She was justified in her reaction. That was all.

To his pleasant surprise, Etienne Martan and Darien Issoire were awaiting his presence in the receiving room. The three men shook hands and slapped each other on the back in greeting. Yet Gereinte knew that their presence here could only be for reasons of strategic importance.

"Well? Are you going to keep me waiting all day? I have bags to pack and affairs to complete before we begin our journey back to Carentan," Gereinte said. His two friends looked askance at each other. "I take it you are not just here because you thought I could do with a bit of company on the road."

"We have uncovered some intelligence on the movement of the Chevaliers," Etienne said, he smiled with his usual cheery confidence, despite the nervous glance at Darien.

"And, we are hoping to divert your attention away from Carentan for a little while," Darien said, picking up the thread. "We should sit down."

The three friends sat around the meeting table and Gereinte's heart sank as they began to discuss the Chevaliers, knowing that his business would take him away from Carentan and away from Jehanna for longer than he had anticipated. He focused on what Etienne was saying and thoughts of Jehanna slowly dissipated as his attention was gripped.

"We are nearly certain that their focus has been drawn to Sarlat." Etienne smiled and opened his hands as though handing Gereinte a meal on a platter. Gereinte was confused.

"Why Sarlat? Surely it has to be a ruse?" he said.

"That was what we first thought," Darien said. "The cabinet has met in your absence in Carentan to discuss this matter and concluded that we should take a party to Sarlat. We should also leave a significant presence in Carentan should events transpire in Vermondie."

Gereinte thought about the situation. According to Etienne's sources, the Chevalier Supreme was still in Vermondie, despite the fact that most of his compatriots had returned to Arrontierre. He was staying with Abiel Morda; another reason not to trust any circumstances on the face of it. That priest was a dangerous hindrance. He knew too much and would undoubtedly stop at nothing in his ambition to bring his own brand of religious order to the Western Isles. He wondered about Sarlat. They couldn't afford to take their eyes off Vermondie; he owed that much to Rann and Lirra.

"There has been a presence noted off the coast of Tordre," Etienne said. His normally cheerful disposition was tempered by the circumstances.

"Heading towards?" Gereinte said.

"Well now, there's the thing," Darien said. "There is a small schooner heading towards Sarlat and a fleet in waiting off the coast of northern Arrontierre, which at the moment is dormant but could be deployed at a moment's notice."

"I see," Gereinte said. It was most likely a trick, to distract their attention away from Vermondie. "And what did the cabinet decide in my absence?"

"We call their bluff. Spring the trap in Sarlat, but have our troops waiting to march on Vermondie at the first sign of trouble," Darien said. "Warmaster Alaric is working on strategy with Jehan, even as we speak." Gereinte let Darien's words sink in and looked at the worried glance that flickered between Darien and Etienne.

"Good," he said finally. "Once you are both fed and rested, we shall depart for Sarlat." He tried to make it sound measured and optimistic, but he knew in his heart that they were not ready to take on the Chevaliers. With only the additional troops from Dern, it was not enough. He had yet to make his case to King Rudelle in Malvas and Alvar Correze in Sarlat. It appeared that his trip to Sarlat had been expedited, but even with a positive outcome from the Sarlatians, it might be too late. They stood to lose it all in one fell swoop if his misgivings about the Chevaliers' latest movement proved to be true.

CHAPTER THIRTY-ONE

Phillip Rudelle, King of Malvas glanced around the conference table in his official meeting room at the collection of barons, knights and their usual hangers-on. The barons and landowners were mostly a discontented bunch of troublemakers who resisted all attempts by Rudelle to create a stable, just and fair regime. The meeting was ostensibly to discuss the future of Malvatian foreign policy, but the reality as Rudelle knew very well was to force him to agree with his Council to launch a military strike against Carentan whilst they were preoccupied with their foray into Tennengaul.

Rudelle sighed. How had it come to this? Since the deterioration of his health, he had spent less time tending to the political affairs of Malvas and trusted his Council to make the right decisions to build a stronger nation. It was unfortunate that they had taken it upon themselves to assume a kind of leadership that instead of drawing strength from their allies, threatened to destroy the relationships Rudelle himself had taken such pains to develop. One of those key relationships was that with Carentan. The very same that they now sought to destroy.

Rudelle was a measured man, a seasoned socialite who was adept at reading the subtleties of court behaviour. Over the years, his slender frame had become emaciated with the fatigue of his failing limbs. It was unfortunate that the very social aptitude he was known for was now denied by the limits of his physical capability. All he really wanted now was a quiet life and the satisfaction of seeing Malvas ruled in accordance with his deepest ideals. Unfortunately, as he looked around the table and his eyes came to rest upon Baron Jorge Delat, his life looked set to become anything but quiet.

Delat was a powerful, rich landowner and an aristocrat, to whom Rudelle had mistakenly given a position on his Council as a diplomat of foreign affairs. It had been a proud day for Rudelle when he had first invited Delat to join their ranks and enjoy the privileges that came with the authority. Now, he looked upon those ducal features with disgust. Disgust at his own choices, disgust at his own self-deceiving notions of loyalty.

"We have both a problem and an opportunity right now," Delat said, addressing the room at large with his expansive gestures. His clothes reflected the richness of the hedonistic culture that had been enjoyed by Malvatians for decades and threatened now to be their undoing. The rubies sparkled from his rings and the crimson cloth of his jerkin looked plush against the conservative and functional clothes that Rudelle favoured. Rudelle sighed. He supposed he had only himself to blame for being misled by this man in the past. He only wanted the best for his people and had always given Delat the benefit of the doubt, thinking that one day he might occupy that space left by an absent heir.

"You are the one who met with Ambassador Issoire from Carentan," Rudelle said. "Please do enlighten us."

"As I was saying," Delat looked irritated by Rudelle's interruption and ironic tone. "We can deduce from Ambassador Issoire's remarks that Carentan has ambitions to expand into other

208

territories of the Isles. I don't know about you folk, but I refuse to become a Carentan lackey. We also know that Gereinte and a large part of his armed forces have just embarked on a journey to Tennengaul."

Rudelle winced at the dismissive tone attributed to Issoire and the casual use of the King of Carentan's given name.

"Absolutely so," one of the lesser barons said. "Let's show these Carentans that they can't dominate us." Delat nodded approvingly.

Grief, thought Rudelle. He didn't like the way this discussion was going. Truth to tell, the closest he had come to finding the kind of man he would feel even remotely comfortable leaving in charge of ruling Malvas was the very person his ill-informed Council sought to destroy; Gereinte Andolin. During his visit over a year ago, the young prince had confided in Rudelle about his ideal to create a Citizen's Charter on his ascendancy to the throne. It was such a simple idea and yet a powerful political tool; a public declaration of a ruler's commitment to his people. Rudelle had always prided himself in being the people's king, but he had indeed been shown the way by the young Prince of Carentan, who had left a lasting impression on the old king.

Perhaps in Carentan it had been easier to accomplish. The Malvatians were far too full of their own importance and forever in pursuit of a life that was decadent even in the quietest of times. Perhaps it was too much to hope that he might effect change in a nation that had been too long going down the wrong track. It might be too late for Rudelle himself; he was too old and ill, though not as infirm as he led his Council to believe. What this country needed was a fresh start, new blood and a gentle change of direction.

"I have my elite troops on standby waiting for the word," Delat said with a smile of exultation. "We can move as soon as we like." There were murmurs and nods of approval from all around the table.

The cynic in Rudelle smiled to himself. Elite troops indeed. More like a bunch of layabouts who spend their days drinking and whoring. He felt sorry for the untrained and ill-equipped freeholder levies, press-ganged into serving with the baron's Elite troops.

Sitting there, listening to his Council plan a war against the only ally in the Western Isles that Rudelle trusted and admired seemed ironic to say the least, not to mention suicidal in all reality. From what he had heard about Gereinte's current fighting force, their troops might be best advised to surrender before the battle had begun. But then, perhaps it was just the opportunity they needed to sweep out the dead roots and plant some new trees. New life, new hope for a lost generation of Malvatians who did nothing wrong, save follow their forefathers. It was harsh. But then, war always was.

"Gentlemen, you are very convincing," he said. "And who am I to argue with your case?" He cringed at his own pious tone. "You will have to excuse me, however. I am not as you know in a physical condition fit for a field campaign." Some nodded with sympathy. Most smiled patronisingly. Rudelle's arthritic knees were well known as was his reliance on two sticks and the strong arm of his seneschal to walk anywhere. What none of them realised was that his physical problems, though real, were considerably exaggerated.

Rudelle rose clumsily to his feet and said, "Well my friends I will leave you to your planning of this campaign, which I am sure will be supremely successful." On that confident note, he limped away. With some good fortune, few of them will survive King Gereinte's new army. He would then be able to rule over a sensible society and welcome Carentan with open arms when they arrived, as undoubtedly they would.

CHAPTER THIRTY-TWO

Jehanna had settled in to her own room in the garrison at Castle Helmstedt. It was small, yet functional and more than adequate for her needs. She had been offered a kennel for Fang, which she had politely refused remembering the last time she had tried to keep Fang in a kennel at Castle Lendholm. The neighbouring occupants of the rooms in the garrison had viewed her with suspicion at first when she had moved in with a large wolfhound, but they had soon become used to the dog's presence. The castle itself and the surrounding area were quite different to Castle Lendholm. It was larger and the outer circle reached as far as the edge of the Forest of Dreams, which she had been longing to explore on horseback. She had been advised, however, not to venture further than the perimeter of the middle circle without a chaperone. There were all kinds of brigands operating outside the laws that governed Carentan, not to mention the continual threat from wild animals.

The castle was built on the promontory of a lake called Mariac, located just north of the village of Canrac. The view from the walls was idyllic with three sides bounded by the lake. The fourth side, revealed the sinister and precipitous cliffs of the towering Helm mountain range. Every time Jehanna looked out at the Helm, she felt an inexplicable urge to climb.

"What lies beyond the Helm?" she asked Alliane one day.

"Malvas. The Helm is the only thing that is keeping Carentan at a safe distance," Alliane said, following Jehanna's eyes up to the mountain range.

"I wasn't aware of any threat. The Gaullians have always had good relations with Malvas," Jehanna said.

"The close proximity of Klagenstill to the border of Tennengaul has necessitated an alliance between Malvas and Tennengaul, to keep the barbarian raiders at bay. However, there has always been an uneasy alliance between Carentan and Malvas. Mainly due to envy; Carentan has always been a prosperous country and there have been attempts in the past to penetrate the Helm and invade from the north," Alliane said.

"Really?" Jehanna said. "I should think that would be a suicide mission." She shuddered as they looked up at the formidable mountains, the peaks invisible to the eye as they disappeared into the grey mist of clouds in the sky.

As a result of the castle grounds being so far spread, there was less of a community feel about the grounds, compared to Castle Lendholm which thrived on its community spirit. Alliane had promised to take Jehanna on a tour of Canrac and enticed her with the idea of accompanying the Forest Rangers one day on one of their border patrols. The rangers fascinated Jehanna. She had only once had occasion to see them; when they accompanied Gereinte on his trip to Dern. Dressed in greens and browns that blended with their natural forest environment, they had appeared a little out of place in the palace, but were quick to move in to protect their king at the first sign of a threat. She

213

had never before witnessed a bow and arrow being nocked with such speed and fluidity.

The Carentans were a nation of relaxed and genteel people. Open minded and tolerant, unlike the Gaullians who were quite an envious race and would stop at nothing to level the playing field if they thought someone was unfairly receiving favours. This mostly manifested itself in the continual bickering and underhand manoeuvring that went on within the barony. By comparison, there appeared to be an air of genial agreement pervading the castle, its inhabitants and its continual stream of visitors.

Jehanna had leapt at the chance to see Jehan. They had spent a whole afternoon ensconced in Jehanna's little room, just chatting and catching up on lost time. They had never before been apart for so long and she felt like an excited little child again. They exchanged stories and news, their words tumbling out, as though afraid they might miss something.

They fell silent for the first time in two hours and just looked at each other, then burst out laughing.

"To be serious," Jehan said. "There are some people here that I must introduce you to. People from our homeland. They have been teaching me some of the old traditions and the language."

"Curious," Jehanna said. "Perhaps we can find out more about where we came from." She noted the wary look in Jehan's eyes.

"There is something they know that they are not revealing. I can sense it. But every time I broach the subject, they just re-direct the conversation. It is very suspicious."

"Who are they?" Jehanna said.

"As far as I know, they are princes from the Eastern Lands, sent by their Sheikh to ensure that Western Isles remain neutral and to fight off any attack from Arrontierre. It seems that their cooperation with Carentan is a long-standing arrangement with the previous king, founded on their mutual interests."

"If they know something, I will get it out of them eventually," Jehanna said with a sly smile. Jehan laughed.

"I don't doubt you will, sister. I don't doubt you will." Jehan looked around the room and frowned.

"What's wrong?" Jehanna said.

"He won't like it, you know."

"Who won't, and why?" But in her heart she knew of whom he was talking. Jehan gave her one of his looks and she gave him a resigned sigh.

"He sent instructions back from Dern with the messenger. You were to be given a room in the inner ward, close to the family and under the protection of the inner gate and keep. He won't be happy when he finds out you are in the garrison."

"Oh," Jehanna said. She felt very strange about the situation. He was treating her like a visiting dignitary, or even a close family member. But she was here to do a job, as much as Jehan. "But you have a room here. We have always worked together, close to the troops. It is part of what has made us successful."

"True," Jehan said. "I'm only telling you what I have been told. Alliane will probably try to get you to change your mind."

"Well, until Gereinte returns to Carentan, I intend to stay here. There is work to be done in the garrison and as you well know, I am not one to sit idly by and watch everyone else do all the hard work." Jehan nodded, resigned to his sister's logic. Besides, she felt uncomfortable at the thought of staying in the inner ward. It seemed somehow intrusive, like she didn't really belong and had no right to be there. Especially feeling, as she did, so unsure about how her relationship with King Gereinte would unfold. Or even, if there was a relationship. She was terrified that he would come back from Dern and finding her ensconced within his personal circle of family and friends, take exception to her assumption that there was anything but a mutual friendship between them. That thought horrified her more than having to deal with his angst that she had taken a room in the garrison. No. She would stay where she was and be happy that she was back with Jehan and they had a purpose in being there.

CHAPTER THIRTY-THREE

Jehanna tugged gently on the reins of her gelding. It slowed to a walk as she felt its hooves start to skitter and slide across the rough track leading up into the heights of the Helm. She saw the back end of Jehan's horse disappear around the next corner just ahead and paused for a moment while the loose chips from his descent tumbled down into her path. Looking down the nearside of the mountain range, she could just make out the turrets of the castle peering over the skyline. She didn't need to wonder why Castle Helmstedt had been built in such a strategically advantageous position or why it had been so aptly named. After all, who in their right mind would try to march an army up or down this range that marked the border between Carentan and Malvas?

She flicked the reins and began moving back up the slope directly behind Jehan. Their purpose was to assess the possible threat of invasion from that most unlikely angle. Or was it Warmaster Alaric's subtle way of keeping them occupied while he planned for the possibility of a war in Vermondie?

With one final burst of energy, the gelding pushed itself to the top of the track, its hooves sliding back again before gaining purchase on the ground. She passed around a sharp corner, which was concealed on either side by tall shrubs before the track gave way to a plateau of grassy land stretching off into the distant hills. Jehan was trotting around the plateau looking out into the distance. He saw her emerge from the undergrowth and beckoned. Jehanna took a deep breath and urged the gelding into a trot to catch up with Jehan.

"You took your time," he said.

"You can't possibly think that anyone would attempt to breach the castle grounds from here, do you? No wonder they call it Hell's Pass," Jehanna said, breathless with the effort of riding in such inhospitable terrain. Jehan just laughed.

"We have to look at all angles. There is no telling what the Chevaliers are up to. We may have to station a camp on this ground, just to be on the safe side. Once we take the battle to Vermondie, the last thing we want is to be left open to attack," he said, sizing up the ground. He dismounted and started to walk around, stamping his feet at regular intervals. Jehanna slid from her saddle and let the gelding graze and rest for a while.

"Are you sure it's not just Alaric trying to keep us out of his way?" she said.

"Well," Jehan said, ignoring her irony. "If the Chevaliers really are sending a schooner towards Sarlat, then who knows what they could be planning?"

"A schooner full of Chevaliers is not going to pose much of a threat to Sarlat," Jehanna said. "I would guess it is as much a diversion as anything else."

"My thoughts exactly," Jehan said. "Which brings me to wonder what it is we are being diverted from?"

"Vermondie?"

"Perhaps. I mean that is the most likely scenario," Jehan said. "And yet, I have an uneasy feeling about this." The hairs on Jehanna's neck

218

prickled. Jehan's instinct was usually right. It was the one reliable thing that had kept them alive for so long when by all accounts, they should be dead. As Jehan continued to inspect the ground, Jehanna caught a flicker of movement out of the corner of her eye. She held a hand out towards Jehan to still his movement and he stopped what he was doing to follow her line of sight. Jehan frowned and squinted, then his eyes widened as he saw what she saw. The bushes at far end of the plateau were moving despite the lack of wind in the air. Jehan's skin beneath her touch pulsed with adrenaline. They were still for a moment. Then a split second passed, before they both launched into a run. Jehanna ran for her horse and leapt onto its back urging the animal first into a trot, then a canter. Jehan was already mounted and moving his horse like it was flying on the air.

In the distance, the bushes exploded into frantic movement as a figure shot out of the undergrowth and launched into a sprint. It was man. A soldier by the look of it, with soft armoured limbs, which impeded his movement. It was not a uniform that Jehanna recognised, the insignia gold on grey and boldly embroidered onto the back of his heavy-weight jerkin. Jehanna wasn't sure where he thought he was going, especially being pursued by two people on horseback. But the instinct to run was there, which meant that he was almost certainly up to no good.

They had almost caught up with the man, when he disappeared over the top of the horizon where the plateau crested into a hillock, taking the landscape into a graded descent down towards the Malvatian border. Jehanna slowed her mount, but Jehan thundered on, oblivious. She had a sick sense of foreboding.

"Jehan," she called, but it was too late. He disappeared over the edge of the plateau in a flurry of detritus whipped up by the horse's hooves.

Jehanna paused for an instant, then edged her gelding towards the lip of the plateau. The closer she came, the more clearly she could see what was beyond the ledge. She stopped and gasped as she took in the view in front of her. Jehan had stilled his mount a few hundred yards from where she was. He was standing up in the stirrups with his hands cupped over his eyes, straining to see. The errant soldier had found his own horse and was now galloping away in the direction of what looked like a massive dust storm. At first, Jehanna thought that the hills were moving. Then when her eyes began to settle, she could see that it was indeed a dust cloud of sorts. But a dust cloud that was being stirred up by the movement of a great many people and horses. She could see clearly now that it was an army. An army of some significant size on the move. On the move towards Hells Pass. Towards Carentan.

Jehan looked around at his sister and Jehanna could feel his angst, rising in waves from his skin. His expression changed from one of disbelief at first when he seemed to realise what they were looking at, to one of grim determination. He turned his horse around and trotted back up the hill to join Jehanna.

"Malvas," he said. "I almost had him, but as I crested the hill, I faltered for an instant. Long enough to allow him time to make it back to his horse. Long enough to make out the Malvatian insignia on the back of his jerkin." Jehanna looked back at the slowly advancing mass of soldiers, horses and what looked like crude stone throwing machines, similar to the trebuchets they had at the castle.

She swore under her breath. "How many of them do you think there are?"

"About four hundred, maybe five," Jehan said, shrugging as though clearly unimpressed. "I reckon they'll be here in about two hours, give or take. Less, if they stick to following the river Stavan, which will bring them right up here beneath this ledge. Just think. If we had been two hours later in our trip, we would be facing an entire army, just the two of us." He smiled grimly. "That would have been an interesting initiation into the warfare of the Western Isles." Jehanna frowned at her brother for making light of the situation.

"How do they hope to march an army through Hells Pass?" she said.

"Perhaps," Jehan said. "They are hoping that we will bring the fight to them. The two of them sat atop their horses and looked into the distance. They sighed in unison, before Jehanna tugged the reins of her horse, turning back towards Hells Pass.

"Come on, then," she said. "We'd better not disappoint them."

CHAPTER THIRTY-FOUR

Gereinte felt particularly uneasy about returning to Sarlat. It had been a year or more since his last visit. Although he had established some common ground between Carentan and Sarlat, he had not gained much favour with the King's daughter, Princess Fiamina. She, on the other hand, had formed quite an attachment to Darien, who had since returned to Sarlat and established his presence not only with the Princess but also in King Correze's court. Gereinte was painfully aware that when he had last left Sarlat, the Princess had given him more than a few scathing words for deceiving her on two separate occasions into believing he was someone he was not. Firstly during a rather prolonged adventure at sea when he had helped her to escape the clutches of her father's enemies. Then just a year ago when he had travelled incognito across the Western Isles on his grand tour.

Darien, Etienne and Gereinte waited to be announced into the court of Sarlat. Gereinte looked at his friends, flanking him on either side, fidgeting with impatience. Darien was clearly impatient to see the Princess and Etienne impatient to impart to the King his knowledge of the Southerners' latest antics. As for Gereinte, he would quite like to have been somewhere else at that precise moment in time.

In true Sarlatian flamboyance, the trumpeters made a racket bugling their entrance, then the announcer called their names in order of importance to the room at large. All heads turned towards the three of them when the King of Carentan was announced on his first official visit to Sarlat since his coronation. He only wished he had simply been there for a social visit.

"King Gereinte," Alvar Correze said, like a father to his long-lost son. "You bring me the absolute pleasure of your company and not a moment too soon, I might add." Gereinte was all beaming smiles and handshakes, prudently dismissing the sardonic tone of the Sarlatian King.

"King Alvar," Gereinte said, warmly greeting him. Alvar was a short and stoutly built man with a darkness to his colouring that made him look as though he spent more time in the sun than entertaining at court. Although Gereinte trusted Alvar Correze and they had indeed built a lasting relationship over the years, he still couldn't help that twinge of doubt that instinctively brushed over him as he pulled himself back from the handshake. Alvar's mouth twitched as though he was holding back a smirk and Gereinte had to fight the impulse to check his hand. Sarlatians were well known for their tricky and sometimes downright dishonourable dealings. There was a famous saying about Sarlatians, 'when you shake hands with a Sarlat, don't bother counting your fingers, just make sure you still have a hand.' Alvar's eyes were so dark, they were almost black and gave him a distinctly sinister look. He peered at Gereinte, as though challenging him to comment. But Gereinte knew better. He had learnt a thing or two about decorum in his travels. Seeing that he was going to be disappointed, Alvar turned his attention to Darien, who was scanning the room with a purpose.

"Yes, yes. I daresay my daughter Fiamina will be here soon," he said.

"I daresay Lord Issoire might be swayed towards a private meeting with you, your Majesty," Gereinte said, nudging Darien in the ribs. "We have some rather pressing business to discuss with you before availing ourselves of your customary hospitality."

"Errr, yes. Exactly," Darien said snapping back to the moment and grasping Alvar's proffered hand.

"And Etienne Martan, spymaster extraordinaire," Alvar said, shaking hands with Etienne.

"Your Majesty," Etienne said, bowing his head and accepting the King's greeting.

"In that case," Alvar said, "to business." He turned on his heel and strode across the great hall to the doors at the far end. Courtiers moved aside, nodding and bowing, while Gereinte and his party followed in his wake.

Just as they were leaving the hall via one exit, the Princess Fiamina was making a grand entrance at another. Gereinte caught sight of the longing glance she cast towards Darien, then her expression fell as she noted the company he was keeping. Gereinte was duly rewarded with a look of scathing hostility, such that he had come to expect from Sarlat's royal princess.

"I see that Fiamina has not softened in her attitude," Gereinte said as they settled themselves around a conference table in the palace's council chamber.

"Oh don't you worry about her," Alvar said, waving a hand dismissively. "She'll come around.

You know what they say - no fury like a Sarlatian woman scorned. I'm sure our good friend Darien Issoire can keep her out of your way."

"No doubt," Gereinte said, casting a weary sideways glance at his friend.

"Well then. King Gereinte. Tell me what business you have that cannot wait upon a few social niceties," Alvar said. Gereinte looked towards Etienne and nodded. "Ah. The spymaster. I might have guessed."

"Your Majesty," Etienne said. "In Carentan we rely on the trust of our barons and nobles. Sometimes in-house bickering is inevitable, but on the whole we stand united as a nation."

"Hmnn." Alvar grunted in reluctant acknowledgement.

"I acknowlege," Gereinte said, "that it has taken some years to reach that stage."

"And only, I might add," Alvar said, smiling, "at the expense of making a very public example of a certain noble house." Gereinte knew that he was referring to his fight with Borsa that had earned him the respect not only as king but as a warrior and leader not to be underestimated. "Your point, Meister Etienne?"

"Can you say the same of Sarlat?" Etienne looked at Alvar, then turned to look first at Darien, then at Gereinte, as though seeking support. Gereinte raised an eyebrow at the king. Alvar looked nonplussed and returned Etienne's gaze, before settling his attention on Gereinte.

"What a ridiculous thing to ask," Alvar said. "This is Sarlat, dear boy. The nobles here have never been satisfied with my rule. The dim clowns have been in a state of rebellion for years. Their latest plot – which I know all about incidentally – will come to nothing more than they have ever achieved."

"Quite," Etienne said. "However, perhaps you might not know who is stimulating, and more importantly, funding their latest scheme?" Alvar looked puzzled for a moment, then raised an eyebrow quizzically. "The Chevaliers of Arrontierre," Etienne said.

"My lords of darkness. Are you quite sure?" Alvar looked stunned.

"Recently, we have managed to penetrate their secret service," Etienne said.

"Which was deemed necessary, after they sent a trade delegation to Vermondie," Gereinte said. "It would seem that our suspicions were not without foundation. Though I admit, I am rather surprised that they have set their sights on Sarlat." Alvar looked around the table at each of them in turn, almost as though he were looking for one of them to crack and admit that it was all a big joke. But neither Gereinte, nor his companions were laughing.

They briefed King Alvar Correze on the plan to catch the saboteurs from Arrontierre before they could lay siege to the Sarlatian navy.

"They must have had some inside help, I would think. There is no other way the Chevaliers could get into Holmport without being captured," Alvar said.

"We will need a list of likely suspects and where they will be in the next few days," Gereinte said.

"I can tell you who are the most likely candidates but as far as their movement is concerned, your guess is as good as mine," Alvar said. "Most of them are even now, drinking and dancing behind that very door." He nodded to the closed double doors, which lead back to the palace's great hall.

"How far reaching do you think their influence will be within the navy?" Etienne said. Alvar Correze frowned.

"A Sarlatian will always be swayed by money," Alvar said. "Find out how much the Chevaliers are paying them, then double it. That should resolve the inside influences."

"We have about two days," Gereinte said, "to find the prime movers, infiltrate their ring, then subvert their alliance with the Chevaliers."

"How much in the way of funds do we have to play with?" Darien said, fixing Etienne with a challenging gaze. Etienne smiled and shook his head.

"Try to think beyond money, Issoire. There are other means to swaying a man's loyalty," Etienne said.

"What, you mean other than sex and power?" Darien smiled.

"Gentlemen," Gereinte said. "There is too much at stake here to worry about cost. We have to do what it takes. What choice do we have?"

Alvar nodded several times and pursed his lips. "Much as it pains me to offer, but whatever you can afford, I will match and double." Gereinte and his companions fell silent. It was rare indeed for the King of Sarlat to offer his own funds in support of a foreign campaign, despite the fact that is was occurring not only on his soil but also as a result of his own conniving nobles.

"In that case, I believe we have work to do. Darien," Gereinte nodded towards the door to the great hall. "I am sure that the Princess Fiamina would be delighted with your company this evening. Please don't neglect all the courtiers and hangers-on that such a perfect couple is inclined to attract." Darien nodded. If there was information in that room regarding the Chevaliers, there was no one other than Darien more likely to sniff it out. "In the meantime, Etienne and I will start talking to the navy troops."

They all rose. Etienne and Darien walked ahead, talking softly to one another as they made their way back to the hall.

"Tell me," Alvar said turning aside to Gereinte. "Do you really believe that these Chevaliers pose a credible threat to the stability of the Western Isles?" Gereinte held eye contact with Alvar.

"Even as we speak, the Chevalier Supreme is colluding with the Arch Bishop, Abiel Morda to bring down Vermondie," Gereinte said. Alvar's face paled.

"I see," he said. "In that case, if you pull this off, you will have the Sarlatian navy at your disposal." Gereinte nodded thankfully, bowing his head as they returned to the bustle and noise of the great hall.

Alvar's hit list proved to be exact. Gereinte and Etienne had no trouble finding links between the nobles courted by the likes of Darien and Princess Fiamina and the leading navy contacts. The

Chevaliers had severely underestimated the guile and greed of the Sarlatians. On this occasion, it was something Gereinte was most profoundly grateful for. Only two days later, a small sloop sailed into view in the darkness of the late evening just off the coastline of Sarn. It was spotted almost immediately by the crew of one of the Sarlatian navy frigates that were lying in wait.

After a concentrated discussion with the navy generals, Gereinte had agreed with them not to attack the vessel, but to allow the Chevaliers the opportunity to descend, giving the Sarlatians ample justification for taking the offenders into custody. Several Chevaliers rotting in a jail in Sarn could give the Western Isles a bargaining tool somewhere down the line.

The rowboat from the sloop was allowed to go to ground in the bay, at which point the six Chevaliers were pounced upon by the waiting marines. Surrounded and outnumbered, the Arrontierre saboteurs surrendered. Gereinte watched from his vantage point on board one of the war galleys, which promptly descended upon the hapless sloop. Those left on board were faced with the navy's best crossbow men, arrows nocked and trained on every one of them. Gereinte had never seen a group of sailors haul down their flag and surrender quite as fast. He smiled to himself. It had all seemed far too easy. There was something he was missing. On board the sloop, they found tools and explosives that would have been needed to carry out the planned attack on the navy ships. But there were nowhere near enough to bring down the entire Sarlatian force. Almost as if they were there just for show, to prove to someone that the intention was there, if not the resources.

It was only when Gereinte returned to the palace to bring the news of their success to Alvar that he realised they had been cleverly misled. The Chevaliers who were duly ensconced in the city jail were merely collateral damage in a war that had barely begun. He had never seen Alvar's face so pale and serious.

"My Lord King, what it is?" Gereinte had a sick feeling in his stomach.

"We have just received a message from Carentan." Alvar nodded towards a messenger wearing Carentan livery, who clearly had ridden without rest and was hardly able to stand, let alone deliver his message. Alvar waved a hand and allowed the man to be taken away for recuperation. "His horse is lame. I doubt it will be able to go anywhere now." Etienne and Darien burst into the room, ashen faced. Gereinte's heart sank. He had known it all along. It was a ruse to distract their attention from Vermondie.

"It's Malvas," Darien said.

"An unexpected attack on Carentan," Etienne said. "We must ride back now."

"What? Wait," Gereinte said, his mind swirling with confusion. "Malvas? But, Rudelle..."

"Has attacked Helmstedt and attempted to take our army at Hells Pass," Darien said. "There are casualties."

"How many casualties?" Gereinte said.

"At this stage, we don't know. The messenger was dispatched before any conclusion was drawn," Darien said. His answer did not quell the sickness that gripped Gereinte. He thought of Jehanna and wished to any god who might be listening that she had not ventured anywhere near the battle with her mercenaries.

"Are you ready to go?" Gereinte looked to his companions.

"Everything is packed," Etienne said.

"We need to move now while we have the cover of darkness on our side." Gereinte turned to face Alvar. "I am only sorry that we have to cut this visit so short." Alvar shrugged.

"Needs must. Just remember, King Gereinte," he said. "The Sarlatian navy awaits your word."

"And that word may come sooner than any of us would have otherwise liked," Gereinte said. The gravity of his tone was not lost on those present.

"The cover of darkness?" Darien said. "I don't think we are likely to meet any Malvatian troops on our way to Carentan."

"That's because," Etienne said with a faint smile. "We are not going to Carentan." Gereinte nodded, appreciating that his friend had second-guessed his next move.

"You are going to Malvas," Alvar said, nodding with approval. "Well, I bid you good luck with Rudelle. Long have I tried to cement an alliance between our nations. It seems not even blood is a bond thick enough to bind us." Gereinte exchanged a glance with Etienne and the spymaster nodded as though reading his thoughts. "You are a better player than I," continued Alvar, "if you manage to secure an agreement between Malvas and Carentan."

"With Tennengaul and Sarlat in alliance, we have a stronger offer on the table," Gereinte said. "Let's just hope we are not too late." Alvar accompanied the Carentans to their horses. "Your Majesty," Gereinte said, "perhaps you could tell us more about those blood ties."

CHAPTER THIRTY-FIVE

They stood on top of the plateau. Four hundred soldiers including forest rangers poised with their weapons, ready to face an army of unknown quality or quantity marching towards them from Malvas. It had taken some persuasion on the part of Jehanna and Jehan to convince Warmaster Alaric to drop his plans to take the Carentan army south to Vermondie and instead to march them up the side of the Helm to Hells Pass to await un unknown fate. To give him credit, Alaric had come with Jehanna himself to view the unmistakable cloud of movement as it snaked its way alongside the river Stavan towards Carentan.

"Are you sure?" Alaric had said, as though he still did not believe his eyes.

"We nearly caught one of their scouts. He had the Malvatian insignia on his back," Jehanna said. Alaric swore.

"In two hours we would have been on our way to Vermondie. The army is mobilised and ready to move, we just have to move them in a different direction. Vermondie's fate lies with the gods now." He turned his horse and Jehanna let out a long sigh of relief. They had wasted precious time already.

Jehanna now sat on horseback behind the ranks of soldiers. She was co-ordinating the newer troops from Dern, who were lined up to flank the main body of the army. Behind Jehanna's contingent, there were a number of crossbow men. These weapons had not yet been tried and tested in battle. The soldiers wielding them looked apprehensive, but she guessed that it was as good a time as any to test out their new strategy. Hiding in the undergrowth behind the ranks of soldiers were the forest rangers. Although she could not readily make them out, Jehanna was aware of their presence blending into the background, longbows at the ready. Although the furthest away, these soldiers would be the first to attack. At the front of the army, Warmaster Alaric and Jehan sat on horseback, waiting for the Malvatians to crest the plateau. Alaric held a monocular scope to his eye and sat very still, viewing the horizon. All eyes were on Jehan, the chief officer issuing the battle orders.

The air was uncommonly still. This was the first conflict the new united army of the Western Isles had seen. The first time Jehan and Jehanna had tested their skills in a battle of sizeable proportions. The only sounds were the horses blowing air from their nostrils and the distant rumble of a great many hooves and heavily booted feet on the move. It had taken Jehan less than an hour to mobilise their forces and get into formation in readiness for a situation that had been both unexpected and unprovoked. Jehanna had a sudden pang of anxiety as she thought of Gereinte, dealing with the threat from the Chevaliers in Sarlat. As far as he knew, the troops were on their way to Vermondie to support King Rann and Princess Lirra.

As the rumble of the Malvatian army grew closer, Jehanna began to see signs of the Malvatian frontline peering over the edge of the plateau. The first soldiers began to amass haphazardly across the breadth of the open space, waiting at a distance for their leaders to come to the fore and signal movement. From Jehanna's distance it was hard to tell how many there were, but as the minutes dragged on, more lines of soldiers arranged themselves in some kind of formation that begged to be organised. Maybe they had marched all of the energy out of themselves. She could feel her own troops gather confidence from the way the Malvatian army lacked form and leadership. Jehanna squinted into the distance as the siege weapons rolled into view. She wondered if the poor soul who had dragged them all the way from Malvas had any energy left to fight. Every soldier was armed, but they brandished some unusual weapons. She could not be sure but some appeared to have forked spears, not unlike a kind of farming tool she had seen used to pitch hay.

A single rider trotted into view and rode out into the centre of the ground that lay between Carentan and Malvas. Warmaster Alaric lowered his eyeglass, nodded curtly to Jehan, then trotted out to meet the Malvatian ambassador. They exchanged words in a peaceable fashion, before Alaric started gesturing and pointing his finger aggressively towards the Malvatian. The two parties, turned at the same time and rode back to their original positions. Jehan and Alaric exchanged a few words, but whatever they discussed became redundant as the Malvatian forces surged forward at surprising speed considering their long march. Jehan and Alaric sped back towards the Carentan army, turning to face the Malvatian force.

Jehan held his hand aloft for all to see. As the Malvatians thundered forwards, Jehan let his hand drop. All shields were lifted on the Carentan side as the entire army dropped to the ground and a volley of arrows sailed over their heads. A few seconds passed in the instant before impact, then the screaming started. Dozens of Malvatians dropped to the ground, stampeded by the remaining frontline as the soldiers thundered onward towards their target. As the Malvatians gained ground, the crossbows were released and dispatched another dozen or so targets, but not enough to make a significant difference to the numbers advancing. Then the Carentan frontline emerged from beneath their shields and charged forward to meet the Malvatian frontline.

The impact was swift and sanguine. The Carentans had a force of experienced fighters who cut through the Malvatian foot soldiers like a knife through silk. Jehanna winced as she witnessed inexperienced Malvatian fighters try to defend themselves with little more than farming implements. She shuddered to think what the leaders of Malvas had used to justify this painful attempt at overthrowing Carentan. They were clearly outmatched.

"These are just the foot soldiers," Jehan said, appearing at her side. "Their more experienced troops will come in the second wave." She nodded. That made sense.

"What do you make of that?" she said pointing to the rear of the enemy vanguard. Several groups of fighters had broken away and seemed to be attempting to retreat or find another way around the Carentan army. Just as a second wave of troops surged forwards, the splinter groups disappeared from view.

"You take the right and I'll take the left," Jehan said, snapping the reins of his mount and cantering away. She banked her horse to the right and took ten of her troop with her, riding hard across the open ground then disappearing from the battle view. The undergrowth opened out into a small clearing where she met the Malvatian soldiers head on. Perhaps they had been hoping to creep through the undergrowth and infiltrate Carentan while the army was otherwise occupied.

"Not on my watch, you don't," she muttered to herself, drawing her long sword from its sheath.

Jehanna's troop took the fight to the Malvatians. She was the only one on horseback, so took advantage by sweeping her sword through the masses as she rode on through, leaving a fountain of blood in her wake. She wheeled around, noted one of her men on his knees, then rode through again sinking her sword into the body of the attacker. The Malvatian toppled over screaming, but it was too late for her man, whose eyes rolled to the back of his skull before he sank headfirst into the mud. She screamed her anger, realising too late that they were no longer dealing with the amateurs sent forth in the first attack.

Then her horse faltered. Its legs gave way and she sprang from the saddle just in time as the great beast groaned with pain and crashed to the ground. The Malvatian that had attacked the animal was crushed beneath its fall, giving Jehanna the time she needed to retrieve her sword and take stock.

The troops were just managing to hold off the Malvatians, but more of them were starting to appear through the undergrowth as they realised that

237

their peers had discovered a weakness in the Carentan army wall. She wondered briefly how Jehan was faring on the other side, before her attention was captured by a tall, gaudily dressed man riding a chestnut gelding who burst into the clearing brandishing a long sword. Most likely a general and most likely from a noble background.

Jehanna bolted for the bushes, hoping to draft in more of her troops, but the Malvatian general had already second-guessed her plan and was riding hard to cut off her exit. His horse skittered to a stop and he drew himself up tall in the saddle. With a derisive smile, he waggled a finger in front of his face.

"Not so fast, little sister," he said. Jehanna was pulled up short, almost skidding to a standstill before the general. "What's a beautiful girl like you doing on the battlefield, eh? I heard rumours that the boy king had recruited female mercenaries, but dismissed it as conjecture. I stand corrected." Jehanna eyed the general, her sword in guard position. The general was so confident in himself that he had foolishly sheathed his weapon and was set to dismount. "You'll make an interesting bed fellow when all is done," he said, keeping his eyes fixed on his prize. "If you live that long."

There was a perfect opportunity to take him just as he dismounted, but Jehanna withheld, knowing that the horse would take a wound from her killing thrust. The general dropped to the ground, his hand crossing to withdraw his weapon. Jehanna whipped her sword around in an arc. The general stared at her for a brief instant before the pain registered on his face. A bloody hand dropped to the battlefield and he staggered sideways. Jehanna watched him curiously, then slapped the rump of his horse, sending it flying beyond the boundary of the clearing and hopefully to safety. She lifted her knee and thrust her booted heel forwards, kicking the general in the sternum. He staggered back looking down at his chest. At the same instant, a group of mercenary soldiers emerged from the undergrowth behind the general. The general looked at Jehanna uncomprehendingly, then down at his chest, which had the point of a sword sticking out from beneath his ribs. He toppled and fell to the side. The mercenaries swarmed into the clearing and quickly dispatched the remaining Malvatian invaders.

Jehan appeared in front of Jehanna, then leaned over placing a boot on the general's immobile form and withdrew his sword.

"Really, how many times do I have to tell you not to play with your opponents," he said.

"I could have handled him. Look," Jehanna said, turning the body over. "He is a soft noble with too much time and money on his hands." She pulled a ruby ring from the general's finger and threw it back at him with disgust.

"Come on. It's time to withdraw and let the troops clear up the mess," Jehan said turning.

Jehanna followed him back onto the main battlefield, which was a scene of carnage. Bodies, broken and bleeding were strewn across the plateau and it was hard to tell at first which side had suffered the most casualties. That was until Jehanna noticed the Malvatians being herded into groups by the Carentan troops. Once it became apparent that their leaders had been killed in the skirmishes, the

Malvatians were quick to lay down their arms and surrender.

The forest rangers had emerged from the undergrowth and formed a semi-circle around the Carentan army, longbows explicitly trained on the enemy. They waited for resurgence from the Malvation forces or deserters from their ranks, but none came. Even their trebuchets, towering above the lip of the plateau like forgotten battle toys, lay empty and unused. Such was the speed with which the Carentan army had despatched the threat.

"We're marching them right back to the Capital of Malvas," Jehan said, launching himself into the saddle of his gelding. "Alaric has sent a messenger to Sarlat for the King. In the meantime, we intend to begin negotiations with King Rudelle. It is hard to say how he will respond, so we plan to place the city under martial law until Gereinte can join us."

"Well, it looks like they have little left in the way of defence," Jehanna said looking around at the bodies.

"True, but we can't be too sure that this was the best they had to offer. It could yet be a trap. I have no choice but to take an army with me." Jehan looked at her and frowned with a little shake of his head. "There is nothing we can do for Vermondie now."

Jehanna nodded. "I'll do what I can here," she said. "I've brought supplies for the wounded." Jehan turned his horse and cantered away to join Alaric.

She looked around at the dead and the dying, engulfed with a sense of hopelessness. It all seemed so unnecessary. They should all be fighting on the same side, what with the threat from the Southern Lands. And yet, here they were, fighting amongst themselves. To outside eyes it would seem all too easy to manipulate the Westerners into their own wars, whilst slipping in unnoticed to take over the running of a small country.

Retrieving her supplies, she went first to the troops that had helped her in the clearing. Those that were able to walk made their way back to the edges of Hells Pass, where a team of medics were on hand to treat the wounded. She lingered for a while over the body of her dead horse, checking beyond hope for signs of life, but the wound it had sustained hit a vital organ. She looked around at the scattered bodies, checked the few of her own men who had fallen, before rising to make her way back. No life there. No hope. As she turned away, a small groan emerged from beneath her dead horse. She swung around and stalked back to where the horse lay. The groans became more frantic as she approached.

"Please... help," someone spoke in Etanese laced with a heavy northern accent. No soldier of hers. The memory of a Malvatian soldier thrusting his sword into the flank of her horse flitted across her mind. Her initial instinct was to leave him there to die, trapped beneath the very beast he had killed. However, she returned to her horse and gently stroking the beast's side, rolled the dead animal away from the soldier enough so that he was able to wriggle free. He was clearly injured and would need some help to get to the medics.

"Thank you," he said. "I'm so sorry..."

241

Before she had even had time to contemplate his meaning, Jehanna felt a sharp pain. She looked down and saw a sword sticking in her side. It had missed her stomach and neatly skewered her from front to back just below her left rib cage. She could not believe how foolish she was to have thought that the soldier posed no threat. His expression was forlorn and apologetic. As though this one last feat had taken all his strength away, his eyes rolled back and he slumped back down to the ground, his hand falling away from the sword. Jehanna tried to stand, but her legs would not hold her. There was a dark patch of blood seeping across her tunic. As her heart laboured, her body weakened and a black curtain drew across her consciousness. She fell to her knees and surrendered to the darkness.

CHAPTER THIRTY-SIX

Deep in the dungeons of the royal palace at Verton, Abiel Morda stalked down the dismal passageway, lifting his white robes clear of the streams of filth that ran down the walls and pooled on the stone floors. The environment would certainly do very well for his Inquisitors once he had established his presence in Vermondie. And that was just the beginning. The Chevalier Supreme had promised him influence that reached even beyond the Western Isles into Arrontierre, where the One God was worshipped on a grander scale.

The guard at the entrance to Marcus Dassan's holding cell dropped his spear across the archway in front of Morda.

"No one enters," he said eyeing the archbishop warily. Dassan had been imprisoned on charges of treason. After the old King Haveritas had died, his son, Rann, had claimed the throne and immediately put Dassan into custody. It had been a smart move on the part of Rann. Morda was aware of the lengths that Marcus Dassan would go to in order to subvert the ascension to power of the royal twins in his own favour. Indeed, Dassan was just the kind of ally that Morda needed to begin building his own power base. The old king had understood the need to keep control over the people, as much as Dassan had understood the need to control the monarchy. Morda pulled himself up to his full height and lifted his chin.

"King Rann himself has decreed that I speak with the prisoner. It is only God who will save him now," Morda said, his tone of voice sounding out

Dassan's impending doom. The guard did not look convinced, so Morda reached inside his robe and pulled out the forged document from Rann, giving him access to speak to Dassan. It was authentically sealed with the royal insignia embossed in wax. Incredible how resourceful the palace thieves could be if paid enough. The guard studied it for a few moments, before withdrawing his spear and allowing Morda to pass.

Even as he reached Dassan's cell, he could hear the sounds of a revolution beginning to stir on the floors above. Dassan was sitting on a stool, his filthy robes wrapped around his stick thin body. The scowl never left his face as his eyes followed Morda's movements from behind the bars of his cell. Morda stopped in front of the locked door.

"Hypothetically speaking," he said in a low voice. "If you were to miraculously find God, how might your saviour be rewarded?" Dassan's scowl deepened. He grunted, unimpressed, then turned his head away from Morda to face the dank walls. As he did so, Morda carefully slid a key into the lock of his cell. There was an audible click and Dassan returned his gaze to Morda and narrowed his eyes. "Even as we speak, there is a revolution happening in Vermondie. With the help of a few... friends, we may yet stake a claim in the outcome." His smile was ingratiating. Dassan looked up to the ceiling as the sound of shouts and running footsteps echoed above.

"Who do you work for, priest?" Dassan spat his words out in a cracked voice. Morda bristled at the common address, but kept his own counsel. He needed Marcus Dassan.

"We need someone with the capability to win over the people. I believe that you have proved this possible in the past," Morda said, ignoring the question. Dassan scrutinised Morda. For a moment, Morda thought that the fool might not take the bait. But who in this God forsaken place would want to be left rotting in a stinking cell when the promise of freedom beckoned, whatever the cost? Dassan rose shakily to his feet.

"Then I am your man," he said, smiling from behind blackened and broken teeth. Morda rewarded the former chancellor with an obsequious bow, then swung open the cell door. As they made their way out of the dungeons, the noise levels from above increased. Other occupants in the adjacent cells had started to bang on their doors and shout. A filthy arm shot out from between the bars of a cell and grabbed onto Morda's robe.

"Hey," said a dirty-faced man with his face pressed up against the bars. "I can believe in any god you like, if you get me out of here." Morda grasped the little finger of the hand and snapped it back. There was an audible pop and a scream as the arm shot back into its cell.

"Don't fret, my fellow. You soon will be," Morda said.

At the entrance to the dungeons, the guard was lying in a pool of his own blood, the perpetrators long gone. Dassan stepped carefully over the body and cast an appraising glance at Morda.

"I suppose you're going to want a seat on the Council for this," Dassan said. Morda turned his back, leading the way out and smiled to himself.

"Your generosity overwhelms me, Chancellor. That would do nicely." For starters.

***

Mercadier watched the turmoil unfold as his Chevaliers swept into Vermondie and held the city of Verton to ransom. The bombs had been strategically placed to cause the least amount of damage but the most amount of chaos. It was easy enough then to disarm the so-called perpetrators, spread the necessary propaganda, then watch the royal twins flee as their people turned against them. The Chevaliers of Arrontierre would be heroes by sundown; and now that Dassan had been sprung from jail, the commoners would have a familiar face to trust.

Mercadier stepped around the rubble at the Palace entrance and was relieved to see that his own chevaliers were now stationed at the door. He glanced back once to see the fire and fighting still raging across the city, before stepping over the threshold and into his new domain. Two of his best men flanked him on either side.

"Any news of Prince Rann?" Mercadier said to the guards.

"Seigneur Chevalier, he was last seen fleeing the palace on horseback," said the guard on the left with a salute. Mercadier nodded to himself and turned to one of his men.

"I want his head on a pike by the end of the day," he said. Without flinching, the chevalier saluted, turned on his heel and ran back out of the palace issuing orders to the group of men cleaning up the palace grounds. Mercadier watched him go, then stalked down the main corridor towards the wide steps that lead to the great hall. It was all very dull and grey looking. He was going to have to do something about that. It was time to set up a new court of judgement for the people of Vermondie. One much more in keeping with the ideals of the Southern Lands; which was where the Archbishop would have his uses.

He took the steps two at a time, then looked behind to make sure his men were keeping pace. Three more had fallen in behind to support their leader; better to be safe than sorry. As he reached for the door into the great hall, he noticed that it was slightly ajar. His hand hovered for a brief moment on the wooden handle, before he strode into the room.

Upended chairs and littered scrolls spoke of an abandoned meeting. Half-eaten loaves and wedges of cheese lay abandoned in the centre of the oblong table. Someone had left in a hurry.

A rustle of fabric caught his attention and Mercadier swung around to see the Princess Lirra scurry across the floor, attempting to escape via the open door. He raised his hand and the chevaliers darted to block her exit, crossing spears across the width of the double doors. Like a frightened rabbit, Lirra's hand shook as she held it to her mouth. She looked to Mercadier, pleading with her eyes. He moved over to her and jutted his chin forward, peering into her face. Her eyes widened and her face was streaked with tears.

"Not so careless to look down your patrician nose at me now," he said with a grunt. The princess had a vacant look in her eye. A sob caught in her throat and she looked down at the floor. "I wonder," he continued, unconcerned about whether or not she understood, "how much you are worth to the King of Carentan." He leaned in closer and sniffed the air around the princess. He smelt the faint floral scent of her bathing oils, overwhelmed by the stench of fear. Fear was good. Fear meant that she would do as she was told. The princess recoiled from his close proximity and her head jerked up at the mention of Carentan. Perhaps there was merit in keeping her alive. By now there would a schooner's worth of chevaliers being held at the convenience of Sarlat. He looked at the princess in a new light; his bargaining tool. Although, it had to be said that they were not his best men he had sent to Sarlat. He smiled, sure that he could find a few other interesting uses for her. The princess shrank away from him. "Take her to the dungeons and keep a guard on her cell at all times," he said.

As she was hauled away by the arms, the archbishop was coming up the steps toward the great hall. A withered and dirty man followed his lead. As the two parties passed, Mercadier heard the princess hiss in disgust.

"Dassan," she said, spitting out his name, "I might have guessed." Having been kept in captivity in such atrocious conditions for so long, Dassan made a passable attempt to straighten his back and smooth down his hair before grinning from behind his rotting teeth.

"Princess... so lovely to see you too," he said, "enjoy your stay. I can highly recommend the decor; I am sure it will be favourable to one with

248

such discerning taste." The archbishop cast a withering look at Dassan and entered the hall.

"Well, well, my ambitious cleric. Let's hear what you have promised the dirty, heathen rat." Mercadier smiled. Dassan and Morda exchanged a blank look. Mercadier sighed. "Abiel Morda, Marcus Dassan. Shall we?" He said in a passable version of Langan. He began to straighten some chairs to make the place resemble a makeshift meeting room for the new state of Vermondie.

CHAPTER THIRTY-SEVEN

Jehanna's body was lifted as she drifted in and out of consciousness. The howling pain in her side returned with every little movement. They were attempting to move her into a position where they could remove the sword. Dozens of hands seemed to be prodding her and rolling her this way and that. It sounded like the buzzing of a hundred bees in her ears as the conversations overlapped and people shouted at each other.

"Take her this way... no that way!"

"Gods but that is deep."

"Keep her upright."

"No, move her onto her side, then we can remove the sword."

"Cloths. I need lots of cloths and water. No, spirits. Someone fetch some strong wine from the supplies. And water."

"Arrurrg...," Jehanna groaned.

"She coming back to us, may the gods protect her."

She listened to the conversations, taking her cues for when to brace herself and when to relax. As the sword was removed from her side, the pain shot through her like hot fire. She bit her lip and tasted her own coppery blood but the medics were too engrossed in stemming the blood flow in her side to notice. She winced, as some liquid was poured over her wound and the burning increased. Then, almost as an afterthought, someone raised a bottle to her lips and dribbled some sweet wine into her mouth. It slid down her throat and warmed her insides, helping to numb the pain. After a while, she could

250

barely feel her side at all. The medics pressed down on her wound and started to pad it with wads of cloth, then wrap her up like a swaddled babe.

Satisfied with their work, they rolled her onto a makeshift litter. She felt, rather than saw, herself being carried across the battlefield and wondered vaguely how they were proposing to get her down the mountainside and back to castle Helmstedt. In the end, the problem was not hers to worry about, as the pain sent her back into darkness.

When she next opened her eyes, she saw the dark grey of a ceiling; her ceiling – she recognised the cracks. She was in her bed, in the garrison. In a moment of panic, she couldn't feel her legs, then realised that the weight pressing down on them was in fact Fang curled up asleep. She nudged him and his huge head shot up and stared at her. He made a little whimpering noise, then licked her hand repeatedly.

"Arrgh," she croaked, trying to encourage Fang to shift to the side of the bed so that she could feel her legs again. There was movement to her left and she rolled her head to the side. A female medic poured her a cup of liquid. She was an older woman, slightly plump around the middle and with a wise smile. She reminded Jehanna of the herb mistress in Dern.

"I tried to get him to sit on the floor but he just kept growling and snapping at me," she said holding a cup to Jehanna's lips. The wine smelt strong and heavily laced with spices. Her head was spinning just inhaling the fumes. She took a small sip and grimaced. No wonder she had been out cold.

"I haven't seen you before," Jehanna said. She was familiar with all the castle medics. The woman smiled.

"I'm Rina. We nearly lost you a couple of times. It's been a rough few days. The castle medics brought me here from Canrac." She placed a hand across Jehanna's forehead and Jehanna suddenly felt a wave of comfort from her soft touch.

"You have healing hands," Jehanna said.

"And you still have a fever, my Lady." Rina held the cup to Jehanna's lips again and Jehanna reluctantly took another sip.

"How did I get here?" she said.

"Believe me, you'd rather not know. I've been tending to the bruises ever since," Rina said with a wry smile. Jehanna visualised the treacherous downhill ride from Hells Pass to the castle and all the bumps along the way.

"Slung over the back of a pack pony would probably have been the only way," she said frowning and suddenly feeling all the accompanying aches and pains that would have meant.

"Something like that," Rina said, rinsing a wet cloth and placing it across Jehanna's forehead.

"How long have I been sleeping?" Jehanna said.

"Three days, my Lady. Four if you include the day they brought you in," Rina said. Jehanna thought about that. Within that time, Jehan would have reached Malvas, Gereinte would have received news of the battle and Vermondie…

She tried to raise herself up on her elbows but Rina gently pushed her back down. She didn't have

252

the energy to resist and slumped back down to the bed, cursing herself as every muscle in her body shrieked in response.

"You'll not be going anywhere for a few days yet, my Lady," Rina said. "But if there is something or someone I can get for you, just let me know."

"Alliane. Princess Alliane," she said through her exhaustion. "And get this dog off my legs. I can't feel my feet." Rina laughed, then started to make attempts to shoo Fang off the bed, to which she was rewarded with a low throaty growl. "Fang, off," Jehanna said, trying to sound commanding through her pain. Reluctantly, Fang jumped down and promptly took up position at the foot of the bed, casting a wary eye at Rina.

"There now," Rina said, satisfied. "I suggest you sleep now and I'll have the Princess look in on you soon." Jehanna closed her eyes. The wound in her side had begun to throb anew with the effort of moving. Slowly she surrendered to the fog that accompanied the draft that Rina had made her drink. The pain, thankfully, slid away with sleep.

The next time she woke, Princess Alliane was sitting beside her bed, peering anxiously at her. Fang was curled up by her feet. Alliane smiled when she noticed Jehanna's eyes open, then reached down to ruffle Fang's ears.

"This dog, has not left your side for five days. Rina has had to bring in scraps for him and send him out to the patch of grass outside your window, as he would not go further afield." Jehanna smiled.

"He can be quite obstinate," she said. Her throat hurt and her voice came out a bit croaky, but she felt much better. She remembered why she was lying there. "What is going on, Ally?" Jehanna saw a look of restraint flit across Alliane's face, before she took a deep breath, then puffed the air out of her mouth in a deep sigh.

"You mean in Carentan, Malvas, or the rest of the world?"

"Start with Malvas," Jehanna said. Alliane nodded, almost to herself.

"Jehan reached Malvas with no further incident. He was joined a day later by Gereinte. A messenger arrived this morning."

"Vermondie?" Jehanna said. Alliane paused.

"As far as I know," she said, "the city of Verton has fallen to the chevaliers." Jehanna's heart sank. They could have done something, if not for this stupid business with Malvas. At least Gereinte and Jehan were safe. For now.

"I'm not looking forward to Gereinte's return, though," Alliane said. She paused, waiting for some reaction, but Jehanna continued to stare blankly at her. A flutter of excitement made her stomach cramp when his name was mentioned. "I was supposed to be looking out for you. He is going to be furious." Jehanna frowned at Alliane. "I was given one task and one task only and I messed that up. You were supposed to be settled into the keep with the rest of the family, not holed up here in the garrison, running off to battle. It's all my fault."

Jehanna had not thought for one moment that someone might care enough about her to want her to stay out of harm's way. For years, it had been just Jehan and herself, looking out for one another, covering each other's backs. Jehan knew she could look after herself, but even Jehan would not have

254

thought she could have been so careless to get nearly skewered by an enemy sword when the battle was over. She reached out and took Alliane's hand.

"Don't worry. We'll think of something. It's not your fault that I'm so stubborn. I've been on my own for so long, I'm not used to having anyone other than Jay looking out for me." Jehanna shifted her weight and inched her body into a sitting position. The throbbing in her side had reduced to a dull ache, which had now been superseded by the ache of hunger.

***

Within two days, Jehanna was up and about, albeit with limited movement. She divided her time between the castle infirmary and the training grounds. Staying cooped up in her room was the worst kind of punishment she could have possibly endured. Much better to do something useful, whether it was helping to heal the wounded or smoothing the integration of the mercenaries into the army. Less time to think. Less time to worry about those who were absent.

She was sitting on the benches that edged the circular training ground, watching the weapons training and wishing she were fit enough to join in, when Fang lifted his head and sniffed into the air. He then began a soft low growl, which grew in intensity as Jehanna heard a commotion near the keep. The castle guards were shouting instructions at each other and she could just make out the seneschal stalking up and down the parapets, issuing orders. Some of the troops had stopped their

255

sparring, to look up in the direction of the noise. She gazed out towards the middle circle and saw that a contingent of the King's Guard was riding out towards a lone rider. Jehanna couldn't decide whether the horse or the rider was the worse for wear as both looked like they were about to drop. She rose carefully to her feet. It would not be long before the rider would wind up, one way or another, in the infirmary.

By the time she reached the inner circle, the chaos had followed the rider from the gate, to the keep and finally, the infirmary. Pageboys and servants rushed back and forth carrying pitchers and platters, towels and bundles of clothing. She caught sight of Alliane, who stopped and ushered Jehanna towards the room where the rider lay, travel worn and exhausted.

"I knew you wouldn't be able to keep away," Alliane said. "You've barely recovered yourself, shouldn't you be resting?" Jehanna ignored Alliane's concern and peered into the room.

"Who is he?" she said.

"It is Prince Rann. He looks like he has been on the road for days with little rest or sustenance. He hasn't spoken a word yet. He's barely conscious," Alliane said.

"Perhaps I can help," Jehanna said. She sailed past the medics and sat next to the bed where he lay. The medics ceased fussing and allowed her the room she needed. She glanced back at Alliane who rolled her eyes towards the ceiling.

As the attendants bustled in and out with cloths, water, clean clothes, combs and soap, she watched a prince emerge from the dirty ragged figure that lay immobile on the bed. Someone dribbled wine onto his lips, which ran down his chin like a streak of blood. A pot of salts were waved underneath his nose. Jehanna held her palm to his forehead and concentrated, trying to read his aura. A steady low thrum of energy pulsed inside him. She batted away the medics and the attendants with their prodding and their potions.

"You won't bring him around. Not yet," she said. A hush fell over the room and the tumult of moments before slowed to a gentle flow of movement in and out of the room. Despite their misgivings, the medics listened to her. They recognised her healing skill. They may not have understood or liked it much, but appreciated her help. Besides, she had come with the authority of the Andolin family, which for most was enough.

She sat for a while, just absorbing Rann's aura and feeding him with her own energy. Perhaps she was being optimistic, but it seemed that his face began to glow with a little more colour. Jehanna barely noticed the people who came and went from the room, so when she finally looked up, she was surprised to see Alliane's sister, Roda and the two easterners, Jabir and Kemal, standing at the foot of the bed watching her.

"Will he live?" Roda said. Jehanna nodded and smiled.

"He is exhausted. But nothing that a few days rest wouldn't fix." The relief in the room was palpable. The two easterners were watching her.

"You are not like your brother," Jabir said. He was the scholarly one who seemed often to speak on behalf of them both. The other one, Kemal, sort of grunted in affirmation. She found herself warming more to Kemal, who had hidden depths; she would love to have seen him out on the battlefield. "Though your strengths complement his perfectly. Quite a formidable pair you are. I can see why certain leaders might perceive that as a threat." Jehanna glanced at Roda, looking for a reaction. There was something bothering Roda. The easterners were gazing now at Jehanna and Roda shot them an irritated look. Jehanna looked back at the sleeping prince, who was already starting to look rested.

"I don't mean to pose a threat. I am here to help in any way I can. The king..." she didn't really know what to say about Gereinte. His words, his kiss. It was all like a distant memory. She could no longer be sure if he had any feelings at all for her.

"That's not quite...," Jabir said.

"For goodness sake, leave the girl alone." Roda cut him off mid-sentence. "Come on. Let's take some refreshments while we wait for the prince to recover. We have lots to talk about." She steered Jehanna out of the room, followed by the easterners who started to jabber away in Hassian. Jehanna wished, not for the first time in the last few days, that Jehan were there.

CHAPTER THIRTY-EIGHT

Molton was the capital of Malvas. But Gereinte could have been forgiven for thinking he had just ridden into Carentan. Soldiers wearing Carentan livery marshalled the city gates. A mixture of the mercenary's black and gold and the King's purple colours adorned the main thoroughfare leading to the palace.

"I see your new chief of staff has settled in nicely," Etienne said. On their approach to the city gates, a bugle was sounded, followed by shouts from one lookout to another that ran along the city wall as unstoppable as an ocean wave.

"The King of Carentan has arrived, inform the guards."

"The King of Carentan, guards."

"...the king is here."

"...the king."

"...king."

Within minutes a personal guard had jumped to attention to accompany Gereinte and his companions to the palace. It was more than a little disconcerting to see so few Malvatians on the streets. Every so often, Gereinte caught a flicker of movement from the corner of his eye. He was surprised, though reassured when Allard and Bolt, appeared at his side.

"I might have guessed I'd find you two at the heart of all the action," Gereinte said. The forest rangers just grinned, slung their bows over their shoulders and fell into step alongside the horses.

On arrival at the palace, they were shown into a meeting room with barely a chance to catch breath, much less wash and refresh themselves after their journey. Alaric and Jehan were the first to arrive and fill them in on events at Hells Pass. Gereinte was stricken by how pale Jehan was looking.

"Were you injured in the battle?" he said.

"No," Jehan said. "Shortly after leaving Carentan, I developed a pain in my side. It is probably just a result of straining too much in the saddle." There was something odd about his manner, something he didn't want to say.

"Was Jehanna injured in the battle?" Gereinte had hoped that Jehanna had not gone anywhere near the battle, but realistically knew that it was like hoping the chevaliers would not invade Vermondie. He only hoped his pig-headed sister, Alliane had the sense to stay out of trouble. Jehan's eyes had a distant look.

"When I left, she was tending to the wounded," Jehan said. But his discomfort gave rise to Gereinte's concern and a new urgency settled on his shoulders. There were issues to be dealt with before he could return to Carentan. But he could at least send Jehan back with little delay.

King Rudelle stepped into the room, accompanied by his seneschal and various attendants.

"My apologies, your Majesty, for the abruptness of this meeting. I can at least offer you some refreshments while we talk." He waved a hand and the servants began laying the table with pitchers of wine and food platters. The old king looked frail as he lowered himself into a seat with the aid of a stick and the firm arm of his seneschal. Quite a deterioration since the last time Gereinte had seen him.

"Your Majesty," Gereinte said, bowing low. Etienne and Darien followed his lead, then they settled around the table. Rudelle stared at him for a long moment.

"That is quite a formidable force you have developed in Carentan," he said. Gereinte acknowledged this with a nod, eyes flickering to Jehan and Alaric, both of whom remained impassive. "Not that I thought for one moment that the Malvatian army had one jot of hope." He smiled.

"Your Majesty?" Gereinte had expected some resistance or at least resignation, but Rudelle seemed almost offhand. He shook his head as though an explanation seemed unnecessary.

"I remember your Citizen's Charter. You discussed your ideas with me over a year ago, when neither of us knew or dared to hope that you would have the opportunity or even the guts to implement it so soon."

"I am a little baffled by your actions, your Majesty, if as you say, you had no faith in a successful outcome from this battle," Gereinte said.

Rudelle paused for a moment as though weighing up the possible consequence of his words.

"There are ways and means of exacting change in a society that has long since lost its way. Granted, this was a little draconian, and I have sacrificed more than you could possibly know or understand," he said, "but I feel lighter with the knowledge that Malvas will be governed fairly in my absence with a chance at a stable future." Rudelle looked at Jehan and Alaric. "If indeed we have a future with the current threat from the south."

Gereinte looked at the gravity on the faces around the table.

"Vermondie?" he said.

"Your Majesty," Jehan said, "we have just received a message from Carentan. Vermondie has fallen to the chevaliers."

The news made everything that had happened in Sarlat, then Malvas over the last few days fall into place. His army and resources had been misled and misdirected on two accounts. He wondered how much influence the chevaliers had had in the current unrest in Malvas. Considering how they managed to infiltrate the Sarlatian navy, it would not be surprising to find some influence at the highest levels in Malvas. They had been outsmarted. Outmanoeuvred.

"I know what you are thinking," Rudelle said. "While I cannot wholeheartedly say that there were no outside influences in this affair, I can assure you that this latest quest was instigated at the hand of my rather ill chosen, foreign minister," Rudelle glanced warily at Jehan, "who I am led to believe did not survive the battle of Hells Pass."

Exhausted though he was, Gereinte stood up and began to pace around the room. He could think more clearly when he was moving.

"Whatever the outcome of the last few days, we need to be working together now," Gereinte said. "I would welcome your co-operation and input on our war council for the Western Isles."

Rudelle was shaking his head before Gereinte had even finished his sentence.

"I am too old and tired to be of much use to you now," he said. "Why do you think I provided no opposition to my own council when they decided to take action against Carentan? No, I will be happy to advise in any capacity I can, but I suggest we begin to think about a future monarchy for Malvas. I have no heir, only distant family ties, fled to Sarlat a long time ago. As it is, you have what is left of my army at your disposal."

Gereinte looked up at the mention of Sarlat, then continued pacing.

"We are in a stronger position now with Sarlat and Malvas joining our forces, though we could have done without the distraction of battling each other," he said. "Etienne. Tap into your networks, see what you can find out about the situation in Vermondie." Etienne bowed his head. "And…," he waved a hand, "that other matter we talked about." His eyes darted towards Darien, who frowned.

"Your Majesty," Alaric said. "Given the current instability in Vermondie, I suggest a prompt return to Carentan with re-enforcements a priority."

"Yes," Gereinte said. "Of course. Prepare to move the army south at first light." He stopped mid-pace. It may already be too late. If the chevaliers launched an attack within the next few days, they would not be able to respond in time. Unless...

"Darien," he said, "I need a messenger, the fastest you can find. How long do you think it would take someone to get to Tordre by land or sea?"

Darien paused.

"Four days, but they would have to ensure swift passage onto a frigate in Sarn. The Sarlatians are the only ones who have ships fast enough to make that journey in two days," Darien said.

"Good," Gereinte said. "I want you on that frigate. The King of Tordre may not accept the news from a stranger. There is something else we need you to do en route." There was a moment of silence as the room weighed up his words, but Gereinte continued pacing. There were too many variables, too much at stake. And yet, if he sat there in Malvas and did nothing, he was condemning the entire Western Isles to a war that could leave every country, every corner of their land decimated and subjugated to southern rulers.

"Jehan?" His chief of staff looked up at him. "We need a strategy. You, Alaric, Rudelle and myself will work this out now. We have until morning, then we must leave."

"And the matter of a successor in Malvas?" Rudelle said.

"I have an idea about that," Gereinte said. "But there are individuals concerned that I need to speak to first before I can share it." There were a few frowns around the room, but they knew better than to push the issue. Once Gereinte had made his mind up about something, he usually followed it through.

He sat down, suddenly feeling the drain on his energy and the effects of the hard ride from Sarlat. A dizzy haze settled behind his eyes and he rubbed the bridge of his nose with his thumb and forefinger. Someone handed him a cup of wine and chunk of bread. He took a sip of the heavily spiced wine and chewed on the bread. His companions took their cues from him and helped themselves to the food and drink. He let the wine warm his insides and closed his eyes for a moment, listening to the soft hum of conversation in the room. Each one, planning their next move. It would be a long night, but they would be ready by morning to make the journey back to Carentan and face their fate.

"Etienne," he said. "I'm going to need that intelligence." Gereinte looked up, but the spymaster had already gone.

CHAPTER THIRTY-NINE

News soon reached the inner circle of Castle Helmstedt that the army had returned to Carentan. Jehanna all but leapt from her seat opposite Roda in the receiving room when the messenger delivered his words. She winced as a stab of pain shot through her side and down her leg. Roda held onto her arm to prevent her falling as she swayed a little.

"Jehanna," Roda said. "Watch your step or you'll be right back in your bed and you won't be able to see anyone." Jehanna sighed. Roda had taken an uncommon interest in her ever since her recuperation. She kept asking her what she knew of Gereinte's intentions and talked incessantly about her missing baby brother, Josselin. Between Roda, her sister Alliane and the two easterners, she had been fending off uninvited attention every moment of the day. The arrival of Prince Rann had merely caused a welcome distraction. Roda had succeeded, where Alliane failed, in persuading Jehanna to take a room in the inner circle with the family. There was something about Roda that made it very difficult to say no. Jehanna still had her room in the garrison, just in case the family got fed up with Fang, who was also being overprotective since her return from the battle.

Fang sensed that something was going on and started leaping and bounding around Jehanna, which didn't help her stay on two feet. She flopped back down into her seat with a weary sigh. As it turned out, she didn't have too long to wait before the door burst open. She was expecting to see Gereinte stride into the room and didn't know whether to be

266

relieved or disappointed when Alaric came in, followed closely by a melee of attendants and hangers-on. Her disappointment turned to relief as Jehan edged his way through the people towards her, his face creased with anxiety. Jehanna didn't attempt to get up. Roda took one look at Jehan and moved towards Alaric and the group of advisers that had sprung up around him.

"I'll leave you to it, my dear. No doubt Alaric or Etienne will fill me in on the news," Roda said. She sniffed, as though unimpressed by all the fuss and turned away. Jehan knelt down and touched a hand to her wounded side. She winced at little, but covered his hand with her palm and held it there, relieved at the touch.

"What happened?" Jehan said.

"It was my own fault," she said. "I was taken by surprise, thinking he was dead." She relayed her moments leading up to the point when she was skewered on the dying Malvatian's sword. Jehan shook his head.

"Have you any idea how hard it was to keep riding on towards Malvas, with a stabbing pain in my side and not knowing if you were dead or alive?" he said. Jehanna's response was every bit as rueful as his comment.

"Forgive me for not empathising, I was somewhat indisposed," she said. He drew her into his arms and hugged her gently. They withdrew reluctantly from each other.

"Gereinte has returned to Sarlat," Jehan said. She wondered why he felt the need to tell her that. "He has some business to attend to, apparently something to do with the future of the monarchy in Malvas."

"Oh?" Jehanna had thought that Gereinte would naturally assume the crown in Malvas. It made most sense to expand his leadership, especially given the outcome of the Malvatian's untimely invasion. The political circumstances were ideal. After all, Carentan had only been defending itself; they could not be held responsible for the Malvatians' lack of self-management. Malvas had taken the battle to Carentan.

"There was some talk of establishing a new line in the Malvatian monarchy," Jehan said. He was speaking slowly, watching her face all the time. She felt sick.

"Is there something you don't want to tell me?" Her heart began to thud and her cheeks tingled with a blush.

"It's probably nothing, but I just wanted you to know. I don't know or understand any more than that," Jehan said. She understood now that he just wanted to protect her. But could it be true? Jess had once intimated that there had once been an expectation that Carentan would be wed to Sarlat, one way or another. She had heard rumours about the beauty of Princess Fiamina and how she was destined to rule as Queen one day. But Queen of Malvas? The thought of Gereinte married to another woman filled her with a hot rage she had never before thought herself capable.

"Sis," Jehan shook her gently by the shoulders. "Whatever happens, it is for the future of the Western Isles. Monarchies are brought up to know and understand that. It is a question of duty."

Jehanna looked blankly over Jehan's shoulder at the easterners, Kemal and Jabir, in earnest discussion with Alaric. She shook her head, hoping to clear the shadows creeping on the edges of her vision.

"I know," she said, "I know all about duty." Jehan followed her gaze, then grimaced.

"Jabir and Kemal have been keeping you entertained then?" he said. She smiled, put her palms together and dipped her head in parody of the easterners' customary greeting.

"We've had to get through worse," she said, "and no doubt, there is worse to come."

CHAPTER FORTY

"How could things possibly get any worse?" Princess Fiamina said, looking Gereinte straight in the eye. Gereinte struggled against the impulse to grab her by the shoulders and shake some sense into her.

"I thought you would be happy... but of course, if it is not what you want." He gritted his teeth. What sort of a fool had she played him for? Granted, they had had their run-ins, but he had believed her to be genuinely attracted to Darien. This should have been much easier and now it was looking likely that Malvas was not going to have the new beginning it deserved. They had discussed the political import of the match and the timing of the betrothal, but none of it had softened the steely look she cast him. Gereinte had no idea what he was going to say to Darien. It had been the perfect solution. A match made by the gods. But apparently, Princess Fiamina of Sarlat had other ideas.

When he had suggested the idea of marriage, Fiamina had looked at him with such horror, his words had trailed off until he sat there looking at her not quite sure if she were about to explode or rip his head off. So he had tried to pacify her with all the benefits of being Queen of her own country and the status that went with such responsibility. To no avail. She was indeed a feisty lady; he couldn't think of anyone better than Darien to pacify her.

"But I can't marry you. You lied to me," Fiamina said. "Twice." Gereinte opened his mouth to speak then snapped closed it when words failed him. "First you dragged me out to some gods-forsaken island to escape my father's enemies, all the time pretending to be a slave boy on board a Coustiller ship." All right. Guilty as charged... but only because he really thought his life might be in danger if he had revealed his true identity. "Then, after years left wondering if I were going mad thinking you were someone you were not, because, let's face it I knew there was something not right about the whole 'slave boy' thing, you turned up in Sarlat at my father's court pretending to be some Count of 'I don't know where'." True. All true, but then her father, the King had known his true identity and it was traditional to travel incognito on a grand tour. It was not his fault that her father only chose to tell her the truth after several days of socialising at court functions. "The only redeeming factor in all of this sorry charade," she said, "was the fact that you brought along the only man that I would ever agree to marry." There it was. He was right. The only person capable of melting the heart of the Princess of Sarlat.

"Fiamina," said Gereinte. "I am not asking you to marry me. Darien would make a fine King and I certainly don't need any more countries to rule. You and he together would rule over Malvas and continue the royal bloodline." It was Fiamina's turn to look at him open-mouthed.

"Oh," she said, seemly unruffled. "Well, that's all right then. Of course I'll marry him." Gereinte breathed an inward sigh of relief and excused himself to break the good news to Darien, who was at that moment in time, preparing to set sail for Tordre.

271

Mercadier stood with his back to the Archbishop, looking out of a long rectangular window that gave him a perfect view of the city of Verton. In the distance, fires still blazed and the rubble of the fallen city walls was strewn across the surrounding space with wilful abandon. Perhaps the explosives had been a little too enthusiastic. It would take time to clean up the city and restore faith in its citizens.

"Dassan has been speaking to the people. It is quite amazing what a bath and a clean shave can do for a man," Archbishop Morda said. Mercadier's skin crawled at the grating sound of his voice. He hated being indebted to anyone, especially when it came to politics and power. "Already, I have inquisitors on the streets of Verton and soon, the dungeons will ring out with the sounds of obeisance.

"Who will clean up this damned mess?" Mercadier swung around and glared at Morda, revealing his irritation with instant regret. Morda looked surprised for a moment before he drew the mask of indifference back over his face, then smiled.

"Why, the people, of course. I will see to it. Before the end of the day, the people will be fully committed to cleaning up the city."

"And where is Dassan?" Mercadier said. "We need space and supplies for the incoming chevaliers."

272

"I believe," Morda said, "that the chancellor is putting a strategy in place for expanding the campaign northward. Towards Carentan."

Mercadier quietly seethed. Did the naked ambition of this man know no bounds?

"Impossible. How can we launch an attack with nothing here to defend the ground we have only just gained?" By the light of the One God, he was going to have to teach these barbarians something about strategy.

"The timing cannot have been more fortuitous, my Lord." Morda sidled up to Mercadier as though his equal, which made Mercadier bristle all the more. "Thanks to our careful interventions, the Carentans are too busy battling with the Malvatians and foiling sabotage plots in Sarlat."

Though it irritated him to admit it, the Archbishop had a point.

"We have to wait for re-enforcements from Arrontierre," Mercadier said. "Then we shall take the fight to the Carentans. We cannot afford for them to launch a siege on the city of Verton. It its current state of affairs we would be lucky to hold off an army of peasants, let alone the combined forces of the Western Isles."

"Remember, my Lord," Morda licked his lips and Mercadier felt sickened. "We still have a bargaining tool."

"The Princess Lirra," Mercadier said.

CHAPTER FORTY-ONE

Gereinte spent the next three days riding hard in a bid to reach Carentan before Warmaster Alaric and Jehan marched the army off to Vermondie. He had cautioned against a reactionary counter attack that would lead to being caught unprepared and without back up. Until forces had arrived from Sarlat and Tordre, their numbers were too small to take on the chevaliers. Etienne had managed to glean more information about the situation in Vermondie from his networks in Sarlat than in Malvas. So it was with a heavy heart and meagre expectations that they rode into the outer circle of Castle Helmstedt late in the evening, three days after seeing Darien aboard a frigate in Sarn.

Darien carried his message to Nerys Andolin, Gereinte's sister and Queen of Tordre. Gereinte didn't doubt that Morra Dreidan, the King of Tordre would be swift in sending re-enforcements. Despite the country bordering Vermondie, the capital city of T'sar was geographically isolated from the rest of the Western Isles, only accessible by sea from the coast of Sarlat or boat down the river Caren. There was no time for an army to realistically re-group in Carentan before they would have to march on Vermondie. He only hoped that the King of Tordre would go along with the plan that he sent with Darien.

The castle guards at Helmstedt only recognised Gereinte once he had dismounted and approached the gates on foot. With no standard flying and no guards surrounding him, it was almost unheard of for their King to just appear out of thin air like that.

Only Etienne and the two rangers, Allard and Bolt, accompanied him, much to the consternation of the King's Guard on patrol at the castle walls. By the time Gereinte's party reached the inner circle, they had a dozen or more advisers, courtiers and knights fussing around them.

He walked his horse into the cobbled yard and handed the reins to the stable boy. Someone handed him a flagon of something liquid that tasted suspiciously like watered down ale, but he wasn't complaining. He made straight for the great hall and flung the doors open, expecting to find only a few die-hard members of his war cabinet. He was surprised to see that the room had been effectively transformed into a strategic war office. The oblong table had been set up in the centre of the room, which was littered with scrolls and pencils, used cups and plates.

All eyes looked up.

Jehan stopped talking, mid-sentence and Alaric clapped his hands together in a mixture of relief and call to action. Servants appeared with fresh platters and pitchers of drink.

"Your Majesty," Alaric said. Jehan just smiled and nodded. Over the other side of the room, he caught a stir of movement and noticed Jehanna rise to her feet.

Gods, but he had forgotten how beautiful she was. He faltered for a moment, then frowned when he noticed how pale she looked. She had a sad, worried look on her face and was leaning slightly to her left. She shrugged ever so slightly, as though to tell him it was nothing.

"We have little time to waste, your Majesty," Alaric said. Gereinte looked back to the table and noticed Prince Rann for the first time. He bowed his head in acknowledgement and turned his attention to the assembled advisors. Apart from Jehan and Alaric, Kemal and Jabir were present. Prince Rann sat next to Baron Issoire, who was deep in conversation with Chancellor Lorquin. Roda sat back with Jehanna and Alliane, apparently at ease with the company she kept. Etienne and Gereinte joined the conversation and the atmosphere around the table lifted with an air of renewed confidence.

"Princess Lirra?" Gereinte said. Rann paled and shook his head, lowering his eyes to the table.

"As far as we know," Jehan said, "she has been captured. We can only wait now for news of whether she is alive."

"My sources in Sarlat and Malvas tell me that not only has Dassan been sprung from jail, but that Abiel Morda is working in collaboration with the chevaliers," Etienne said.

Gereinte let out a long slow breath. Just the mention of Abiel Morda was enough to set his pulse racing with fury. Rann's expression registered at first shock and his head shot up. A little smile curled at the corner of his mouth.

"Perhaps, then," Rann said. "Lirra will be alive." He looked at the blank expressions around the table. "Dassan always had a soft spot for Lirra. He was forever trying to get our father to agree to a betrothal. 'Over Lirra's dead body' were father's exact words, though I hope it won't come to that. But it might just keep her alive long enough." Gereinte knew if it were his sister, he would have

276

laid an entire city to waste in order to get her back. He glanced at Roda and Alliane, who had sidled near to the table in order to hear the news. Jehanna held onto Roda's arm for support and he frowned at her, putting off the questions that he burned to ask.

"Rann. If we are marching on the city, there is a very real chance that if she is alive, she may not survive the siege," Gereinte said. Rann stared back at him with empty eyes. It had to be said. He would do everything in his power to return Lirra to her brother, but he had to prepare Rann for the worst.

"The city is at its weakest. We cannot leave it much longer before we attack. If the chevaliers have any sense, they will have sent for more forces," Alaric said.

"Or," Gereinte said. "They will bring the battle to us. Draw us away from the city. That's what I would do."

"How long before we can expect re-enforcements from Sarlat and Tordre?" Jehan said. Gereinte shook his head.

"Two or three days. We cannot rely on them. I am confident the help will come, but when and how many I can't be sure. Darien is handling the Tordre end, Alvar Correze is directing the troops from Sarlat. That much I can say," Gereinte said. There was a moment of silence around the table as his words sunk in.

"We have no choice," Alaric said. "We have to make a move independently, assuming in the worst possible scenario, that the extra troops may be too late, too early or not arrive at all." He unrolled a large scroll and set it in the middle of the table, weighing down each corner with a flat stone.

Gereinte hoped that the warmaster had a substantial plan, because he had done about as much as he could.

***

Jehanna listened as Alaric relayed his ideas, pointing out various strategic areas on the map. It felt odd to be so close to Gereinte and yet so far away. His attention was utterly absorbed by the plans for attack on Vermondie. But she had seen that frown on his brow as he took in her appearance. Was it disapproval, disgust, surprise? He may have expected to find her here, but ensconced within the heart of his family? Perhaps the news of her injury had not yet reached him. Maybe that was what it was. Or maybe, his visit to Sarlat had indeed cemented an alliance between the two nations. Maybe he had changed his mind about her. Maybe it was Fiamina who dominated his thoughts now. Frustration mounted at her continued inability to read his emotions. Then he had said those unkind words to Rann. Just when the man had been given a thread of hope that his sister might be still alive. Her indignation grew to the point where she made herself a promise. Come what may, she intended to ride out with the troops and sneak into Verton herself if necessary to get the Princess out. Whilst nursing Rann back to health, they had shared some rare moments of understanding; sometimes it took a twin to understand another twin's plight.

The noise of discussion grew more confident as the evening wore on. Before the night was out, they had been over the plan in as much detail as humanly possible. The meeting dissolved and the conversation dispersed into splinter groups around the room. When she next looked up, Gereinte was gone.

She stood and excused herself from the presence of Gereinte's sisters.

"You are not going back to the garrison, tonight are you?" Roda said. Jehanna faltered by the door.

"There are some things I need to attend to before the troops leave in the morning," Jehanna said. Roda's expression reminded her too much of Gereinte.

"I shall see you in the morning?" Roda said. It was more like a statement than a question. Jehanna smiled, almost to herself and nodded. You didn't say 'no' to Roda. Even Alliane seemed powerless to intervene when her sister had spoken.

Back in her room, she sat on the bed wondering how she was going to get away in the morning without anyone noticing. Even Fang looked at her with suspicion in his eyes.

There was a loud rap on her door and Fang barked.

Then he was standing there, looking all regal and proud. She stood shakily, felt her left knee buckle and he was suddenly at her side holding onto her arm and supporting her weight. Damn the wretched injury.

"Are you all right?" Gereinte said, "I knew something was wrong, but I didn't dare ask Jehan. I'm sorry it took me so long to get back here." The blood pulsed through her veins and rushed to her face. With one arm around her waist, he leaned in closer and brushed a stray lock of hair away from

279

her brow. They just stood and looked at each other for what seemed like an eternity. He leaned in closer and she felt the heat of his breath on her cheek. Then he lowered her back down and sat beside her. He looked around the room, seeing it for the first time and she could sense his displeasure.

"Why have you been staying here?" he said. For a moment she wasn't quite sure how to answer him, so sat there like a dumbstruck servant, while he pierced her with his eyes.

"I... needed to be close to the troops, to do something useful with my time, anything to fill the bare hours until..." Gereinte looked at her, expecting more, but receiving only silence. Then he seemed to understand and nodded to himself.

"Tell me what happened," he said. Jehanna told him about the battle and events that led up to her injury. He smiled, then grunted when she got to the part about the Malvatian nobleman, raised his eyes to the ceiling when she told him about how Jehan had stepped in. His expression darkened when she reached the part about the soldier, presumed dead, trapped beneath her horse. It was hard to tell how he felt about that, but he was certainly not smiling.

When she had finished, they sat once again looking at each other.

"Tell me about your travels," she said. But his mood had turned black as he churned over her words. He barely even heard her.

"I don't want you anywhere near any more battles," he said, "especially not Vermondie."

She blinked. Took in his words, delivered with absolute conviction that she would do as he pleased. She was transported back to that time in the orchard of the palace of Dern. That moment in time she would rather forget. How could he make assumptions and demands of her as though she were a child, or worse, some kind of possession? How dare he, when he had only just returned from courting the future Queen of Malvas? Her face flushed again, though for a different reason. It was raw anger now that coursed through her veins.

"Who are you to make demands like that on me?" Along with her anger, confusion ran rampant. "It is not even like we are a couple. You just sent me here, told me to take a room in the inner circle with your family. What am I supposed to think? One minute you're holding me in your arms, the next you are forbidding me to use the skills that I thought Jehan and I were hired for in the first place. Then you rush off to Sarlat with proposals for the Princess..." She had said too much. Gereinte's eyes were wide; he had the same look on his face that he had just after she slapped him in the orchard. She cringed at that memory. "Where I come from the women are not trussed up in flouncy dresses in castles, expected to only speak when spoken to. They are warrior queens who rule the Sheikdoms and raise their children on the battlefield."

Gereinte was silent. He looked away, looked around the room again, then looked back at her. Had she once again acted out of place, out of turn? Just when she thought she had mastered one set of Western customs, another popped up to surprise her. Women didn't habitually speak back to the men and certainly not to their monarch. Oh grief, what had she done? He looked like a little boy again, lost on a battlefield of conflicting emotions. On impulse, she reached out and took his hand. He flinched at first, then relaxed and allowed her to curl her fingers around his and absorb his warmth. He felt good, he felt calm.

"I'm not very good at this, am I?" he said.

"I'm sorry, it's me who should apologise. I take your words too much to heart. Usually I can read emotion and intention, but with you... you are like a blank canvas to me. I have to get used to that." Jehanna felt the tension in the room dissipate. Gereinte traced a line across the back of her hand with his fingertip and she shivered in response.

"I don't want you to get hurt," he said, looking her square in the face, defying her to argue back.

"I can look after myself," Jehanna said lifting her chin a little. Gereinte grimaced.

"Evidently," he said.

The anger rushed up to meet her again, but she quashed it when she saw the twinkle of mischief in his eye. "You've been talking to Jabir and Kemal, haven't you?" Gereinte said. She shrugged. "I've had the stories about the Eastern Lands as well, you know. Alliane practically feeds on their every word, using it as ammunition to change the customs here."

"But you have done so much, already. I've read the Charter," Jehanna said. Gereinte looked up, eyes narrowed. "When I was in Dern... Jess let me see it." The mention of Princess Jessamine seemed explanation enough.

He looked at her, thoughtful but at the same time, torn. Soon he would tell her that it had all been a misunderstanding. That he had a duty to marry a Princess and cement the future of the Western Isles.

282

"I need someone like you," her heart skipped a beat, "to lead the way," he said. Her heart plummeted. All that was left was the fight and the possibility of helping Rann to bring back Lirra.

"Let me come to Vermondie," Jehanna said.

"My mother would be turning in her grave," Gereinte said. She squeezed his hand and he smiled, though his eyes looked distant. Perhaps this was the last time she would enjoy his company, enjoy the pretence that she could ever have been his queen.

"Some people say that Roda resembles your mother a great deal," she said. They were silent for a moment and Jehanna was not sure how far she could push the next question. "Roda talks a lot about your baby brother, Josselin." He looked up and a profound sadness crossed his face. She wished then that she could take those words back. It was too soon, she didn't know him well enough. He inched a little closer to her and she felt reassured.

He shook his head sadly.

"Josselin is like an unsolved mystery," Gereinte said. "Roda keeps on hoping that one day he will just turn up." Jehanna dared to lean in a little closer to him. His warmth and aura was strong now and made her dizzy. He responded by drawing her into his arms. She lifted her face to his.

"You don't have to always be the protector," she said. "Sometimes it is okay to let someone else protect you." Something she had learnt from an early age. She wasn't sure if he absorbed her words, or ignored them. The next thing she knew he leaned forward and pressed his lips to her. He kissed her then, with their mouths slightly parted. Her whole body filled with light from the tips of her toes to the end of her nose.

CHAPTER FORTY-TWO

The next morning, Jehanna was up and ready with the troops. Jehan and just about everyone else had advised her to stay put and rest her injury, but she could not just stay in Carentan when those she loved most were out defending all of their freedoms. Jehan understood, though he didn't much like it. Besides, she had made a promise to Rann. It seemed like he was the only one prepared to take her seriously and she had meant every word when she told him she would do everything in her power to help him find Lirra.

The army had finally been mobilised to make a start on their journey, with Jehan and Alaric at the helm, leading the way. Gereinte appeared by her side and her heart sank when she saw the look on his face.

"Do I have to lay myself down on the ground in front of you to stop you from endangering yourself?" he said. She rode on without a word, head held high. "Is it not enough that I have had everybody who means anything to you try to tell you this is not a good idea?" Oh. So no one really cared about her, it is all his doing that everyone advised against her going to Vermondie. He settled his horse into a steady walk in rhythm with her own mount. She scowled at him and said nothing. "Is this how it is always going to be between us?" he said. She could not compromise her values, her integrity and her skill for the sake of his peace of mind. Besides, he had the Queen of Malvas to be thinking of now.

"So be it," he said and jerked the reins of his horse. He cantered off to the head of the march.

***

"Two days?" Mercadier said. The messenger withered under his gaze. What was the Emperor thinking?

"I... can only pass on the message, Seigneur," the messenger said. Mercadier's anger brewed beneath his indignation. "There is trouble in the Eastern Lands."

"Get out and don't return until you bring me news of the arrival of the additional chevaliers," Mercadier said. The messenger nodded and backed out of the great hall, evidently relieved to have survived another day. Mercadier turned to look at Morda and Dassan, who were spread out around the table with a selection of his best chevaliers. Morda looked as obsequious as always, sickening him ever more. Why did he think to bring the slimy cleric in on this deal in the first place? Dassan, although useful in bringing about confidence from the people of Vermondie, was proving to be a thorn in his side when it came to making sensible decisions. He wondered if the man was really subverting the course of events in his own favour somehow. He wasn't quite sure how he was doing it, but the nagging doubt was there, nonetheless. He also spent far too much time visiting Princess Lirra in the dungeons. Was he gloating, or did he indeed have a soft spot for her? Damn them all. He needed those extra chevaliers.

"There is no way that we can withstand an attack from the rest of the Western Isles without some sort of reinforcement," Dassan said. "The city is in ruins and we are barely keeping civil order. It could all erupt in the face of a siege." Dassan's appearance had completely changed, now that he had eaten some decent meals and raided the palace wardrobes for some regal robes. Not forgetting what a difference a long hot bath could make to a man's state.

"I have it on good authority that the Carentan army have left Helmstedt. They will arrive in the borderlands within a day, Seigneur Chevalier," Morda said. "If we are to survive this attack, we must take all the troops that we have and march out to meet them. It is the only option."

"By which time," Dassan said. "Your additional Chevaliers will have arrived to protect the city." Mercadier stood silent for a moment, thinking. He knew this had been coming, it was only a question of time.

"How many does he have?" He said. Dassan looked at Morda, then back at Mercadier. God damn that heathen rat, if he didn't look pleased with himself.

"With the depleted ranks from Malvas, we estimate, four or five hundred at most," Dassan said. "According to my sources, there is no movement as yet from Sarlat or Tordre."

"Good. Good," Mercadier said. "Let us hope that the boy king has failed in his attempts to gain support from those regions."

"Though, one might expect some reaction from Tordre, given that an Andolin is wed to the king," Morda said.

"A woman?" Mercadier said. Wonders never ceased. "I doubt that an army could be raised by a woman's influence." Mercadier noted the look of unease that flitted between Morda and Dassan, while his own chevaliers nodded in agreement. Mercadier waved his hands in dismissal.

"Even with additional help from Tordre, we still outnumber them. Once more chevaliers arrive from Arrontierre, there will be little the Western Isles can do to stop us," Mercadier said. "We ride out at first light to meet this so-called threat from Carentan."

"And the Princess Lirra?" Dassan said, trying to sound casual, but betraying his unnatural interest. The princess could rot in her cell for all Mercadier cared. He paused for thought.

"If anything should go wrong, we still have her as a bargaining tool," he said. Was that relief that washed over Dassan's face? "Perhaps, Chancellor, you should take her into your own personal care?" Mercadier smiled. He had Dassan now and he knew it. Dassan nodded and smiled, trying to hide his eager expression.

"Gentlemen," Mercadier said. "My chevaliers are experienced in warfare. Let us take the battle to the Carentans and show them how to rule a nation." Reputation aside, he had no doubt that the Carentan army would either wither under their attack or surrender their arms. The boy king's head would sit on a pike on the city wall of Verton by sundown tomorrow and the gates to the Western Isles would be open.

CHAPTER FORTY-THREE

Jehanna rode with her troops, who kept a close eye on her and were a little too eager to close ranks around her. No need to wonder where that instruction came from. All the time, she rode with her head held high, one eye on the road and the other on the front of the battalion, where Gereinte and Jehan rode. Rann also rode up front and was planning to break away on arrival at Vermondie to find Lirra while the troops kept the Chevaliers occupied. She hoped that Gereinte would be too busy ordering battle formations to even consider that she might retreat to help Rann.

They stopped after the first day of travel to make camp, eat, drink and rest. The campfire was banked early after eating; no one wanted to be caught too soon and without adequate preparation. One more day of hard travelling, one more night of rest before they would descend upon the Vermondie border and march towards the city. It was expected that the chevaliers would meet them head on, before they even made it to the capital.

The tents were erected with speed and precision, her men not allowing her to strain herself on account of the injury. She felt slighted but at the same time a bit relieved as the pain in her side had begun to throb after her body had been bounced around in the saddle for the last day. She had been given her own small corner of tent with screens for modesty, but still she was kept awake by the chatter of the soldiers, excited at the prospect of flexing their muscles. She hoped that their anticipation would be met and that they were a match for the reputed chevaliers of Arrontierre. If not, all that training and effort had been for nought.

Sleep was a long time coming for Jehanna, as she stared at the sky through the slit in the tent on her side. It was clear enough to see the sparkling of the stars behind the black blanket of the night.

Morning came all too quick and the campsite was deconstructed. Back in the saddle, still sore from the previous day's ride, Jehanna rode with apprehension. Her side still ached, but at least the wound was healing. All she had now to deal with was the residual pain and the unnecessary attention she attracted from those who claimed only to be looking out for her interests.

Morning rolled into afternoon, into evening. As they drew ever closer to the Vermondien border, their presence would surely draw attention from the chevaliers. They eventually reached the plains of Aergon, just north of the Verton Delta. It was a wide-open space, which stretched for miles, then dropped suddenly from a promontory. The descent rolled down towards Vermondie and stretched west towards the city of Verton. The walls were visible from their vantage point, so any possible movement from the chevaliers would be seen.

Troops dismounted, horses were led to water and left to graze, groups splintered off to rest, eat, recuperate. A small core including Gereinte, Jehan, Alaric and the battalion leaders grouped near the centre of the plain. Jehanna longed to join them, get the inside word on the strategy, but she held back, hoping to make herself seem invisible. It would not be long before each battalion was briefed. She had appointed Brastac their leader, unwilling herself to take charge of the attack. Everyone else thought it due to her injury and wishing to stay out of the front line, but she had other plans.

It all happened in an instant. Had Gereinte and Jehan expected the attack? One moment, they were all fairly relaxed - apprehensive yes, but prepared. The next moment, Brastac was running towards them signalling with both hands; mount and fight or sit as ducks and die. The army split into two separate factions as the leaders reached their battalions. That could not have been by chance alone.

She caught a few shouts and cries on wind before the ground beneath them erupted with a massive cruumpptt, scattering soldiers everywhere. Then the chevaliers appeared from the settling dust with their gaudy uniforms and their jewel encrusted long swords. They rose up from behind the Carentan ranks as though they had been beneath the earth itself; heads up, eyes screwed in concentration and frowning in ugly supposition. The chevaliers were all pumping arms and legs, emerging from the cocoon of their camouflage. They picked off the troops that were not fast enough to reach their horses and disabled the horses that were not fast enough to escape their swords. They were swift and business-like, not dwelling for long on the fallen or falling, but intent on quashing the invading threat from the north.

Jehanna made it to her horse and for a moment was torn between the two sides of the Carentan force that had split down the middle. This had to be part of Gereinte's plan, it was too regimented, too swift. But Brastac had not reached his battalion in time, so she had no forewarning about the formations. She had a split second to decide whether to follow the rest of her battalion, which had reined up behind Brastac and were galloping after the half of the army that had broken away and were heading east. What was going on? That was away from Vermondie, towards Tordre. The chevaliers must have assumed they were retreating as only a handful went in pursuit, the rest were intent on disabling the remaining half of the army, which stood their ground and fought on the open plains.

The pointed golden helmet of a Chevalier popped up beside her horse, its occupant snarling in a language she neither understood nor cared to interpret. She bent her knee and kicked her boot into his face before he had a chance to harm either Jehanna herself or her horse. The man reeled back clutching a bloody nose, then fell over before being run through with a broad sword. The bloody face of Rann looked up at her and grinned, withdrawing his weapon from the dead chevalier.

"Lost my horse, somewhere in there," he said. She reached down and clasped his forearm, heaving him to his feet. Then he vaulted onto the back of her horse and she galloped around the melee of swords and soldiers spreading out across the plain. "Verton?" he said. She nodded and spurred the horse on.

CHAPTER FORTY-FOUR

Gereinte was plunged into darkness when the earth beneath his feet rumbled and a dozen shields were thrown over him. One or two of the soldiers fell away, leaving a chink of light in the cover, others were bleeding but remained steadfast.

"Move out, now!" He had to force his way out before they realised the detriment to all of their lives if they stayed there in middle of the battlefield beneath that canopy of shields.

He blinked, surveyed the damage, the bloody and broken bodies and then saw the chevaliers rise up from the periphery of his vision to attack his army. To give them credit, most of the battalion leaders had issued the order to break formation just seconds before the ground erupted.

Damn those chevaliers and their bloody explosives.

That was one trick he had not factored into their strategy. It had drawn the chevaliers right into their hands, but had left the Carentan army equally at peril.

Two horses were galloping towards him with no sign of stopping. One was riderless, the other had Jehan bearing down, shield and sword in hand. Was it dust from the explosion or was there really steam coming from the nostrils of those war horses? Jehan slowed just enough to allow Gereinte to grab his helping hand into the saddle, then they both bolted towards to the edge of the clearing. Two chevaliers on horseback pulled up in front of them, attempting to cut off their escape. Gereinte drew his sword, its hue made his hand look as though it were on fire with its strange blue glow. The chevaliers hesitated long enough for him to drive his thrust through the first one. The chevalier's chest heaved, his scream pierced the air, then he fell sideways from his great war horse. Jehan had made quick work of the second chevalier, who lay in a bloody heap.

Just as they reached the edge of the clearing, the Carentan longbow men launched their attack. Most of their men, having lived and trained as forest rangers, had a lifetime's training with the longbow. They picked off the chevaliers one by one in the melee leaving barely a scratch on the Carentan troops who were still struggling in the centre of the battlefield. The chevaliers were so arrogant that they wore the most distinguishing and brightly coloured livery Gereinte had ever seen, making it easier for the rangers to target.

"Where are their crossbow men?" Gereinte said. Jehan was scanning the horizon. It seemed the chevaliers either had no strategy at all or they had something extra up their sleeves. There were no foot soldiers, no Vermondien labourers to absorb the frontline attack. They had sent in their seasoned warriors to be slain by the Carentan longbow men. He would have expected somewhere to see a wave of crossbows, but where were they?

Jehan was issuing orders to the remaining troops, as the chevaliers fell back. They re-grouped and re-directed their movement towards Verton. Gereinte fell back and looked into the distance for evidence of the other half of the army, which had broken away just as the ground exploded. By now, they should have made enough distance to outrun the chevaliers and launch their co-ordinated attack on Verton from the South, mopping up the villages and towns as they went. Jehan reined up beside Gereinte.

"We better hope that Alaric joins up with the Tordrean contingent, otherwise we don't stand a hope of launching any significant attack on Verton," he said. Gereinte nodded. The battlefield was littered with bodies. As far as he could see, mostly Carentans with a few peacock feathered chevaliers in between. He had an uneasy feeling about the speed with which the chevaliers had withdrawn.

"Get our troops out of there. Fall back now," Gereinte said. Jehan galloped off issuing orders, but it had come too late. He heard the arrows singing on the breeze before he saw the wave of crossbow men from the enemy rise up from the lip of the promontory. Their own crossbow men did not have the distance to be able to counter and the rangers could not react with enough speed to pick off enough of the enemy bowmen to make a difference. The Carentan force started to drop like autumn leaves; dead or dying before they even hit the ground. They were sunk. May the gods protect them and the citizens of Verton. Before they were finished here, there would be no army to march on Vermondie. Jehan came streaming out of the melee.

"We have to move our crossbow men into position, they are too far away," he said, then cantered past Gereinte. Stick to the plan. Gereinte reined in past the ring of men making ready to attack, before the order was issued. They marched forwards, aimed and fired above the masses in the centre of the field, towards the chevaliers. A few bolts hit home, but not enough to quell the onslaught.

"Again," Jehan said. He raised his hand, beckoned the troop forward, then paused while they loaded their weapons. He dropped his hand and a volley of crossbow bolts cut through the battlefield. It was a calculated risk, they could have hit some of their own men, but it was the only way to reach the enemy and beat them at their own game. A few more chevaliers fell, along with a few Carentans. Yet still, the chevaliers seemed to have a never-ending supply of men and weapons. Gereinte reined up beside Jehan.

"Get the longbows into position, take them around the back, down the side of the promontory, there." He pointed to an area that seemed almost impossible to penetrate. Jehan frowned as he tried to follow Gereinte's train of thought. "Trust me, they can do it." Jehan nodded and pulled back behind the line of crossbow men.

CHAPTER FORTY-FIVE

Jehanna galloped away from the battlefield, towards Verton. She could just about make out the wall that surrounded the city, so she put her head down and pushed the horse forward without a backward glance at either Rann or those she left behind. A sick, aching pressure in her chest pulsed when an image flashed across her mind of Gereinte being buried beneath a pile of dirt, soldiers and shields. There was nothing she could do. To ride into the middle of it all would have been suicide. Better to concentrate on something she could do. Jehan would look after Gereinte.

Rann was clinging to the saddle, his body pushing into her back with every stride of the horse. Fortunate that she was so slim; the saddles were not made for two and it proved an uncomfortable ride for them both. Despite that, Rann shouted directions at her at every turn, taking them deep into the heart of the city without encountering a single chevalier or palace guard. There was no way in this world that she would have been able to navigate her way so quickly into Verton without Rann's help.

They slowed finally and came to a stop at an inn inside the city, on the outskirts of the palace walls. Rann was quick to bustle Jehanna off the horse and into the relative anonymity of the public lounge. She was surprised when the innkeeper descended upon them both and drew them into a back room. She let out a long slow breath, felt the sickness rush to her core and for the first time realised she was shaking. Rann didn't look much better. His face was streaked with dirt and his arms were bloody and raw. He had a sword slash on his left upper arm where his tunic had been ripped and was flapping around the open wound. Jehanna clutched her stomach and groaned as the bile rose in her throat. A warm friendly arm reached from behind her and placed a bowl beneath her face and comforting hand across her forehead. She looked up in surprise at a plump rosy-faced woman in a serving apron.

"Marcie will take care of you now," the innkeeper said. Lines of worry creased the man's brow but he had a strong, determined face. He returned quickly to the front room, allaying suspicion about the strange, dirty-faced travellers that had suddenly appeared on his doorstep. Marcie left the room for a brief moment. Jehanna sat with her head over the bowl and Rann stared at the wall; the pair of them shocked into silence. Marcie returned with a bundle of clothes and a maid in tow with a tray of refreshments.

"In due time, you'll be wanting to clean yourselves up and change out of that livery. That is, if you want to walk unseen through the streets of Verton and not like some exiled enemy of the state," Marcie said, with a glint of mischief in her eye. Rann stood up.

"Lirra," he said, stalking towards the door. The innkeeper's wife stood between him and his exit with her arms folded across her chest.

"The princess is safe for now. But she won't be if you go running off to the palace in your current state," she said. Seeing the wisdom of her words, Rann slumped back into his seat and allowed the woman to fuss around them with food, washing rags and fresh clothes.

They whispered to one another, Rann drawing a visual picture of the palace in Jehanna's mind, Jehanna fighting her desire to jump back on the horse and gallop back to Gereinte. What will be, will be. Their most immediate concern was how to get into and out of the palace unseen.

"This place is a safe house," Rann said. "I have known Ertan and Marcie for many years. They worked at the palace while we were growing up and have always provided a safe haven for me and Lirra." Jehanna frowned.

"It's not looking good, Rann. Without re-enforcements, Jehan is unlikely to be able to take Verton with the remaining troops. It will be difficult getting back out, even with your knowledge of the area." Rann was looking at her strangely when she mentioned Jehan. "It's okay, he's still alive. I would know otherwise," she said. He nodded, understanding. Jehanna felt some of his tension ease.

"If they stick to the plan, Alaric's half of the army will attack from the south west, with Jehan and Gereinte attacking from the north ea..." His words trailed off. Jehanna leaned over the bowl and retched, the tears springing to her eyes. Well at least she could pretend it was the sickness that was making her cry. She pulled herself upright, took some deep breaths and tried to brush it off, but Rann was looking at her curiously.

"Did you see something, back there?" Rann said. Jehanna smiled weakly and shook her head, but was unable to stop her tears.

"I don't know," she said, "if the king is still alive."

Rann's eyes widened. Jehanna kept a straight face and shrugged her shoulders as though it were nothing. But she had already given enough away.

CHAPTER FORTY-SIX

Gereinte led what was left of his half of the army across the Verton Delta and into Vermondie. The rangers had eventually picked off enough chevaliers to worry them into retreat and now, the remaining Carentans were effectively herding the chevaliers back to Verton. Gereinte's numbers had been seriously reduced and he doubted whether they could make enough of an impact without the rest of their numbers. Once the fleeing chevaliers had met up with their regiments, Gereinte's army would be just like an annoying buzz in their ears. Jehan rode beside him, eyes forward, frowning in resolute determination.

Gereinte tried not to think of Jehanna and he knew from experience that whenever something was wrong with her, Jehan started behaving strangely. He figured she must have escaped with Rann just after the explosion and hoped that was the case. He could not bring himself to even contemplate the alternative.

It took less than an hour to reach the borders of Vermondie and a further hour to penetrate deeply enough into the city before they came to a wall. Jehan commanded their troops into some kind of formation, spanning as much of the open ground they could, providing a shield for the bowmen who waited behind the front line. The most they could hope for was to puff themselves up enough to appear bigger than they really were and wait for Alaric to come in from the south with re-enforcements.

They stood still. Waiting on the front line.

The air was light and breezy, drifting in from the south coast. There was a distant hum, as though life rumbled on in Verton without a care to the battles raging outside its walls. Any moment, Gereinte was expecting a revitalised troop of chevaliers to spring up from the walls and launch a targeted missile attack. There was no way that the attack on the Verton Delta was the sum of all their men. It was odd, now that he thought of it, that the chevaliers had just drifted away, absorbed by the city like a ghostly apparition. It all seemed so unreal to him now, sat on his horse staring at an empty outpost.

Gereinte and Jehan glanced at one another, then Jehan nudged his horse forward and trotted towards the nearest gate. Jehan reached the wall and pushed the wooden gate. It appeared to give and he edged his horse forward, disappearing. Gereinte held his breath. Jehan could look after himself, but one man against a troop of chevaliers was not good odds. He prepared himself to gallop into the fray, then Jehan's head peered around from the other side of the wall. He beckoned. Gereinte led the troops cautiously forwards.

The entire north side of Verton was deserted, save for one ill-positioned chevalier who now had his hands tied behind his back and knife held to his throat. Jehan looked up and grinned.

"Verton is under attack from the south. It appears our friend here was put on lookout for us. There were others, but they escaped, so we need to move quickly," Jehan said.

Gereinte gave a small hand signal and the troops surged forwards, pouring over the mouth of the wall and through whichever gate would yield to their pressure. They swept through the north of the city, mopping up any stragglers along the way. Fires burned and bodies littered the streets, but most sensible Vermondiens stayed locked behind their doors. As they reached the south side, it became apparent that the chevaliers were having difficulty holding off the onslaught from the Carentan army.

No.

Not Carentans alone. Gereinte was heartened to see a mixture of Western Isles nations peppering the battlefield. The black and gold uniform that signified his united forces was now speckled with the light blue and white livery of a Tordrean troop.

Yes.

Darien had made it in time. In amongst the melee, the stark crimson sashes of the Sarlatian navy's foot soldiers weaved in and out like streaks of fire in a forest bush.

Jehan took one look at Gereinte, then grinned and moved their half of the army forward to bolster the attack from the north. As they marched forwards, Gereinte could feel the rangers in their company disperse with the wind, running alongside their march, at the same time hiding above and behind any structure that got in their way. Arrows were loosed with the precision of the sun's own time keeping, finding their targets more often than not. The south side troops hollered and roared their approval when they saw the incoming troops from the north. Gereinte watched with an increasing sense of pride as he realised that the combined forces of the Western Isles had now formed a circle around the threat from Arrontierre. The chevaliers were fast being depleted and Gereinte took the opportunity to drop back from the front line and double back.

He left his forces to finish the job, only one thing now on his mind. Find Rann. Because he had sneaking suspicion that if he could find Rann, he would find Lirra and Jehanna was certain to be close by. He cursed himself for allowing her to join the campaign; she was in no fit state to be riding and no fit state to be fighting. Gereinte slipped away from the fight. No one noticed his departure, so absorbed were the troops.

The palace lay in ruinous abandon, to the west of the battleground. One or two chevaliers were standing guard, but it looked like most had been drafted into the battle. He dismounted and ran along the inside of the wall, keeping close to the shadows. As he sprung up to take the first guard by surprise, he faltered and dropped back when the bulky form of the chevalier rocked forwards and tumbled down the steps in front of him.

A knife was sticking out of the back of his neck.

It was when he stepped over the body to deal with the second guard that he noticed the thin line of blood that ran down the second chevalier's chest and formed a pool at his feet. The only thing holding him up was the weight of the broadsword that had skewered him to the wooden door. The sword was of Vermondien stock, the royal insignia embossed on its hilt.

Rann.

With sword in hand, Gereinte crept forwards, took a cursory look at the dead chevaliers, then

305

sprinted for the stairs. As memory served him, Dassan liked to reside in the highest room of the palace and that was where he expected to find Lirra.

He took the steps two at a time and reached the first landing. Two more dead chevaliers lay in a bloody heap in the middle of the floor. As he passed over them, he sensed rather than saw a flicker of movement behind him. He turned and within a split second of being sliced with a long sword, he parried the attack. The chevalier's clothes were ripped and torn, streaks of blood ran down his face, arms and chest. Yet he wielded that sword as though it were the only thing keeping him from death's clutches. When the chevalier saw the glow of Gereinte's sword, he faltered, perhaps believing that death had already come, but it was enough for Gereinte to thrust into his chest and complete the task. The chevalier looked at him with disbelieving eyes, then slumped back on top of his compatriot.

Gereinte, rather belatedly, checked both men to make sure they really were dead. He extracted a small throwing knife from the second man's throat and a bubble of blood and trapped air escaped, animating the dead man for a brief second. He turned the knife over in his hand, feeling its weight, assessing its throwing trajectory.

Jehanna.

He tucked it away and leapt up the next flight of steps. Portraits of the dynasty of royal lineage in Vermondie adorned the landing walls. Were they holding Lirra here, or should he be going down towards the dungeons? No. Something had lead Rann and Jehanna this far, his instincts were right. Then he heard muffled voices coming from further

306

up. He peered beyond the landing to a small circular winding staircase that lead, he presumed to the balcony. The steps were barely wide enough for one person, let alone two and he could not imagine how Rann and Jehanna had both managed the climb without putting themselves in danger. As he reached the summit, there was a small window, which opened out onto a long rectangular balcony that appeared to run across the length of the palace roof. He stepped out onto the balcony, feet first and ducking his head to squeeze his body through the small opening.

"Ah. The boy king, at last," a voice said from the edge of the parapet.

The first thing Gereinte noticed was Jehanna stretched at an impossible angle over the edge of the palace roof. Her face was turned away, as though looking down to greet her fate. Her body flinched at the words and he knew then that she was still conscious. The man was holding a knife at the back of her neck with one hand and using his knee to apply pressure to her wounded side. He was evidently a chevalier, possibly the Chevalier Supreme. His high status had not improved his dress sense. Perhaps the gaudy colours helped to distract their enemies. Jehanna emitted a small whimper and the chevalier pushed his knee harder into her side. She screamed and the chevalier laughed.

Gereinte sprang forward with his sword raised, but the chevalier just tipped Jehanna fowards a little more. She was only just hanging on to the edge, one more push would send her falling. No one could

307

survive a fall from that height. Gereinte stopped in mid-stride.

"What do you want?" he said.

"Look," the chevalier said, nodding to the horizon. Gereinte followed his gaze, expecting to see the last remnants of the southern usurpers disappearing under the might of the united Western Isles.

His knees buckled and he dropped his guard.

It was all over.

A sea of lurid uniformed chevaliers rose from the South and swarmed towards Gereinte's army. Once the chevaliers hit the city wall, the Western Isles didn't stand a chance.

The Chevalier Supreme was laughing.

"Well, my boy king," he now had one hand underneath Jehanna's legs, ready to tip her over the edge, "you have walked right into my world, did you expect to just rescue the girl and walk back out again?"

What was the bastard waiting for? Vermondie was sunk. He could do nothing. What was the point in prolonging the inevitable?

"For years I have looked across the sea at the coast of Vermondie and dreamed of owning this land," the chevalier said.

Ah, there it was. He wanted to gloat. It wasn't enough to win this battle, he wanted to glory in it. He was waiting for his audience to arrive. "It is true, I could just kill you both here and now and claim the throne, claim the Western Isles. But I feel your people need to be taught a lesson. A lesson in humility. Something you could well have learnt

308

before you attempted to banish the One God from your nation."

The Archbishop.

The chevalier was becoming distracted. Good. Gereinte took a faltering step forwards and gripped the sword at his side a little tighter. His throat constricted. Jehanna's aura washed over him, giving him strength.

"I have always advocated religious tolerance. It was the messenger I banished, not the god," Gereinte said. The chevalier had caught his movement and tightened his hold on Jehanna. The blue glow of his sword welded the weapon to his skin in fiery steel. "Let her go," Gereinte said. His voice carried an edge of warning. The chevalier looked at first surprised, then slowly he began to smile. He casually lifted his arm and Jehanna's legs tipped over her head and she was gone. There was a faint scream, then silence.

CHAPTER FORTY-SEVEN

"No!" Gereinte sprang to the edge of the balcony and looked down. There was no sign of Jehanna. He turned to face the chevalier, who was circling him with his sword drawn.

"That's it, little boy king, let the anger pour forth. Let me show you how a real chevalier fights." The goading did nothing; Gereinte was cold inside, detached. As he brought his sword into the guard position, his entire body filled with the light of the steel. The chevalier's eyes flickered in momentary surprise, then his expression fixed into grim determination.

Gereinte didn't know what he would do without Jehanna. He didn't know what he would do without an army. But he did know that he needed to rid the world of the parasite in front of him. Come what may.

The chevalier made a faint to left and stepped inside Gereinte's guard with a dummy thrust. Gereinte parried at the last moment. The air rang with the clash of steel on steel. They stood toe to toe for a moment, locked together, before the chevalier pushed Gereinte away, attemping to slice him on the retreat. The sword caught his upper arm and the sting of the cut made him wince. The chevalier smiled. Gods, he was fast.

Gereinte always fought better on the defence, but at the same time it was a weakness when confronted with a tactical fighter. It was how Kemal beat him almost every time in their sparring sessions. He watched and waited, circling the chevalier, looking for an opening or a crack in his defence line. But the chevalier was good. He held tight to the line of attack, never deviating an inch. Gereinte took a gamble, stepped left, then snapped back to the right, weaving inside the Chevalier's defence. The chevalier's sword wavered for a fraction of a second and Gereinte seized his moment with a thrust to his chest. The chevalier parried the attack and came forwards as Gereinte was on the retreat, just nicking his shoulder.

He could not afford to let this go on for too long. The longer they crossed swords, the greater advantage the chevalier would have. He was bigger than Gereinte, clearly fit as he had barely broken sweat and he was fresh. Gereinte had come straight from the battlefield after days of travelling and fighting, his breath was labouring and the cuts on his arms were dripping with blood. The chevalier knew this and would try to string this out for as long as possible. Gods, give him strength. His sword filled him up with its glow.

Gereinte saw an opening and pushed forwards. The chevalier broke his line of attack, slashing wildly to stave off the attack, but Gereinte kept pushing forwards, left, right, left, forwards. He caught the chevalier in the upper thigh with a flesh wound. The chevalier barely registered the hit but kept Gereinte at bay with his parries. Gereinte kept up the attack. Small movements, to push him back, to confuse him with combinations. It was working. The chevalier was running out of space, moving back and back towards the palace wall. The chevalier's eyes registered doubt for an instant. Then Gereinte knew he had him.

He pushed forwards, ignoring the stinging blows that the chevalier was issuing with each defensive thrust. Gereinte had more injuries than him, more cuts, but the chevalier could not hold him off for much longer. Live or die, Gereinte no longer cared. He stepped one more time inside the defence, took a step back, then thrust his sword up through the chevalier's chest, missing the rib cage and aiming for his heart.

The chevalier's eyes widened. His breath faltered. His sword hand dropped and he was flailing for a hold on the wall behind him. Gereinte withdrew his sword, then gave him a gentle push. The chevalier toppled over the edge of the wall and screamed as he fell to his death. Gereinte heard the thump as his body hit the ground below.

He slumped down to his knees, using his sword to prop himself up. His breath laboured in and out, his whole body howled with pain. The blood from his cuts streaked down his arms. He wanted to just lie down and die, but the vision of Jehanna tumbling over the edge of the wall and the painful memory of her screams forced him to his feet. He had to see. Whatever state her body was in, he had to see her one last time. He edged himself towards the wall and looked over.

There she was.

Not the broken and bloody corpse he expected to see, but alive and dangling from the edge of a parapet that jutted from the palace wall one level below. She looked up, her almond shaped eyes beseeching his help. Her hands were bloody with the effort of hanging on.

312

Gereinte's fatigue disappeared and he dangled himself headfirst over the balcony, hooking his boots into a crack in the wall to hold himself in place. He could just reach her hand. Their fingertips touched and he stretched forwards, nearly losing his footing, but just pulling back in time.

He reached again, this time grasping one of her hands and began to pull. She released her other hand and used her feet to facilitate the upward pull. But the blood and sweat on them both made her hand slip from his grasp. Gereinte adjusted his grip and circled her wrist, pulling harder and faster with a desperation that was ripping him apart inside.

She crept up the wall, seeking footholds. When she reached Gereinte, she used his body as a human ladder. Her arms reached the top of the wall, just as Gereinte's body slipped from his foothold. She grabbed his foot and this time, it was Gereinte dangling over the edge. Inch by painful inch, she helped him to crawl backwards up to the top, reining him in by his leg. They both heaved over the edge and fell into a heap onto the stone floor on the palace balcony. Jehanna fell into Gereinte's arms and he held her tightly, as though afraid to let her go again. She shuddered in his arms and he let her sob, allowing her shaking body the time to adjust.

After a while, he pulled away a little and looked at her face. Shocked, injured, but alive and despite the streaks of blood and dirt, still the most beautiful woman in the world. He pressed his lips to hers and she responded with a passion that filled him with heat. He kissed her lips, her eyes, her cheeks, her neck. He felt the rhythm of her pulse racing beneath his touch and he wanted to stay there forever, locked in her embrace. Reluctantly, he pulled away.

"Marry me, be my queen," Gereinte said. Then she started to laugh, but it was not in happiness. It was a desperate laugh, a laugh of defeat. Then he saw she was crying.

"I would gladly be your wife, but queen? We have no nation to rule," Jehanna said. He shook his head.

"If we get out of here alive, I'll build a new nation, a new army," Gereinte said. She smiled and nodded. He got the feeling she was getting to know him.

Then they heard the clear, clean note of a horn in the distance and looked blankly at one another. Gereinte didn't remember the chevaliers having horns and his army certainly didn't use them in battle. They rose to their feet and looked out over the edge of the wall.

Gereinte had half expected to see a battle raging between the chevaliers and the Western Isles, but what he saw both confused and elated him. Jehanna squeezed his hand.

"My people," she whispered to herself.

The chevaliers had not even reached the city walls before being overrun by another army. What kind of army gave their enemies due warning that they were about to attack? Then he realised. It wasn't a warning to the enemy, but a warning to the western army. Alaric and Jehan called the combined forces of Tordre, Sarlat and Carenten into a retreat from the city of Vermondie. A few troops were left to mop up the remaining chevaliers, while the vast mass of able-bodied soldiers turned their wrath upon the incoming chevaliers who were caught in the middle between the east and the west.

The easterners wore elegant flowing robes in deep, rich colours and scarves across their heads in black, red and gold. They rode ugly beasts that hissed and spat at their opponents and frightened the horses of the chevaliers. Many of the enemy horses just folded beneath their riders or bolted away from the oncoming beasts. Then the western army descended upon the chevaliers from the other side and the balance of power shifted.

From their vantage point, Gereinte and Jehanna watched in awe as the threat from Arrontierre was extinguished. They were so wrapped up in each other and the scene unfolding before their eyes, that they hardly noticed Rann and Lirra step onto the balcony. Gereinte turned his head when he sensed their approach. Rann looked triumphant and Lirra, although a little worn around the edges, looked relieved. They joined Jehanna and Gereinte to watch the remaining battle.

"Dassan?" Gereinte said. Rann shook his head. Well, at least that was one problem he didn't have to deal with. He wondered where the Archbishop was hiding.

CHAPTER FORTY-EIGHT

Jehanna was anxious to see her brother when they rode out to the battlefield. The only horse still left outside the palace was Gereinte's gelding, grazing as though oblivious to the war that was raging around it. Jehanna had to lean on Gereinte's arm to steady herself as the pain of her old wound ripped through her side with renewed vigour. He launched into the saddle and virtually dragged her up behind him. She held onto him, arms wrapped around his waist, for fear she might fall as much as an excuse just to hold him. By the time they reached the edges of the battleground, it became evident that Jehan had taken control of the situation as order was being restored to the ranks.

Jehanna didn't know whether to weep with relief or shame. Relief that Gereinte had followed her and ultimately saved her from falling from the palace roof, or shame at having got herself into that situation in the first place. She had hung from that balcony praying to whatever god might listen that Gereinte would survive, while her arm was slowly being wrenched from its socket and her grip on the edge of the balcony was slipping. Then he had appeared over the top and her strength re-doubled. When she finally fell into his arms it was as though everything that had gone before, the anger, resentment and misunderstanding were just wiped away. She knew then that whatever the outcome of the battle, she would never again leave his side.

There were bodies being piled up, one side for the Western Isles and one side for Arrontierre. The chevaliers that remained were being held under guard until such a time that they could be extradited.

They dismounted and all around them, easterners pitched in with clearing the scene, herding captive chevaliers and calming the strange foreign animals. It was oddly surreal to see so many people who looked just a bit like her, after living for such a long time as an outsider. There were women too. Unlike the sprinkling of female soldiers in the mercenary troops, the easterners had an even split of female and male warriors. This somehow didn't surprise Jehanna and made her stand a little straighter and rely a little less on Gereinte for support.

Then as they moved towards the centre of activity, she saw Jehan talking to one of the easterners, a woman with a headdress twice the size of any she had seen before. The woman's face was darker than Jehanna's but her eyes were shaped like almonds and had a familiar gaze. An eastern man stood beside her, all but basking in her glory, his face was shrouded with a tasselled headscarf. He was talking to Jabir and Kemal in what she presumed to be Hassian.

Jehan looked up, caught her eye and his relief was palpable. The conversations stopped. Jabir and Kemal were looking at her. The eastern man dropped the scarf from his face, his mouth open in surprise. The woman with the headdress fixed Jehanna with the most adoring gaze she had ever seen anyone offer her, save perhaps Gereinte when he didn't realise she was watching him. Gereinte squeezed in closer to Jehanna, his warmth containing her in a shroud.

317

Then the weirdest thing happened. Gereinte released his hold on Jehanna and stepped forwards. He went down on one knee and uttered something that sounded incomprehensible. The woman reached out and put a hand on his shoulder, repeating some words. Gereinte glanced at Jabir, who nodded and smiled. Then he rose to his feet and turned to face Jehanna.

"Your mother has granted me permission to ask for your hand in marriage," he said. Startled, she stepped back a moment. Looked at Jehan who was beaming at her, then at Jabir who had the grace to look a little guilty. Kemal was just Kemal. Gereinte was waiting for his words to sink in. Now that the man with the headscarf had revealed his face, the resemblance to Jehan was startling. She choked back a sob.

"I'm sorry I couldn't tell you before," Gereinte said. "They wanted to see you both first, to make sure."

"I think," Jabir said. "That it is as plain as the day you both disappeared that you are the heirs apparent to the Sheikdom, Arjat an-Nahr."

Jehanna stared. Not knowing what to say or what the correct protocol was. So she placed her hands together and bowed her head the way that Jabir and Kemal did, then allowed everyone to fuss around her asking questions, hugging, patting, bowing and finally taking her off to see to her injuries.

The rest of the day passed in a haze. A makeshift tent had been put up close to the battlefield to deal with immediate injuries. Gereinte had stopped her from attempting to offer her healing services and sent her back to the palace with an eastern entourage. Jehan remained on the field to see to the clean-up operation and Gereinte was ensconced with eastern leaders, Jabir there as a translator. They had insisted on remaining near to their people and a magnificent tent had been put up for their comfort.

Jehanna still had some difficulty thinking of them as her kin, let alone her birth parents and wondered if she would ever get used to that notion. She had very little memory of them and had an ingrained image in her mind of her early years having been spent surrounded by a sea of attendants, brightly coloured cloth and heat. She remembered being dearly loved but could not recall any faces. Their auras felt good and familiar. Jehan had been quick to trust them and since she trusted Jehan, she guessed it was okay to feel the same way.

Rann and Lirra had begun to put some order back into the running of the palace and the people were reluctantly emerging from their houses as the news went around that the chevaliers had been defeated. The Vermondiens looked a little dazed, as though someone had just woken them up from a bad dream. Fires were still burning across the city where the chevaliers had used their explosives to ward off the enemy. A renewed community spirit began to spread as people took stock of their situation and rallied together to put out fires and clear the streets.

Gereinte's name was being whispered amid the crowds as their 'liberator'. Jehanna had been so close to Gereinte in the past few days, it was easy to now see him as the man who had engineered this victory.

Lirra had insisted on Jehanna taking a guest suite in the palace, which was lavishly adorned for visiting dignitaries from far off lands. When she had started to complain, saying a smaller room would do just as well, Rann had stepped in.

"This will do well enough for the future Queen of Carentan and warrior daughter of Arjat an-Nahr," he said. Jehanna opened her mouth to protest, "Don't even think about it, believe me, after the day we've had..." So she just kept quiet, but was unable to hide the blush that rushed up her neck and flushed her cheeks. She guessed she would have to get used to it.

Had she agreed to be Gereinte's wife? She supposed she had and now that it had been made so public, how could she deny how she felt about him? It felt right. A warm glow lit her up inside when she pictured his face, his earnest expression, asking her to marry him. Then his relief when she said yes, and his consternation when she began to cry. Why was that? Happiness, relief, fear. After those last moments on top of the palace walls, when she thought she would die and then they both looked likely to die together, they had become inescapably wedded to one another. Wed in a deeper way. Two futures, tied to each other so closely, physically and emotionally.

She could feel him now in a way that she had not previously been able to. It was bit like the bond she had with Jehan, but different. With Jehan, she could reach out to him and sense if he was upset, angry or hurt. Gereinte's aura was like thick shroud that wrapped her up and held her close. It was almost stifling, but somehow a comfort to know he was always there. The other difference was, she didn't appear to be able to switch it off, like she could with other people. For so long, it had perplexed her that she could not read Gereinte and now she could not avoid reading him.

Without the energy to oppose it, she allowed the attendants to fuss around her, washing, dressing and seeing to her injuries. She lay back, closed her eyes and could almost imagine her four-year-old self, surrounded by colour, cloth and a never-ending supply of warmth.

CHAPTER FORTY-NINE

Gereinte watched Jehanna being whisked away by her compatriots and longed to go with her. He turned and looked at the Queen of Arjat an-Nahr and saw his longing reflected in her eyes. Those deep, almond shaped eyes that so resembled her daughter's.

Kemal was quick to arrange provisions and a large tent for the easterners and before long, they met around a makeshift table with refreshments; a mixture of western fare and eastern delicacies.

Darien had appeared to Gereinte's utmost relief, though he looked battle weary but probably not half as bloody as Gereinte himself. He hugged his friend and not just at the relief at his bringing a whole army with him from Tordre. The attendants kept intervening with wet cloths and salves for their cuts, but they were both too pleased with the outcome of the battle to care about their appearances and kept batting the attendants away like annoying flies. When eventually they managed to sit and assess the situation, a group of dignitaries had assembled around the easterners, which included Jehan, Jabir and Kemal, Alaric and assorted advisors and battalion leaders. Before long, Rann had joined them bringing news from the city and the palace.

"Lirra is making preparations for a celebratory feast. As soon as the palace and the streets have been cleared, we would like to extend our invitation to you all," Rann said. A few indecipherable words were exchanged between Jabir and the Queen before she nodded and smiled her assent. There was only one person Gereinte was really interested in seeing at the palace, but duty demanded his present attention.

There was more conversation between the easterners, then Jabir said, "Queen Taliah would like to know what you plan to do with the prisoners." Gereinte looked back at the Queen and was sucked into her fathomless gaze. She appraised him with her eyes, as though searching for a crack in his armour. Did she want to know how he intended to treat her daughter? He wondered how Jehanna would adapt to her life, now that she was caught between her western upbringing and her eastern heritage.

"We will send them back," Gereinte said, "with a strong message to their leaders. We will not tolerate violation of our national sovereignty and as they can see, we have both the will and the means to respond appropriately to such action." He locked eyes with the Queen, who kept his gaze while Jabir translated his words. She nodded her approval. Without realising he had been holding his breath, Gereinte let out a long sigh.

"Let's not be too quick to point a finger of blame at the Emperor," Rann said. "We should deny a state of war with Arrontierre and paint a picture of misadventure on the part of the chevaliers. The Emperor may then decide to disassociate himself with the action, leaving open further negotiations." There were nods of approval around the table.

"Piracy," Alaric said. "A case of piracy on the part of a group of ill-advised chevaliers. Yes, I like it. It won't sit well with the Emperor to admit to such an offense, especially given how badly it went on their part, but still... preferable to admitting culpability for an act of war."

Gereinte turned to Rann. "Round them up and bring them here. It should be you who sends them back with their tails between their legs." Rann smiled and issued the order. "Oh, and Rann..." Rann turned back to look at Gereinte. "Let's be sure to tell them what we do with pirates that are caught in our waters or on our land."

"Certainly, I will," Rann said. His eyes flicked towards the city walls, invisible in the cover of the tent, where the bodies of their enemies hung in the early evening air.

The celebrations lasted long after the official feast had ended; the people of Vermondie were quick to acknowledge their narrow escape at the hands of the chevaliers and the ill-fated former chancellor, Dassan. Abiel Morda had to all intents and purposes disappeared. A growing suspicion itched at Gereinte's conscience, so he set Etienne off to investigate the Archbishop Morda's whereabouts.

***

Gereinte was relieved when he was finally able to return to Carentan, to the relative comfort of his home, albeit somewhat battered and bruised. Each morning for weeks following their return, he would wake in a panic, wondering if Jehanna would still be there. But every day he was rewarded with her unwavering gaze and lost himself in the deep pools of her eyes. She made true her promise to be his queen, but only on the proviso of having a traditional eastern wedding. It was agreed and the date set when together they would travel to the eastern lands, to Arjat an-Nahr, guests of the Warrior Queen Taliah herself. Jehanna spent most of her days ensconced in the study of eastern culture and the language of Hassian, with a little help from Jabir.

Darien and Fiamina were married in true Sarlatian style and just as Sarlat became wedded to Malvas, the two nations of Malvas and Sarlat became part of the intricate web of alliances that now made up the Western Isles. Gereinte called a meeting of all the leaders of his allied nations to inform and discuss the future.

He paced in front of the large window that gazed out upon what used to be his mother's favourite garden. He wondered what she would have made of his decisions, some of which had very nearly cost them not only Vermondie, but Carentan and threatened to unravel the careful thread of relationships he had forged. He had very nearly lost Jehanna too; the only woman who had truly captured his heart. He shuddered. He put his fingertips to the window and looked out into the little herb garden that Jehanna had now claimed as her own. She was there, on her knees, digging little troughs in which to plant her seeds. He smiled. Try as he might to get her to behave like a queen, she still insisted on taking a hands-on approach to her new found leadership. Though he knew she could more than handle herself on the battlefield, he felt a strong urge to protect her. She looked so vulnerable, toiling away in the garden. She looked up at the window and caught him watching her, then smiled and waved before returning to her task. She strengthened his resolve to bring about change to the Western Isles, fundamental change that the key leaders might not necessarily agree with.

There was a loud rap at the door and he turned to face the judgement of his closest friends and allies. As the room began to fill, the servants bustled in and out with refreshments and platters of meat, loaves of bread and great bowls of cheese, fruits and sweets. As was customary, the visitors bowed and shook hands with Gereinte before taking their place around the large oval table.

First came the Sarlatian contingent, Alvar Correze with his daughter, Fiamina who along with Darien would be representing Malvas. Baron Issoire slipped into the room, quiet and enigmatic as ever.

"Gereinte," Jessamine said, as she flew to his side, embracing him. "Where is Jehanna? I'm just dying to catch up." He laughed.

"She'll be here. Just finishing up some... business," he said, eyes flickering to the window. Seth D'Alban, Jessamine's Regent took his place by her side. Jabir, Kemal and Jehan sat together on one side of the table, chatting quietly. Fulk from house Borsa had to duck through the doorframe and Gereinte nearly missed his sister Alliane who was all but lost in his shadow. Fulk proffered a northern greeting, fist across his chest in front of his heart. Alliane smiled and kissed Gereinte on both cheeks.

"Guess who came," she said, stepping back to reveal her twin sister, Nerys.

"Gereinte," Nerys embraced him. He drew her back and looked her up and down.

"Look at you," he said. "The burden of the crown suits you well." Nerys adjusted her bodice and brushed down the nap of her blue velvet gown. She stepped aside to reveal her King, Morra Dreiden. Gereinte clasped King Dreiden's forearm and they shook.

"What can I say?" Gereinte said. "Your troops were there, in our hour of need. My thanks." Dreiden nodded, his guarded expression unwavering.

The room filled and the light conversation carried a buzz of anticipation. Rann and Lirra Haveritas arrived, followed by warmaster Alaric, Etienne and Chancellor Lorquin. At some point, Jehanna slipped into the room. He felt her presence before he noticed her sitting with Jessamine and Alliane, deep in conversation. She looked every bit a future queen in her ermine trimmed claret gown. He smoothed a hand over his brow, trying to hide the warm glow to his skin.

"Gentlemen, ladies..." The idle chatter subsided and Gereinte was aware of the weight of the gaze from the leaders upon him. He willed his nerves not to fail him now. "As you know, I have called you all here today to discuss the future of the Western Isles. I acknowledge that the victory in Vermondie could not have been possible without the co-operation of our six nations."

"Hear, hear," Alaric said, whose words were echoed around the table.

"But even with the support of the easterners, our continued stand against future attacks from the south or even, dare I say it the north, can only be assured by a continued alliance." Gereinte stopped

327

and looked around at the expectant faces. A few were nodding, particularly Morra Dreiden and Rann Haveritas. Fulk's brow was creased. "I speak of the far north, Klagenstill, which remains as wild and unstructured as ever."

"As far as I know," Etienne said, "they have introduced a confederation, if you can call it that, of semi-autonomous clans with little or no formal structure which at the moment appears to be a shambles."

"According to your sources," Alaric said. Etienne sighed.

"Indeed."

"They have a chieftan," Gereinte said, with hope.

"Who seems barely able to control the activities of the clan chiefs, short of encouraging the fighting, drinking and pillaging," Etienne said.

"You cannot possibly think that we could form an alliance with Klagenstill," Morra Dreiden said.

"Perhaps... not," Gereinte said. "I was hoping some of you might be able to suggest an alternative."

"Conquer and occupy each individual clan," Alaric said, folding his arms across his chest.

"We don't have the resources," Jehan said. Gereinte wondered how long it was going to take them to come to the same conclusion he had some months ago.

"Sanctions," Chanac Issoire said. "Restrictions on movement, trade embargoes or otherwise, with all the other countries of the Isles."

"That's all very well," Alaric said. "But their damned warriors are always raiding towns and

328

villages in Tennengaul and Malvas and even further south." Gereinte looked at Jehan.

"What is the current penalty for raiders?" Jehan said.

"For those found guilty," Chancellor Lorquin said. "A minimum of five years hard labour. Unfortunately this does not seem to deter many of them."

"Well that's your answer." Jehan looked at Gereinte, then around the table at the leaders. "Restrictions on entering all other territories outside Klagenstill. The punishment for infringement, depending on crimes committed could lead to a death penalty. If that doesn't deter them nothing will." There was a steely silence.

"Without a fair trial?" Jehanna said.

"You haven't seen what they do on one of these raids," Jessamine said, her face pale.

"That is, if you can catch them," Alaric said with a hurrumph.

"They need to know that we will carry out our threat if our laws are violated," Jehan said.

There were nods of agreement all round the table and Gereinte turned to Etienne.

"Prepare the appropriate proclamation; I will sign it and we publish it immediately."

There was a certain amount of fidgeting around the table as Gereinte handed out copies of the Citizen's Charter. "Many of you will have already seen and perhaps read this document," he nodded in the direction of Seth D'Alban who smiled thinly. "My proposal today is to extend it across the Western Isles and forge a new united alliance to strengthen our position against internal threats, such as Klagenstill and more importantly, external threats from Arrontierre. Although, I have to say that the Emperor has washed his hands of the recent activities of his chevaliers, claiming it to be nothing more than an independent offensive carried out by a group of ill-advised chevaliers. Nothing short of piracy." He raised an eyebrow at Alaric, who was smiling to himself. There were grumbles of dissent around the table. "Despite that, I am prepared to negotiate a peace treaty, but one that comes from a United Western Isles..."

"One that should come from the leader of such a united front," Alaric said. There were mutterings around the table as the leaders leafed through the Charter. Then to Gereinte's astonishment, Morra Dreiden, the King of Tordre, tossed his copy of the Charter into the middle of the table. It landed with a flat slap. He stood up, the chair scraping across the stone floor. All eyes were upon him. He drew his sword, steel chiming against the scabbard. In unison, men reached for their own swords and for a moment, Gereinte had the horrific vision of this turning into a blood bath. He was just about to leap across the table to Jehanna, when Morra Dreidan pointed his sword up to the ceiling.

"Long live, Gereinte Andolin, Emperor of the Western Isles." he said.

As though each and every mind in the room had the same thought at exactly the same moment, there was a chorus of cries that echoed Morra Dreiden and a dozen swords all pointed up towards the ceiling. Gereinte had his hands on the table, ready to launch into action, but then he stood still, mouth open. His eyes caught Jehanna's and her lip curled up in faint smile, her eyebrow raised on one side in a challenge. The hairs prickled up on the back of Gereinte's neck. Jehanna rose to her feet along with the rest of the people in the room. As if all that was not enough, Fulk rose to his feet and drew his massive broad sword, sweeping it in an upward arc and bellowed...

"Andolin rules!"

He looked around the room. It appeared that Gereinte's future had been decided for him.

332